SILENT DEATH

Death Trilogy Book 2

MARIËTTE WHITCOMB

ISBN Paperback: 978-1-991202-95-6
ISBN eBook: 978-1-991202-96-3

I dedicate this novel to the people whose
deaths went mostly unnoticed.
And to those seen as a commodity
and not human beings.
Your life matters.

Chapter 1

"Do you realise how dangerous this is, Maddie? What if one of the women gets caught?" Richard Davenport asked from behind his desk.

The refrigerator door closed with a thud. Madison placed her hand against the cold glass. "I do, and so do they. Don't you think it's worth the risk? Richard, I understand if you don't want to help me. Your involvement comes with risks."

Madison turned to face the only person, apart from the women, who knew what she was doing. She'd found an unlikely ally in her future sister-in-law's father. Their bond had been forged in the depravity of someone else's darkness.

"Maddie, sit down." Richard waited for her to take a seat. When she did, he handed her a cognac. "I understand why you're doing this and you have my full support. However, I'm worried that the person responsible will find out what you're doing. You don't know what he is capable of."

"The police aren't being helpful. I have to do *something*. It has to be one person who is responsible for the disappearances of all the women." Madison lifted the snifter to her lips, savouring the taste of the brown liquid. Richard had introduced her to cognac and taught her to appreciate it. "And no, it's not me trying to make up for my past mistakes. Or seeing a serial killer in every person I pass on the street."

Richard studied her, tilting his head ever so slightly. "We've both made mistakes and have to live with the consequences. It

1

could've ended far worse for us. Have you discussed survivor's guilt with your therapist?"

"Have you?" Madison snapped.

"Yes. Answer my question."

Madison stared at Richard, trying hard to find the right words. This wasn't the first time Richard had wanted to discuss her mental state. She hated it. But respected him too much. "She tried to bring it up … I'm not wired for idle chit-chat. Do I feel guilty for being alive? No."

"Yet you see yourself as gullible and weak for failing to see the monster."

Madison reached for the leather shoulder bag at her feet, placed it on her lap and fidgeted with the buckle. "I came here to put those samples in the fridge, not to rip off scabs. Thank you for your concern. I appreciate it. You've reconnected with Noa and I'm happy for both of you. But with all due respect, Richard, I'm not your daughter. You don't have to worry about my safety."

Richard leaned forward, resting his elbows on the desk. "No, you're not my daughter." He smiled. "What you're doing is both brave and stupid. You need to be very careful and hyper-vigilant, considering who you suspect is behind the women's disappearances."

"I know." Madison focused on the movements of her fingers over the steel buckle. "Tomorrow I'm casting another net. Perhaps this time, he'll get caught up in it."

Richard sighed. "At least tell Clay, so he knows to look out for you."

"I can't tell him, my family or my friends. I've already put you at risk by involving you. Thank you." She patted the bag.

"I'm always here for you if you need to talk, Maddie. You're not the only one who walked out of that cellar. I should've known *who* was involved in Noa's life." Richard shook his head, regret visible in his grey eyes. "I should've been involved in my daughter's life."

Madison walked around the desk and hugged Richard, for

herself, and for him. Two people who'd been held hostage in a serial killer's cellar — a torture chamber — but had survived.

Thursday, 9 December, 6:00 p.m.

The villa was everything he'd said it would be. Vegas placed her suitcase on the marble floor, wondering in which room she'd be able to unpack her things. None of the rooms were for *their* comfort, only the pleasure of others.

Vegas knew what was expected, as did the four women standing next to her. Their expressions ranged from fear to excitement. She knew both triggered the same physiological reaction in the human brain.

Vegas smiled, nodded and made small talk, as the men took turns introducing themselves.

She was all too familiar with this dance and what would follow.

In two weeks, Vegas would either have made enough money to get her through the first two months of the new year, or she'd be dead.

Where are you, Angie?

Thursday, 9 December, 10:45 p.m.

Light filled her bedroom window. Coming here was selfish, but Clay needed Madison. Needed to hear her voice, feel the electricity humming from her and be close enough to touch her. Clay never did, not in the way he wanted to.

If only a countdown timer hung over Madison's head — visible only to him — to show when she'd be ready for him, when she wanted him and not as a friend. Before the day he carried her out of that house, he had never needed anyone. That was, until he met Madison Taylor.

Clay tapped his knuckles against the apartment door,

hoping Madison's roommate was spending the night with her boyfriend.

The door opened. She stared at him with deep blue eyes. He fought the urge to reach for her.

Madison placed her hand against his heart. The gentleness in her touch tugged on his restraint. Clay wanted Madison to wipe the memories of the day from his mind, but he never shared the bad days with her. She battled her own demons.

"It can't be your mother. I saw her today." Madison stepped back and closed the door after Clay entered. Three clicks filled the quiet as she slid the deadbolts in place.

Madison rubbed her hands over the stiff muscles of his back; Clay's head dropped forward. Despite the horrors and the sadness she witnessed as a social worker, Madison's light always drowned out the darkness of his world.

"Work?" Madison asked, her hands still offering solace.

"Yes," Clay whispered.

Madison took his hand, leading him to the kitchen. Without a word, she warmed the Chinese food she'd bought for him earlier in the evening.

Clay forced the food down, knowing she needed to take care of him as much as he needed to be taken care of. He ate enough to satisfy her then followed Madison to the couch. The silence between them enveloped him. It always did when neither of them needed anything more than just to be together. In the past six months, they'd shared many nights filled with quiet and comfort.

I want you, Maddie.

As if hearing his thoughts, Madison turned to him, the glow of the television making her hair blue.

"I'm here. You're safe. Just breathe, Clay." Madison reached for his hand, intertwining their fingers. He held her stare. Concern and understanding filled her eyes. A welcome change to the fear Clay had seen in the children's eyes earlier in the evening.

Those call-outs were the only reason he hated his work

as an officer of Shadow Bay's SWAT team. Give him a drug bust, bank robbery, or any situation other than the one he'd witnessed tonight. The children's vacant stares would haunt him forever, even though they were no longer in danger. At least they were now safe from the *Boogeyman*.

He clung to Madison's hand, absorbing her presence, and dropped his head back to stare at the ceiling. Tonight, he wouldn't sleep. Next to him, Madison yawned. Clay turned his head towards her.

The smile didn't reach her eyes. "You're staying here tonight. When you're ready to talk, or want me to sit with you and share a big mug of hot chocolate, let me know." Madison squeezed his hand and then fetched a pillow and blanket from her bedroom.

When she returned and stood in front of him, Clay grabbed Madison's hips and dragged her closer, pressing his face against her stomach. She ran her fingers through his hair. He breathed in her scent and fought against the images that were seared into his memory forever. Before Madison came into his life, he would've gone home and drank enough beer to make him sleep.

"Thank you," Clay murmured. Madison traced her hands over his shoulders and down his back. Clay increased his hold until she stiffened. "I'm sorry. I didn't mean to hurt you." He kept his cheek against the warmth of her core.

"Tomorrow morning we're going to kickboxing. You need to work this out of your system. One day at a time. Like you always tell me." She bent down, pressing her lips to his hair.

Clay closed his eyes, taking a deep breath. *I'm tired of fighting.*

"I'm in there if you need me."

He released her and watched as walked away. Clay stared at Madison's bedroom door. Tonight, her bed called to him more than any of the other nights he'd stayed over.

Soon, Maddie.

***

Thursday, 9 December, 11:47 p.m.

When Clay's ready, he'll tell me.

When they first became friends, Madison had learned not to push Clay, making him the only person she didn't badger for answers. She understood the reasons Clay didn't share his demons with her. Her own were still fresh in her memory, and his. The next morning's newspaper would answer the question of what tormented him.

Early in their friendship, she had learned to seek answers elsewhere – never to pry but to understand Clay better – and to give him the support he needed. The same way he'd done for her every single day for the past six months.

Light seeped in through her closed curtains. Again, Clay twisted and turned on the couch. At this rate, neither of them would get any sleep. Madison threw off the duvet and got out of bed. She leaned against her bedroom door, watching him. Every part of her ached to chase away the darkness which had followed Clay home.

Madison stepped closer to the couch. The streetlight outside the living room window illuminated her path. Clay turned, looking up at her and the hand she held out towards him.

The warmth of their physical connection spread to every part of her as Clay took her hand. What Madison was about to do would no doubt break her heart, but he needed this. She'd bury her feelings if it meant there was a chance to chase away the darkness.

Tugging on Clay's arm, Madison led him to her bedroom. "Sleep with me," she said, releasing his hand to get into the opposite side of the bed.

Clay did the same, and she pulled the duvet over them. Madison reached for his hand again, covering it with her own. Clay intertwined their fingers.

She ached to rest her head on his chest. Instead, Madison pushed her back into the mattress. A single tear slipped from Madison's eye, tickling her temple.

Clay Davis was in her bed. But a man like him would never want her the way she wanted him.

Chapter 2

Friday, 10 December, 5:00 p.m.

Madison returned the file to her backpack. *What a waste of time.* It took all her self-control to appear interested in Detective Evans' words. No one cared about the missing women, least of all the police.

"I know the type. Women like that never stay in one place for long. There are always newer and fresher ones to compete with on the streets. *Miss* Taylor, you're wasting your time. They've left Shadow Bay, and have taken their business elsewhere."

"Where are Detectives Carmichael and Jones? I spoke to them before. It's not that I don't appreciate your time, but under the circumstances, I think it's best if I keep working with them," Madison said.

"They have their hands full with the thirty children who were rescued last night. And that's not even considering the number of bodies that need to be identified." Detective Evans leaned back in his chair. Madison frowned. "Big paedophile ring bust. Biggest one yet. Right here in our city."

Oh Clay. Madison steeled herself as she remembered another night Clay had come to her with a similar darkness hanging over him. The headline article in the media the following day had also involved children.

"I'm grateful the children were rescued and understand that locating missing sex workers won't be a priority. Please talk to Detectives Carmichael and Jones. The facts can't be ignored." Madison clasped her hands on her lap, remembering the feel of Clay's hand in hers. The desperation with which he'd taken hold of her and held on until sunrise.

"Miss Taylor, you can't be sure these women didn't leave out of their own volition, taking their trade elsewhere. Until we have evidence that a crime was, in fact, committed, there's nothing we can do."

"That's where you are wrong, *Detective*. None of them have anywhere to go. If you refuse to investigate their disappearances, I guess we're done." Madison grabbed her bag and pushed to her feet. "I'll come back when either Detective Jones or Carmichael is available."

Detective Evans rose, placing his hands on the desk. "I understand your frustration, and I commend you for your dedication. But there's nothing we can do."

I can. "Two years ago, five young women went missing. Last year, ten women disappeared. Both years it happened in December. Do you still think this is nothing but a coincidence? What can you tell me about the five bodies that were found in November? Have any of them been identified yet? The newspapers mentioned nothing again after the initial report." Madison swung the bag over her shoulder.

"Miss Taylor, sometimes it's better not to ask questions. Besides, I can't give you information on an active investigation. You know enough about this world and what happens on the streets to understand the dangers. And, like I said, they took their trade elsewhere."

Madison placed a Ziplock bag containing a hairbrush on the desk. "At least compare the DNA from the hair to the bodies of the women who were found in Potters Park. I promised a friend I'd bring it in. Her sister disappeared last December. The least you can do is compare the DNA."

Evans shook his head. "Do you have any idea how bad the backlog is at the lab? Homicide and rape cases are far more important."

Madison straightened her spine. "Will you release the DNA of the five bodies if I arrange for it to be analysed and compared by a private laboratory?"

"Do you have more DNA samples than this hair?"

"I could try to get hold of the missing women's DNA." Inside the refrigerator at Richard Davenport's facility, the DNA samples waited. More samples than just those of the missing women.

"My superior officer won't sign off on it. It won't look good in the media." Evans shrugged.

Madison turned and walked out of the office. Without looking back, she said, "Thank you for your time, Detective." *I will find them.*

Friday, 10 December, 8:00 p.m.

Throughout dinner, the missing women's faces and life stories occupied Madison's thoughts. She didn't laugh when her friends did or join in on the conversation. The food on the plate in front of her remained untouched.

While the others spoke about their plans for the holiday season, Madison focused on the women and girls she worked with. Some of them she'd known for close to a year. Or a lifetime, considering their connection. Madison had met them while completing her master's degree. Now she considered each of them a friend.

Some nights, Madison wondered how she had gotten so lucky to have her family and life. Her new friends didn't deserve the lives they were living. No little girl grows up dreaming of earning a living that way. No one cared about them, not their families nor the authorities.

The friends sitting around the table didn't know the reason she'd thrown herself into her work over the past six months. Madison's family and Clay knew what she wanted them to know. Being on the streets was dangerous, but she didn't care. Besides, she always carried her gun and knife. *It's what most survivors do.*

Madison excused herself and left the restaurant. As she approached her car in the parking lot, Madison removed the keys from the back pocket of her jeans.

Her body slammed into the driver's door.

The force knocked the air from her lungs.

Clawing at her throat, gasping for oxygen, Madison tried to pry the object away from her neck.

A warm breath filled her ear. "Just because one serial killer was soft on you, it doesn't mean the next one will be. No one cares about whores, Madison."

Friday, 10 December, 8:30 p.m.

The oven dinged. Clay headed to the kitchen and removed the pizza. This week had been rough, from the hostage situation on the train to the previous night's bust, the second biggest of his career. Clay grabbed a beer from the fridge. As he twisted off the cap, there was a sound outside his apartment door. Reaching for his SIG-Sauer P228, Clay lifted it towards the door, watching the lock turn.

The intruder's face came into view. Clay lowered the weapon and rushed to her. He slipped the gun into the waist of his jeans, pulling Madison against his chest.

"What happened, Maddie?" he asked, holding her trembling body tighter. Madison wrapped her arms around his waist and took a deep breath. "Maddie, you're scaring me. What happened?"

Madison kept her arms locked around him. Again, her inhale was audible.

Clay stepped back, holding onto her shoulders. A distinct red line was visible around her throat. Without a doubt, the scratch marks were Madison's as she'd tried to fight back. And stay alive. "Who did this to you?"

Madison shook her head.

"Dammit, Maddie, I promised your family I'd look out for

you." Clay grabbed her hand and led her to the couch, waiting for her to sit before he did. "Tell me. Who did this?"

"I have no idea," she whispered when Clay gently touched her back.

"What happened? Start at the beginning."

Madison told him about going to dinner, as she'd planned weeks ago, walking to her car and about the attack. She told him the attacker's exact words.

"It's impossible. No one knows what happened to you in June." Clay pushed to his feet, pacing the short distance between the bed and the kitchen. "The court records refer to you as Miss X. Where were you before you met up with your friends for dinner?"

"The police station. I spoke to Detective Evans about the missing women."

Clay walked to the fridge, removed a beer and handed it to Madison after untwisting the cap. He grabbed his own bottle and brought it to his lips, lowering it without taking a drink. "What missing women?"

"December, two years ago, five women disappeared. Last year in December ten went missing. I asked him about the remains of the five women found in Potters Park, and whether the police are considering if they could be the women I've reported as missing."

"What did Evans say?"

"Nothing, except that they probably packed up and moved on. You know how sex workers are stigmatised by law enforcement and the media? They would've told *someone* if they were leaving Shadow Bay. Only a few items were missing from their rooms – clothes, toiletries, basics, but not all of the few things they own."

Clay placed the beer bottle on the coffee table. "Let me take a look at your neck." With his index finger, he traced the bruise. "That's going to leave a mark."

"Dammit." Madison jumped to her feet and ran to the bathroom.

She leaned against the bathroom door, covering the mark with her hand. "I can't go to the wedding like *this*. If my parents see it, they'll demand I move back home."

"You have more important things to worry about than your parents finding out you've been working the streets at night." He gave her a naughty smile. Humour, Clay had learned, kept Madison's anxiety attacks at bay.

"Not funny, *Slay*. What am I going to do?"

He held a hand out to her and waited for her to return to the couch. Madison snuggled into his arms, resting her head on his chest. For the first time, Madison's skin was on his and her heat spread to every part of him.

Unless Madison asked, he wouldn't touch her in a non-platonic way. To him, their friendship had never been platonic; not since he'd laid eyes on her again, a few days after rescuing her from that cellar. But pushing a woman who'd suffered through what Madison had would be a dick move. And that was one thing Clay refused to do.

The fact that the attacker had referenced Foster Ericson made Clay's blood run cold. "A random pimp won't know about it. Only a handful of police and SWAT officers, the state prosecutor and the judge know. Of course, Foster's defence attorney knows your real name."

She rubbed a hand over his chest and stilled. "Do you think *he* told someone and sent them after me?"

Clay pressed his lips to Madison's blonde curls. "I don't know, but I promise you, I will find out."

Madison lifted her head and stared up at him. Her eyes filled with the same fear Clay had seen the day he'd carried her out of Foster's house. With his thumb, he wiped away the wetness on her cheek, careful not to brush against her lips.

"It's just us," he whispered.

Madison dropped her head back to his chest. Clay held her as the familiar fear and anger tore through her.

Chapter 3

Madison wiped her tears from Clay's bare chest. The patch of fine blonde hair tickled her palm. She bit her lower lip. *I don't want to be your friend.*

"Can I stay here tonight?" Madison asked as her hand still wiping Clay's now dry skin.

"You can take the bed. I'll sleep on the couch." Clay eased her hand from his chest before walking to the kitchen.

Madison pressed her palms to her eyes. How many times had she cried in Clay's arms in the months since they'd met? She was tired of crying. Tired of not throwing her arms around his neck and kissing him until neither of them could breathe. Every time she wanted to reach for him, she remembered how Clay had found her. He'd never be able to see her as anything other than the ignorant woman who'd slept with a serial killer and ended up locked in that cellar.

Waking up next to Clay this morning had been the best and worst morning of her life. Not counting the morning she'd woken up a prisoner, next to Foster Ericson.

Clay returned with two plates and a pizza, placing everything on the coffee table. Madison reached out to him and trailed her fingers along the phoenix tattoo on the left side of his back. Black ink obscured the distinct ridges under her fingertips.

"What happened? I've never seen you without a shirt before. I love the design. It's a work of art."

"Bomb," Clay said.

14

Madison shook her head. Clay rarely spoke about his work. "Where? When? How?" Sometimes her resolve not to push him crumbled.

He glanced over his shoulder. The corner of his mouth lifted; an eyebrow raised. "Madison Taylor, you're an inquisitive woman."

She nodded. "Got me in trouble tonight."

Clay grabbed a shirt from his closet and pulled it over his head. "Have you gone to the police station to open a case?"

Master of deflection. "No."

"Don't. You getting attacked shortly after speaking to Evans might be more than a coincidence." Clay handed her a plate, which she placed on her lap and then stared at the pizza. "You need to eat. One slice still counts as eating."

Madison laughed. "You're the best thing that has ever happened to me. You almost force-fed me when I came back to Shadow Bay. And here you are, still taking care of me."

Sitting down next to her, Clay lifted a slice to his mouth. "I'm glad you still have the key to my apartment. Keep it. If you ever feel unsafe or need to be alone, come here. Even when I'm at work."

"We're practically living together with the amount of time, and nights we've spent in each other's apartments. Thank you." Madison touched his back, even though cotton now obscured her view of his tattoo. *I'm torturing myself.* "At least I'll have the most badass date at the wedding."

Clay leaned back against the couch. "How do you think your brother will feel if he hears you say that? Not to mention your sister. Jamie Edwards is a force to be reckoned with."

"The twins are depleting *the force*, and they aren't even born yet." Madison laughed and took a sip of beer. "For the record, you know Luke respects you as a member of SWAT, but also enough to trust you with me." She picked up another slice of pizza and out of the corner of her eye noticed Clay's full lips smile.

Many nights when the fear of another nightmare kept her

awake, she wondered how his mouth would feel against hers, and his hands on her skin. Whenever thoughts of finding out drove her to walk to Clay's front door, only to turn back as she lifted a fist to knock, she'd put on his SWAT jacket and get back into bed. The jacket no longer smelled like him. She had to wash it after all, but it still brought calm and a sense of protection. Just as the man who'd given it to her did.

They finished eating dinner and carried their plates and empty beer bottles to the kitchen. Madison caught sight of her reflection in the window above the sink and placed her hand against her sore throat.

"How am I going to keep this from my family? Three ex-detectives, a former social worker, and Spencer's calm observant eyes … King probably already knows. I miss that dog."

Clay took the plate from her and washed it. He turned to face her, wiping his hands on a dishcloth. He traced his finger along the mark, and a sigh escaped Madison's lips. Clay lifted his hand to her face and traced her jawline with his thumb. Her entire being trembled under his touch.

"Maybe you should wear the outfit you wore on stage last weekend." He winked.

"Of course, why didn't I think of giving my parents heart attacks? Just what Luke and Noa need at their wedding – all eyes on me."

"You looked sexy. Very rock chick and the slight bulge between your breasts had the crowd going wild."

"Could you really see it?" Madison pressed a hand against the Glock Gen 43 holstered in her bra.

"Not if you didn't know it was there." Clay glanced at his feet; a gesture which had made Madison ache for him since the first time she saw him do it.

"Clay Davis, aka Slay, did you just admit to checking out my boobs?"

"Wasn't that the point of the dress?" The corners of his mouth lifted.

Madison forced her eyes from his beautiful smile and shrugged. "Maybe."

"*Maybe* you can wear the choker you wore with the dress to cover the bruise." He removed two more beers from the fridge and handed one to Madison, smiling when she opened it herself.

"Is this the eighties? I don't think so." She shook her head. "And my dress is low cut. Do you think I can fake a disease and skip my favourite brother's wedding?"

Clay bumped his hip against hers as he walked out of the kitchen. "Your *only* brother, and no. You'll think of something. Are we going to finish our series tonight and call it an early night? Tomorrow is going to be a long day."

Madison loved watching police procedurals and asking Clay what was fact and what was fiction. He never grew tired of answering, unless he fell asleep after a long day keeping the city safe. In Madison's eyes, he'd always be a hero, even when he did nothing more than paperwork on the days when work was thankfully slow.

"You take the bed, I'll take the couch," he said again.

"You're way too tall to sleep on a two-seater. Besides, the leather will wake both of us up every time you change position." Madison stood and headed to the bathroom. "We're adults, and it's not like we haven't slept together before."

Not that either of them had slept much the previous night; too aware of the warm body next to them.

Chapter 4

I can never wake up next to him again. Madison reached to unlock the door to the apartment she'd shared with her best friend, Emma, for the past three years.

Clay grabbed her shoulders, pulling her away from the door. Lifting an index finger to his lips, Clay unholstered his gun.

Madison stared at the door, realising it was ajar. She also reached for her weapon.

"Wait here," he mouthed, easing the door open with the tip of his boot. Clay disappeared inside the apartment.

Madison gripped the gun even harder. She tried to control her breathing; the way her therapist had taught her to do in stressful situations.

Madison peeked around the doorframe. The apartment was in utter chaos. She heard Clay's voice and moved through the rooms, careful of where she stepped.

In her bedroom, Clay stood talking on his phone. He spun around as she approached and pushed her out of the room, sending Madison stumbling back. He wrapped an arm around her waist and lifted her off her feet, carrying her out of the apartment while still speaking on the phone.

Clay hugged her to him, finishing the conversation. He released his hold enough to look into her eyes. "I told you to stay outside."

"It's my home." Madison stepped backwards and tried to move around him.

Clay's fingers wrapped around her arm. "You're not going in there."

"Who were you talking to?" she asked, realising Clay still held his gun. *How did he carry me with one arm while holding a gun and talking on the phone?*

"I called it in."

"A burglary? The police will take hours to get here. We don't have time for that. Not today." Again, Madison tried to get into the apartment, but Clay kept blocking her way.

"I think it's more than a burglary, Maddie." Clay placed a hand on the back of her head, bringing Madison's face to his chest.

"No." Madison's arms wrapped around his waist. "Emma?" she pleaded.

"No, the apartment is empty. But someone left a message on your bedroom wall."

"What message? What does it say?" She tried to step away, but Clay held her to him.

"It says: *Stop.*"

The sound of approaching sirens became unmistakable. Madison retrieved her phone from her bag.

"What are you doing?" Clay reached for her wrist.

"I need to talk to Emma and tell her about the break-in. She invited her cousin to stay here for the weekend."

Clay released her arm. Madison called her oldest friend. She didn't give Emma any specifics, but told her they couldn't sleep there.

Before ending the call, Emma asked to borrow Madison's car.

Saturday, 11 December, 7:35 a.m.

This was what they had all been looking forward to for the past year. Two weeks of sun, sea, sand and a different woman every night. Unlike the previous year, they'd have to take the same woman to bed more than once. Considering the quality of the women, it wouldn't be a hardship.

Torch tapped a thumb against the metal band encircling the fourth finger of his left hand. "Another beautiful day for indulging. Are we going to draw straws or throw their names in a hat?"

"You already have the shortest straw. Let's do the hat thing." Trigger laughed at his own joke. The other men kept their gazes fixed on the women in the swimming pool.

Blade lowered his sunglasses over his eyes and reached for the coffee mug on the table next to him. "What if we change it up this year and stick to one girl each for the duration? It might sweeten the experience."

"If I wanted sex with the same woman every day, I would've stayed home. We're here to create enough memories to last us until next December. Have any of you given our last night some consideration? It's going to be almost impossible to beat last year's final night." Crush rubbed his thighs.

The five men leered at the five women in the water. Two weeks with any of them wouldn't be enough, not with their skills. This was paradise. A fantasy. Their right.

"I wonder what happened to Angel. Wouldn't mind having her again," Blade said.

"Who cares about her? These girls are much better than last year's. Gentlemen, in all my years, I've never met a woman with Tiffany's talents." Archer placed his glass on the floor next to his chair. "If we're considering changing it up this year to one on one for the duration of our stay, I call dibs on her."

Torch rose and turned to Archer. "I need to get rid of the tension in my back ... maybe Tiffany will sort it out." He walked towards the swimming pool and asked Tiffany to join him. Without saying a word, she climbed out of the pool and followed Archer into the house.

"We should call her – Atlantis. Nobody goes down like her." Crush laughed.

Chapter 5

Lamont Estate was closed for business because of a private function; the wedding of the owners' son to the woman he'd fallen in love with six months earlier.

The sound of nails against the hardwood floor welcomed Madison as she opened the front door. Madison entered her parents' home and dropped to her knees. Noa's blue-nosed pit bull, King, came rushing through the house.

"Hello, my gorgeous boy." She rubbed his ears, kissing the top of his head.

King's body stiffened. He turned his head towards the front door. The moment Clay walked into the foyer, King dropped his tail and wiggled out of Madison's arms. He rolled onto his back at Clay's feet, waiting for a belly-rub.

"Were you saying hello to King or to me?" Aaron Taylor asked and held out a hand towards his youngest daughter.

"Hello, Daddy. You haven't been a gorgeous boy in over fifty years. There's your answer." Madison reached for her father's hand, but he yanked it back at her words. She fell backwards and winced.

"What happened to you?" he asked.

Madison forced a shrug. "Kickboxing. We did some sparring yesterday."

Aaron's left eyebrow raised. "I know you're lying, but I don't have time to coax it out of you. Clay," he said as he extended his hand, "what happened to her?"

Clay glanced at Madison and tilted his head. "Who, Maddie? I thought she came out like this? Did she bump her head as a child? It would explain a lot." He shook Aaron's hand.

"Come, put your bags in your rooms. Maddie, you're sleeping in your room. Mom prepared the room across the hall for Clay." Aaron turned to Clay. "I'm a heavy sleeper. Feel free to sneak across the hall during the night."

"Dad." Madison rolled her eyes.

"King is sleeping with you tonight, baby. I don't have to worry about any hanky-panky happening on his watch." Aaron strode off in the kitchen's direction.

Clay picked up their luggage and started for the stairs. "You're cute when you blush. It doesn't happen often enough. Well played. Keep it up and they won't know what happened."

Madison ran up behind him with King on her heels. "I don't know how I'm going to keep it together through the wedding and reception. It doesn't make sense."

Clay waited for Madison to open her bedroom door and placed her suitcase on her bed before doing the same with his suitcase in the bedroom across the hall. He returned to Maddie's room to find her sitting on the floor, her face buried in King's neck. The dog looked up at him and gave Clay his trademark pit bull smile.

Clay crouched down and sat next to her, placing an arm over Madison's shoulder. "If it gets too much, we can go for a walk and talk it through. Tomorrow, I'll start calling in favours to find out what they have found, but the labs are short-staffed and personal crimes take precedence over weekends."

"What if *he* sent someone after me?" Madison lifted her eyes to Clay's, inhaling his scent. Her mind drifted to the memory of waking up in his arms and her heart shattered at the realisation that it could never happen again.

"If it is Foster, why now? And Maddie, I won't let him or anyone else hurt you. I promise to figure out what's going on. Try to focus on Luke and Noa's wedding and share in their joy today. I'm here for you. You're not alone in any of this."

Madison shooed King off her lap, brought her knees to her chest, turning to face Clay. "How am I ever going to repay you for always being here for me?"

"One day, we will think of something." He placed his palm on her cheek.

Madison closed her eyes, drinking in the sensation of his warm skin against hers as she had done this morning.

"Right now, there's nothing you can do, Maddie. Let the police handle the investigation."

Do it. Madison pressed her mouth to his palm and heard his breath catch. "How do you distance yourself from everything you've seen and lived through?"

"Compartmentalisation. Work is work. This is this."

Madison wanted to ask what *this* was, but didn't want to hear that Clay didn't feel the same about her. Waking up in his arms, the warmth of his lips on the curve of her neck, him calling her *babe*. None of it was enough to give her hope. She reasoned Clay said and did the same to every woman he'd woken up next to. The slight pressure of him against her bum didn't erase the fact that she was damaged. No sane man would ever want her. *Friends, nothing more.*

"I knew I should've made Clay book into a guesthouse down the road." Laura Taylor appeared in the doorway and placed her hands on her sides.

Clay jumped to his feet and helped Madison up. "Hello, Laura. Thank you for inviting me to stay with your beautiful family on this glorious and splendid day of love between two people who deserve all the happiness this life has to offer. Have I told you how young you look today? I can see where Jamie gets her remarkable beauty. Wow, you look good for a woman of – how young are you again – forty-five?" Clay gave her a quick peck on the cheek.

"I *like* you. That's it, I'm adopting you. Unless you plan to get *freaky* with my daughter. When I told Luke I wanted to adopt Noa, he said it would be *icky*. Clay Davis, what are your plans with my youngest? I know you love my other two children. How about this one?" Laura wrapped her arms around Madison.

"*Freaky*, Mother? It's a good thing you stopped adopting children after you adopted Luke, otherwise there wouldn't have been room for me. You really should stop joking about adopting grown-ups. The animals you rescue are enough." Madison hugged her mother and fought the tears building in her tear ducts.

"So, you think my sister is beautiful, but not me?" Madison asked Clay.

"You can't handle what I think about you, Madison Taylor. Now, I need to go see a man about a tux. Ladies." Clay moved to walk past them, but Laura pulled him into her and Madison's embrace.

"His scent is … is … I don't have words." Laura pressed her face to Clay's shirt.

"I told you," Madison said, and did the same. With his warmth against her face, she decided that come Monday she'd start easing away from Clay.

He deserved to have time to go on dates. And to find a woman worthy of his love. A woman with better judgement.

"You Taylors are weird people." Clay shook off their arms and left the room.

"Noa said the same and today she officially becomes one of us." Laura called after him, still holding Madison in her arms. "Baby, I know something is wrong. And I realise you want to talk about it but won't because of the wedding." She eased Madison away, keeping hold of her youngest's shoulders. "Tomorrow morning, you and I are going for a ride, and then we'll discuss it. Your horse misses you almost as much as I do. I love the scarf, very bohemian."

Madison ran a hand over the scarf. "Can I borrow one of yours that will match my dress? I'm considering making this my new look."

***

Saturday, 11 December, 2:00 p.m.

He waited outside the apartment complex. Could only twelve hours have passed since he'd left the little bitch a warning? She was too fickle to grasp it, but it had given him a good laugh. He hated people like her, the caring, and out-for-justice kind.

The world consists of takers, and those made for the takers' pleasure.

Madison Taylor was a taker. How else had she survived being in Foster Ericson's clutches?

He understood why Ericson hadn't killed her. Who wouldn't want to keep her chained in a basement as a plaything? Irritating as an STD, but as pretty as they came with her curly blonde hair and hazel eyes. He suspected the blonde came from a bottle, but how a woman made herself look beautiful didn't matter.

The gate opened. Madison's car drove past him. He waited until another car passed and pulled into the lane. There really was nothing like the hunt, and this time, he wouldn't take any chances.

It didn't matter that Madison had a friend with her.

Two is a party.

Chapter 6

Madison leaned against the bar, lifting a tumbler to her lips. Over the rim of the glass, she studied her brother and his wife. Luke and Noa's paths to each other, and to their wedding day, hadn't been easy. Somehow, they made everything look easy.

It was hard to believe that the carefree and compassionate woman – the picture of elegance in her white dress – had endured forty days of psychological and physical torture at the hands of Foster Ericson. The same man who'd abducted Madison had spent over a decade stalking Noa, pretending to be her best friend.

What Madison had lived through wasn't a drop in the bucket compared to Noa's torment.

Clay walked towards her. Madison swallowed hard. It didn't matter if he wore full SWAT gear, nothing but a pair of jeans, or a tuxedo, he was still the most handsome man she'd ever seen. Caring, patient, funny, and the person she'd leaned on most in the past six months.

He ordered a drink before turning to her. Madison pretended to focus on the crowd. "Have I told you?" Clay asked.

"There are many things you haven't told me, Officer Davis. Maybe I'll never know you." Madison tilted her head back to meet his eyes and smiled, despite the crushing realisation she had to distance herself. "Okay, tell me."

He leaned closer, pressing his lips to her ear. "You, Madison Taylor, upstage the bride. And Noa is gorgeous, so what does that tell you?"

Madison downed the last of the liquid in her tumbler. "Are we playing twenty questions, but only you get to ask questions?"

Clay shook his head, taking a seat on a bar stool while Madison ordered another drink. Her hand trembled as she reached for it.

"Do you want to go for a walk?" Clay asked.

"No. I want that." Madison lifted the glass towards the newlyweds, who were kissing, oblivious to the people around them. Madison envied the way Luke and Noa could disappear into their love, even when surrounded by people.

Clay took the tumbler from her and placed it on the bar. He then took Madison's hand, gently pulling her towards the dance floor.

"Clay, we can't dance. They haven't opened the dance floor."

Clay walked up to the bride and groom, giving Luke a quick bro-hug before kissing Noa's cheek. He whispered something in Noa's ear; Madison didn't miss the colour that crept across Noa's cheeks.

"Watch it, Slay. No one does that to my wife except me." Luke placed an arm around Noa with the biggest smile Madison had ever seen on his face. Luke radiated with joy.

I'm jealous. If only she hadn't been stupid and naïve enough to be seduced by a serial killer. Or to have seduced a murderer. Not a day had gone by that Madison didn't remind herself of her mistake, even though her therapist had urged her to move past it.

Madison prided herself on being an excellent judge of character. Well then, psychopaths didn't have character because she hadn't seen Foster for what he was. Again, Madison wished *he* was dead. The room spun. She took a step away from the others, lifting a hand to her mouth.

Clay pulled her against his side, bending his head down and whispered, "I've got you, babe."

Madison yanked her hand from her mouth, her shoulders shaking. "Babe? Am I a pig?"

"You eat like one after kickboxing or when we get back

from the shooting range."

Yes, because I want to devour you. "Fine, Davis, from now on you can cook for yourself."

The corners of Clay's mouth lifted. "Who's going to watch television with you and explain how to restrain someone with Flexi-cuffs?"

Luke cleared his throat. "Why the hell are you two talking about handcuffs?"

Noa rammed an elbow into her husband's ribs. "You, Mister Taylor, don't get to talk about handcuffs. Do you remember our first time?"

Madison gagged. "Serious overshare, sis. I didn't need to know that. Nobody does. Gross."

Ignoring Madison's comment, Noa asked Clay, "What're your intentions with my sister?"

"First Laura, and now you. I need a drink. Luke, do you want to join me?"

Luke crossed his arms over his chest. "As soon as you answer my wife."

Madison did a one-eighty and stormed towards the bar.

Saturday, 11 December, 6:14 p.m.

Noa stared after Madison, and asked, "What's up with Maddie? She hasn't been herself today."

"It's been a rough couple of months for all of you, and I think her thesis isn't going the way she wants it. I'll keep an eye on her. Anyway, what time are you guys leaving tomorrow? I don't want to walk in on any *consummating.*" Clay glanced at Madison before returning his attention to his friends.

"We're leaving for the airport around midday and will be back on the twenty-third. It's our first Christmas as a family. Have you decided whether you'll be joining us?" Luke asked.

"Not yet."

"Clay, when are you going to tell Maddie?" Noa asked.

Luke shot her a questioning look.

"Tonight, after the wedding."

Noa stepped closer, placing her hands on Clay's arms. "You need to tell her about the job offer. Give her a chance to tell you how she feels before you make a decision which will alter both of your lives. You've been her rock and Maddie's scared you don't see her as worthy. She's scared people think she's ignorant because of what happened."

"That's the dumbest thing I've ever heard. How can she not see how magnificent she is? Any man would kill to have her." Clay gazed at Madison and smiled when she caught him watching her.

"Are you that man, Slay?" Luke asked.

"Yes." *I want to be.* "I've known since *that* day, and I tried to give her time. I respect our friendship, Taylor. And won't pursue a relationship with Madison if I don't have your blessing."

"It's easy to see why my mother loves you. She's long past liking you. You're a gentleman, Slay. Let's get a drink. We have a lot to celebrate tonight." Luke patted Clay on the back and steered him towards the bar.

Saturday, 11 December, 10:00 p.m.

Under a broken spotlight he sat, not taking his eyes off the bar's door. This was going to be a long night. He needed a bathroom break. He reached for the empty energy drink bottle on the passenger seat and unzipped his pants. The bar's door opened and Madison and roommate stepped out onto the street. *Dammit.*

This time of year, many people drove while intoxicated. This was going to be easy. He watched the two women make their way to Madison's car, and as he had earlier, he waited for a car to pass before pulling into the street.

In his mind, he mapped their route and remembered their apartment was still sealed off, following the break-in.

Her car turned towards the beach. Half a kilometre ahead was a deadly bend. That was his chance.

In a matter of seconds, he closed the distance between Madison's car and his. As her car entered the bend, he pressed his foot down hard on the accelerator and flashed the headlights. She stayed on the road. *Worth the risk.*

The Toyota's vendor clipped her Ford's bumper and moved ahead of him. He pressed his foot against the floor and twisted the steering wheel.

The Ford lost control, spinning.

He slowed down.

The Ford's rear bumper smashed through the steel barrier. For one glorious moment, the Ford's headlights blinded him before lifting into the dark sky.

"Sorry, Madison, but I warned you."

Chapter 7

Madison returned to their table and kicked off her shoes. She reached for the whiskey tumbler, finding a bottle of water in its place. Even for a small wedding, the dance floor was packed. It was what Noa and Luke had wanted – intimate, filled with laughter and delicious food.

She scanned the dance floor, looking for her date. Clay sat with her mother at their table. The moment she laid eyes on him, Clay looked at her. *How does he do that?*

He touched Laura's shoulder before making his way towards Madison. She loved watching Clay. The confidence in his walk, his hyperawareness, that wicked smile of his which made Madison want to rip off his clothes.

Perhaps it was the whiskey, but she considered walking up to Clay and kissing him. To know what kissing him would be like. *Just once.*

Seven years her senior, Clay had lived through a lot. First, losing his sister in a hostage situation. And now his mother lived in a care facility for people with Alzheimer's. Clay took care of all her bills. What woman wouldn't fall for him? Madison had. Hard.

Clay reached for her hand and pulled Madison to her feet. He dropped his head and stared at her bare feet. "Are you done dancing or may I, at least, have one dance with my date? You've been avoiding me all night." When Madison didn't answer, Clay stepped closer.

31

"Not fair. You can't use your scent to get your way with me." Madison pushed at his chest, but Clay didn't move.

"What can I use then?" He searched her eyes.

Madison lifted a hand to his cheek, exploring the stubble with her fingertips. In Clay's eyes, she saw something she realised she'd always seen, but never grasped. She dropped her hand to her side. Clay took it in his and brought it to his mouth, brushing his lips against her knuckles. "Clay?"

"When you're ready to have what Luke and Noa have – but better, because it's us – I'm right here, Maddie." He lifted her other hand to his chest. "Do you want to dance, or are we going to keep staring at each other for the rest of the night? I'm good either way."

Madison's head moved up and down; the knot in her stomach tightened.

"Words, babe."

"Please don't call me *that*. I'm your *friend*." Madison shook her head, pulling her hands from his. "Sorry, the alcohol is talking for me."

"Neither of us expected to wake up the way we did, but I don't regret it. Maybe our bodies voiced what our mouths have been too afraid to. I've never called another woman *babe* in my entire life. Only you fit the description I have in my mind."

Madison stared at her toes. "You shouldn't want me. You know—"

"This right here, what we've built over the past few months, is all that matters. If this is about *him*, I don't care. It has never affected the way I see you. You are not his. You never were. Maddie, please talk to me." Clay cupped her face between his palms, looking at her with such an intensity Madison lost herself in the blue-green of his eyes.

"I'm tired of talking, thinking, wrestling with myself. All of it."

"Then let's dance, because everything else I'm thinking of doing with you doesn't involve onlookers."

Madison stepped back, placing both hands on her cheeks.

"You're bad for me, Davis. I make people blush, not the other way around."

Clay led her to the dance floor. Placing a hand on the small of her back, he brushed his fingers against Madison's bare skin. A small moan escaped her lips. She arched her back, pressing her chest against his.

Madison felt him against her stomach and pursed her lips. Clay tried to place distance between them; Madison moved with him. "This morning, it wasn't basic biology?" Her stomach clenched at the feel of him against her. She fought the urge to press harder against him.

"No. But holding you this close, and this dress … I can't promise to have the self-control I had this morning."

Madison pressed her body closer to his, revelling when Clay closed his eyes. "You don't want people to see what's clearly meant for me." She stared up at him and drew her bottom lip between her teeth with a smile.

"I want you, Madison Taylor. No matter what lies you told yourself about why I wouldn't, I do, with an intensity that scares me." Clay lowered his head until their foreheads touched.

Saturday, 11 December, 11:30 p.m.

The heat of the flame warmed his face as he held it to the tip of the cigar. He exhaled the smoke with a cough. Another of his vacation indulgences. Since dinner, he'd indulged plenty with Kayla. Footsteps behind him made him tilt his head back. Torch watched a *friend* walk out to join him. He waited for Blade to take a seat before handing him a cigar and holding his Zippo towards Blade.

"Tell me again why we can't have two each? Don't get me wrong, I'm having fun, but there's nothing like a couple of threesomes a day to keep me feeling young," Torch said, rolling the Zippo between his fingers. With his other hand, he brought the cigar to his mouth.

"Your wife no longer indulging your fantasies?" Blade asked.

Torch glared at him. "Just as I don't talk about your wife, you don't talk about mine. It's one of the few rules we have. You know exactly why we can't risk it this year."

"No wife." Blade leaned back in his chair. "The stars are so much brighter here."

"It's all the sex. You think it's brighter here, but it isn't. I'm glad we now have year-round access to this house. I call dibs on using it first. I've already told the one we won't mention that I need to travel for work more often next year. And won't be home for two weeks at a time." Torch reached into the ice bucket at his feet and handed Blade a beer.

"Are we going to discuss what happened last year?" Blade asked, taking a swig from the bottle.

"No. We have rules for this, remember?" Torch crushed the cigar in the ashtray. "Don't bring it up again. The others aren't like us."

"But they are, Torch. Don't you get it? We're all in this."

A scantily clad Kayla came up behind Torch and ran her hands over his chest. She bent down and nipped at his earlobe. "I'm not done with you. Come back to bed. I have a surprise for you."

He grabbed the back of Kayla's head and twisted his neck until his mouth met hers. "I like the sound of that. Life doesn't get any better than this."

They disappeared inside the house. Blade forced a smile as he watched the trail of the full moon on the water's surface. Shadow Bay's lights illuminated the horizon.

After finishing his beer, Blade headed into the house; voices came from the living room. Vegas sat alone on the couch, wiping her eyes. *How did you end up doing this?*
"Are you okay?" he asked.

Vegas jerked her head around, forcing a smile. She tried hiding the tissue clutched in her hand. "This movie gets to me."

He looked at the screen and wondered why a comedy would make her cry. "Do you mind if I watch it with you? It's one of my favourites."

"Sure." Vegas scooted up on the couch and patted the spot next to her. "Can I get you something to drink?"

"How about I go make us some popcorn? I haven't watched a movie with someone in ages. And a movie isn't a movie without popcorn."

"Sit, I'll do it. It's my job to take care of you." Vegas pursed her lips. "What do you want, salted or butter?"

He wanted to ask her what she had meant by *job*, but knew he had to ease into it. "Please, allow me. You ladies have prepared all our meals and snacks. It's the least I can do for you."

Blade returned from the kitchen with a bag of popcorn and two non-alcoholic drinks. He settled next to Vegas; she placed a hand on his thigh.

"No need for that. We're just watching a movie." He patted her hand, giving it a quick squeeze.

Dread filled Vegas' eyes.

They watched the rest of the movie in comfortable silence, except when they both laughed. Vegas didn't wipe her eyes again.

Blade noticed Vegas shake her head at certain medical references. "What's wrong with the cast on his leg?"

"He broke his femur six hours ago, and not a single character mentioned the extensive blood loss he'd have suffered."

"How do you know that?" He reached for the popcorn. Vegas slapped his hand away with a playful grin. She lifted a kernel to his mouth. Blade took it between his teeth, careful not to brush his lips against her fingers.

Vegas returned her attention to the screen. "We all have interests and lives outside of this house."

Chapter 8

The wedding reception ended at midnight. Madison and Clay waited until the last guests had left before walking the short distance to the house. He draped his jacket over Madison's shoulders, holding her hand as they made their way along the cobble-stone footpath.

Madison thought about a conversation she'd had with Noa in June; the day after she was rescued. She'd told Noa that she'd fallen for Foster Ericson because of how he treated her. All the other men she'd dated before had been in their early twenties and few knew how to treat a woman as anything other than a sex toy. She admitted to Noa she'd enjoyed the casual sex, but even before the devil had come into her life, Madison knew she was ready for more. A meaningful relationship and to build a life with someone who would call her *his*.

Clay stopped. "What are you thinking about?"

"How do you do that? It's like you can sense when my mind is somewhere else and focused on something mundane."

"It's a gift. So, what are you thinking about? For the record, you never think of trivial things."

"Not anymore." Madison wrapped her arms around her waist.

Clay stepped closer. Madison's eyes lifted to his. Above Clay's head, fairy lights hung from the majestic oak tree, one she'd loved to climb as a child. "Please, Maddie, don't go there. Not tonight."

"Okay. Are we watching television until we fall asleep? It seems to be our thing."

Clay took her hand and led her up the steps leading to the porch. Without saying another word, he walked straight to Madison's bedroom door.

Her heart clenched when Clay released her.

Clay brushed the hair from her face and ran his fingers through it. "I've wanted to do that since the night at Luke's house when we officially met." He traced her jaw with his thumb.

Madison tilted her head down, touching his thumb with her lips.

Clay moved closer, not removing his thumb from her mouth. "Goodnight, Madison Taylor." Clay kissed her forehead.

Madison reached for his face, raised up on her toes, bringing her mouth to his. Clay lifted her off her feet. Holding her with one arm, he closed the door behind them.

"I can't stay," he whispered.

"Please, I can't kiss you for the first time and not kiss you again." She failed to wrap her legs around his waist. "Damn this tight dress."

Clay smiled against her mouth. "I've been patient for six months. If I stay here tonight ..." He eased Madison down until her feet touched the floor.

"I don't have patience, so we're good." She rubbed her forehead against his chest.

"Not in your parents' house."

"I can be quiet."

"Not with what I have been fantasising about doing to you."

"I want to kiss more than your mouth. There are specific parts of you ..." Madison pressed her stomach against the bulge in his pants. "I want to see you." She glanced down at what pressed against her.

"Dammit, Maddie. Not like this. We both drank tonight. When I make love to you, I don't want you to have any regrets or doubt whether it would've happened if you were sober."

"I'm sober enough." Madison pushed out her bottom lip. "Please."

"Madison Taylor doesn't beg." Clay ran his thumb across her extended lip.

"Because I never had the option of being with *you*." She stepped back and extended her arms, palms up. "Look at you, you're breathtaking. And your heart, voice, smile, eyes. You're everything I've always wanted. Not even your fascination with ice hockey and Shark Week bugs me. I can live with it. To be honest, I watch hockey games on the nights you're at work. The only drawback, Clay Davis – you can't cook. But that's okay because neither can I. We can survive off takeaways. No one should want me after what happened, least of all *you*."

Clay turned away from her, rolling his shoulders. "I never want to hear you say that bullshit ever again. You don't see yourself the way I do. So, what, you made a mistake? A lot of amazing and intelligent people get involved with a criminal without knowing who or what they are. It's time to put it behind you."

Madison ran her hands up Clay's back, exploring the lines of his muscles. "I want to trail the design of your phoenix with my tongue." She tugged his shirt from his pants.

Clay spun around and grabbed her hands. "Our first time won't be in your parents' house. The moment we're alone, I'm going to show you."

"Show me what?" Madison ran her fingers over his abs and trailed a finger along the waist of his pants. Clay braced himself against the bedroom door. "I'm waiting. Show me what?"

Sunday, 12 December, 5:45 a.m.

Detective Gina Larson stood at the edge of the cliff. The mangled wreckage of a blue car lay on the jagged rocks below. She'd been called to the scene forty-five minutes earlier.

"Survivors?" Gina asked, repositioning her sunglasses over

her eyes. The sun was already above the horizon and brought heat with it.

"Two female occupants. Both deceased. Their identification cards name them as Emma Thompson and Jenna Thompson – cousins or sisters. The car is registered to a Madison Taylor," the first responder said. "Fishermen went past here and spotted the wreckage. They called it in."

"I know Madison Taylor. She was in the station on Friday afternoon. Think she spoke to Detective Evans. I'll talk to him and see if I can track her down."

"With the tide this high, it's going to be a bitch to get the wreckage up. I'll send you my report, Detective."

Gina nodded. "Thanks."

How had a social worker's car ended up at the bottom of a cliff? The car wasn't reported as stolen. Why had the deceased been driving it?

Gina turned around, studying the road. No skid marks – the driver hadn't braked. The guardrail should've held, had the driver kept to the speed limit. A toxicology report would confirm the driver's blood alcohol level. This wasn't the first vehicle to end up at the bottom of the cliff because of an intoxicated driver.

Gina walked back to her car, removing the phone from her back pocket. "Good morning. I need contact details for Madison Taylor, the social worker." She spelled Taylor and ended the call. Before opening the car door, she scanned the scene again.

First the break-in at Madison's apartment, and a few hours later, two women died had in her car. Madison Taylor had some explaining to do.

Chapter 9

Clay rapped his knuckles against Madison's bedroom door. Leaving her the previous night was the second hardest thing he'd ever had to do, in his personal capacity. If her parents hadn't been asleep down the passage, he would've had her in all the ways he'd fantasised about for the past six months. *I have to tell her the truth.*

He knocked again. This time, the door opened. A grey streak sped past him. Clay cursed as hot coffee spilled over the rim of the mug he carried and onto his hand.

"That's what I wanted to do with you last night." Madison leaned against the door.

He took in the sight of her, still flushed from her morning shower. Her damp hair curled around her face. Without makeup, she looked innocent, young, and carefree. Two of those things he knew Madison would never be again.

Clay wanted to see Madison smile like this every day for the rest of her life.

"Good morning. Your coffee." He held the mug towards her.

"I don't want coffee. I want you." She grabbed his shirt and pulled Clay into the room, closing the door. Madison took the mug from his hand, placing it on the bedside table.

Clay walked up behind her. "We need to talk." He ran his hands over her bare arms. "Can you please put some clothes on? The idea of you being naked underneath that towel is driving me insane."

40

Madison turned to face him, placing her hands on his chest. "If you want me out of this towel, remove it and dress me. *If* that's what you want."

Clay grabbed her waist and pulled her closer.

"Well, hello to you too," Madison said to his crotch.

Clay smiled, shaking his head. "I've known you for six months and I still can't get used to you saying everything that comes into your mind."

Madison placed her hands on his shoulders and jumped into his arms, wrapping her legs around him. Clay grabbed her thighs and dug his fingers into the exposed flesh. He brought his mouth against hers and teased her lips with the tip of his tongue. Madison hummed and opened her mouth to him.

Clay pulled away from her. "We need to talk, because if I don't say this now, I never will."

"Okay. But I'm not getting down, unless you tell me you didn't mean what you said last night."

Clay rested his forehead against hers. "My ex broke up with me because of my work. I am who I am, and my work is important to me."

Madison cupped his face in her palms and waited for him to look at her. "I know your work is everything to you. It's one of the many reasons I'm crazy about you."

"Maddie, I work shifts. I might not be able to attend things with you, or be there for your shows."

"Have we not spent all our free time together over the past six months? Did you spend the same amount of time with your ex, or have you only been hanging out with me because you feel obligated to keep an eye on me?"

He eased her down onto the bed. Madison kept her legs locked around his waist. Clay didn't dare to look down to see if the towel had moved, exposing her.

He placed his hands on either side of her head. "I like spending time with you. With my ex, I wanted to be home alone after a hard day or go to the shooting range with my friends in my free time. Now, whenever I have a hard day, all

I can think about is seeing you. And how us being together, trying to cook or watching television, makes it all better. Case in point – Thursday night."

"Neither of us are going into this blind, Clay. You have your work and I have mine. We've been able to work around it and I understand some days you just need me to be there and not talk."

Clay lowered his head, brushing his lips against hers. "We'll figure it out. I just needed you to know."

"I'm not your ex. I'm not dumb enough to let you go." Madison arched her back, pressing against his crotch.

Clay pushed her back down on the bed using his body. Madison bit her bottom lip as he thrust against her.

"No towel?" he asked. Madison shook her head. "Get dressed so we can leave. Six months is a very long time to crave you, Madison Taylor."

Clay stepped back as Madison pushed herself onto her elbows, crossing her ankles.

"I have a question. How are you the sweetest, most patient man I've ever met, yet when it comes to doing the nasty, you're very direct? I like it. I'm just curious. You could write the book on why still waters run *hard*."

Clay smiled at her deliberate mistake. "First, there's nothing *nasty* about what we're going to do. Second, I'll show you *deep*."

Madison blushed and averted his eyes with a smile on her beautiful face. On the bedside table, her phone rang. "I don't know this number." She held the phone towards Clay.

"I do." He took it from her. "Good morning, Gina. This is Clay. What can I do for you?"

"Clay? Why do you have Madison Taylor's cell phone?" Detective Larson asked.

"Because she's in the room with me. Why are *you* calling her?" Clay watched Madison walk into the adjoining bathroom. When she dropped the towel to her feet, he turned away. *Strongest man in the world, a coward as well. I need to tell her.*

"Why are you in the same room at this time of the morning?"

"That's none of your business, Gina. Why are you looking for her? Last I heard, you're with homicide."

"We found her car at the bottom of the cliff at Perry Bay. Both occupants are deceased. I believe her roommate was driving. I need to speak to Madison. Where is she?"

"We're at Lamont Estate in River Valley. I don't want to bring her into the station, I'll explain later. Can you meet us at my place? I'll call you when we get back to Shadow Bay."

"Okay. You still living at The Gables? Must be convenient to live in the same complex as your girlfriend. This is urgent, Clay. I need to talk to Madison and I won't allow you to play guard dog for the first time in your life."

"You have no idea what you're talking about, Gina. I'll call you when we get there." Clay ended the call.

Madison leaned against the bathroom door. "Who's Gina?"

"Maddie, please come sit on the bed."

"No. What happened? Who is Gina, and why is she calling me?"

He walked over to Madison, lifted her up, and carried her to the bed. Clay sat down, keeping Madison on his lap. He placed his mouth against her damp hair and kissed the top of her head. "The police found your car at the bottom of the cliff at Perry Bay. The occupants didn't make it."

Madison covered her mouth with her hands and whispered, "Emma?"

Chapter 10

Sunday, 12 December, 8:00 a.m.

The entire family sat at the dining room table, including the newlyweds who couldn't keep their hands off each other. Madison remembered another morning she'd stood in the doorway watching them. That day, a different shadow had hung over them. This morning, Noa's laughter filled the room. The moment she noticed Madison, she pulled away from Luke. An eerie silence replaced Noa and Luke's joy as the family members turned to Madison.

Clay took her hand and stepped towards the table. "I'm right here, babe."

Madison feigned a smile. "Again, with the pig reference."

"I'll explain why I call you *babe* later," Clay whispered as she sat down in the chair he pulled out for her.

"What happened?" Noa reached for Madison's hand.

Madison touched the scarf around her neck. It was sheer luck her mother had a silk scarf to go with the black dress she'd worn to the wedding. She took a deep breath. "Last night, Emma died in a car accident."

Laura's hands shot to her mouth, and she rushed to Madison's side. She dropped to her knees, wrapping her arms around her child. "I'm so sorry, baby. Her parents must be devastated. I'll take them food later."

"What happened?" Luke and Jamie asked at the same time.

Clay looked at Madison, then at her siblings. "She drove off the cliff at Perry Bay in Madison's car. Her cousin didn't survive either."

"Why are your suitcases outside the door, Slay?" Jamie asked, rubbing her extended belly.

"We're heading to Shadow Bay. The lead detective wants to talk to Maddie, and we need to stop by her apartment to pack some things." Clay turned to Luke. "Can she stay with me while you're away?"

Before Luke could answer, Aaron cleared his throat. "Did you sleep in my daughter's room last night?"

"No, sir." Clay intended to never spend another night without Madison.

"Good. Just remember, I can come over at any time. Activate the motion detection cameras so you can be forewarned. I don't want to walk in on anything. The illusion of Maddie being an innocent young lady is something I want to hold on to for as long as possible."

Clay stared at the plate in front of him before looking at Noa for help. "This family's bluntness is worse than you made it out to be."

"Be careful, my friend. It rubs off on you." Noa took a sip of her coffee and winked at Clay.

"If you didn't like the *rubbing*, you wouldn't have married the *rubber*," Madison said, with her face buried in her mother's shoulder.

Laura released her and kissed the top of Madison's head. "I'll pack you some food if you want to leave now." She then pressed her mouth to Clay's forehead, a gesture Laura did with such ease it had baffled Clay the first couple of times she'd done it. The Taylors were good, honest people, and he loved them all. Not that he'd admit loving Luke to his face. They were manly men – the kicking ass and slamming on cuffs type. In the Taylors, Clay found the family he never had growing up, just as Noa had.

"Laura, Maddie won't eat when she's like this. May I please use your kitchen to make her a smoothie?" Clay asked and pushed to his feet.

Laura grabbed his face with both hands. "You're the

best thing to ever happen to her. We've been able to sleep because we know you're there for Madison when we can't be. It's possible you understand her better than we do. How can we ever repay you?" Laura pulled Clay's face down until her mouth reached his cheek.

"Give him permission to pursue her pants off, like I gave Luke to pursue Noa. Look how well that worked out. My best friend is married to my brother," Jamie said and pulled her shirt from her chest. "Hey, boys, don't make me come in there. Those are my ribs and bladder." She pushed her chair back. "I need to pee."

They watched Jamie leave and laughed. Madison shook her head, covering her face with her hands.

Clay squatted next to her chair. "I'm going to make you something for the road, and will put some honey in it if your mother has any. The way you like it."

She turned to look at him and ran her fingers along his jaw. "My mother is right. What will it take to repay you, Officer Davis?"

Next to her ear, he whispered, "You." Clay eased back. "We need to go meet with Detective Larson and pack your stuff."

Clay stood and walked to the kitchen. He declined Laura's offer of assistance, but Luke wasn't as easily deterred.

Sunday, 12 December, 8:22 a.m.

Clay removed the ingredients from the fridge to find Luke leaning against the counter top. His arms were on either side of him, gripping the marble edge.

"Tell me the truth, Slay. What's going on? We're talking about my baby sister here, so don't bullshit me." Luke stepped to the side and removed a knife from the drawer, handing it to Clay.

Clay rinsed strawberries and quartered them as he spoke. "The truth is, I don't have a clue what's going on. I promise I'll protect Maddie and I know the detective. It's not the same one as yesterday, and believe me, I'm going to ensure they share information."

"What happened yesterday?" Luke removed blueberries from the tray and rinsed them.

"There was a break-in at her apartment. Maddie spent Friday night with me." Clay's hands stilled on the lid of the yoghurt tub. "I haven't touched your sister." *Yet.* "You know we spend time together and some nights I'll fall asleep on her couch, and she fell asleep at my place once. Taylor, I promise you, we slept. Nothing happened."

Luke patted Clay's back and exhaled hard. "No one wants to think their baby sister is having sex. But Maddie isn't a baby anymore and you're a great guy, Slay. You'll be good for her. It goes without saying, if you hurt her, I'll hunt you down and kill you if Noa and Jamie don't beat me to it. Is she okay after everything that happened with *him*?"

"As okay as I think she can be. Maddie is strong and courageous and stubborn and brilliant." *And hot as hell.* "It will always be a part of her, but she needs to move on." Clay poured yoghurt into the blender and tossed in the berries. He reached for the honey and smiled as he squeezed the bottle over the blender.

"You've got it bad, man. Good. Then you're serious about her and we both know you've never been into screwing around. Weird conversation for two men to have." Luke faked a shudder.

"Not if you consider what our women have been through." Clay switched on the blender. The sound drowned out the silence but not the dread swirling inside him.

He switched it off and took the glass bottle Luke held out to him. The Taylors were all about recycling, another thing he admired about them.

"What happened to her neck?" Luke asked.

"Focus on your honeymoon and your wife. I'll take care of Maddie." Clay washed the blender, cutting board, and knife and placed them on the drying rack.

"Slay, you better call me, because Noa will be pissed off if something is going on with Maddie and we're not here to help her. Yes, she can stay with you. Just stay out of our room and off *our* couch when you do *stuff* with my sister. Those are words I never thought I would say." Luke grimaced. "We prepared the guestroom for you and the food in the house is yours. You can take care of Maddie better than any of us, so taking care of King will be a breeze. Ask Maddie to help you with the horses. It'll do her good. So much for you being on vacation for the first time in years. Can I throw a spanner into the works? I've been meaning to talk to you about it, but with the wedding, I was a little sidetracked and I didn't know about the job offer you got."

Clay hung the dishcloth on the rack and grabbed a banana from the bowl. "What spanner?"

"I have a job offer of my own for you. Do you remember the private security company who contacted me to train their employees?" Clay nodded; Luke continued, "It came through, but I can't run the shooting range, the self-defence classes and manage the intensive training these guys need to undergo. Jamie helps, of course, but she needs to slow down for the babies. Think about it. The money is good, better than you're getting now. And you won't need to move to Marcel."

They returned to the dining room where Madison rushed into Clay's arms. "I'm right here. Let's go. We need to get to Shadow Bay and get back here to take care of King. Do you want to stop at Emma's parents on the way back?"

"They're visiting her brother in Dubai. They'll be back as soon as they can get a flight."

Clay and Madison did their rounds of hugs and handshakes, which ended in more hugs and left for Shadow Bay. King sat on the backseat of Clay's SUV, as per Luke's orders.

Chapter 11

He stared at the faces on the computer screen, wondering whether they found it as difficult to decide when they came to Shadow Bay every year. Unlike them, he wasn't a stranger to this game. He knew what waited for her. *Worth the risk.*

Using his private phone, he called her to set up a meeting. He told her what to pack and reminded her that discretion was everything. She wasn't allowed to tell anyone about their meeting, or that she'd be out of town for a few days.

He rubbed his throbbing cock.

The study door opened. "Honey, are you in here?"

"What can I do for you today, my darling wife?" Holding a hand towards her, he used the other to close the browser.

She stepped around the desk and sat on his lap, laughing when she felt his erection against her hip. "I think the question is, what can I do for you?"

"This is why I don't want children. Nothing beats starting the day the right way, here on the desk."

"We've been together long enough that you should know how much I hate sex this early in the day." She stood.

He grabbed her arms, lifting her up onto the desk. "Let's play a game. Your name is Madison."

***

49

Sunday, 12 December, 10:00 a.m.

Madison reached for King's leash, letting him out of the SUV. Clay held her hand as they walked up the flight of stairs to his apartment. A gorgeous redhead waited for them; Madison had seen her before.

"Maddie, Detective Gina Larson. Gina, Madison Taylor." Clay made the introductions while unlocking the door.

The reality of Emma's death struck Madison hard. She bent down to remove King's leash, desperate to hide her emotions from Detective Larson. Fear? Anger? Shock? Madison didn't know which one gut-punched her the hardest. But seeing a homicide detective made it all too real. Her best friend was gone. Forever.

King ran into Clay's apartment and jumped on the couch. His blue eyes focused on Madison until she sat down next to him.

Clay knew better than to get between Madison and King, allowing the dog to remain in the middle.

Detective Larson took a seat facing them. "I'm sorry for your loss, Miss Taylor," she said, holding her phone.

"Call me Madison."

"Okay, Madison. Why was Emma driving your car?"

"She borrowed it, as hers is in for repairs."

"Did Emma often drink and drive?"

Madison pursed her lips. "Sure, when we were students, but Emma wouldn't have been drinking last night."

"You're *still* a student." Detective Larson didn't look up from her phone.

"Technically, yes. I'm doing my masters." Madison stroked King's back.

"In social work?"

"Yes. Detective, we've often seen each other at the station whenever I'm there because of my work. Surely, it's a waste of time asking questions you already have the answers to?"

Detective Larson's eyes shifted from her phone and focused

on Clay. "Why didn't you want to meet at the station?"

Clay turned to Madison. She nodded and removed the scarf from her neck. Madison lifted her head, giving Detective Larson a clear view of the scar.

"On Friday, Madison spoke to Detective Evans in Missing Persons, regarding her concerns about the disappearances of several sex workers over the past few years."

"Let her talk, Clay," Detective Larson said. "You've spent a lot of time at the station over the past year talking about missing prostitutes."

"Yes, I have. And no one seems to give a damn because they're *sex workers* and not from rich or powerful families. As Clay mentioned, on Friday I met with Detective Evans. I left the station and had dinner with friends. When I got to my car, I was attacked. A man came out of nowhere, slammed me into my car, choked me with something, and threatened me before he disappeared. It happened so quickly I couldn't get my gun or my knife out."

"You carry a gun and a knife?"

Madison's head tilted to the right. "Don't you?"

Detective Larson smiled, typing on her phone. Madison knew from experience that few detectives still wrote in notebooks. "What did your attacker say?"

"He told me to stop caring about whores. Not a direct quote."

Clay reached for Madison's hand. "You need to tell her." Madison shook her head, staring at their joined hands. "This might be related, Maddie. Gina can do some digging. If it's not him, then at least we'll know."

"What's going on?" Gina placed her phone on a small side table and leaned forward.

"To protect my identity, my name wasn't mentioned during the trial." Madison took a deep breath and exhaled, shaking her head. "My attacker said, 'Just because one serial killer was soft on you, doesn't mean the next one will be. No one cares about whores, Madison.'"

"Only a handful of people know about what happened to Madison six months ago. I believe her attacker is either a police officer or *he* sent someone after Madison," Clay said.

Detective Larson's perfectly shaped eyebrows contracted. "Who is *he?*"

"Foster Ericson, aka Eric Foster." Madison saw the flash of recognition on Detective Larson's face.

"Shit. You're the last woman he abducted."

Clay tried to move King, but the dog snuggled closer to Madison, resting half his body on her lap. "On Friday night, someone broke into Madison's apartment. I think it's related to the attack earlier that evening. And last night her friend died. Was it an accident?"

"Can't say for sure yet. But once the car is recovered, it will be examined and Emma Thompson's blood alcohol level report is, of course, crucial."

Madison shook her head hard. "Emma wouldn't have been drinking."

"Eyewitnesses put her at a bar last night."

"She hasn't touched a drop of alcohol in over three years, not since her boyfriend died in a car crash while intoxicated. Emma was not drinking last night. Ask the waitress, waiter, or the bartender. I don't care who. You'll see when you get her tox screen back. Emma was sober." Madison pushed to her feet. "Are we done here? I need to pack. I can't wait to walk into the apartment I shared with my life-long best friend who died in *my* car."

Madison grabbed King's leash and he rushed to her side without being called. She clipped the leash and kept her head bowed. Tears dripped onto King's head as she bent down to hug him. "I'm going to get a house with a garden and you're coming to stay with me. Noa has Luke now. I need you more than she does," she whispered.

Chapter 12

Blade sat with his feet in the infinity pool. He smiled down at the woman between his legs, her arms resting on his thighs. The wind rustled his hair as the sun warmed his back.

"I'm going to keep you," he said to the woman who called herself Vegas. "What's your real name?"

Vegas rubbed her cheek against his inner thigh. "You know the rules, *Blade*. No real names. Nothing, except this." Her face moved closer to his crotch.

Blade slipped into the water, pulling her closer. "You're more than a lay. Have you forgotten you're a woman who deserves life? Let me take care of you."

Vegas pushed away from him, keeping her hands on his shoulder. "Like a sugar daddy?"

"No. Not a man paying you for sex. Someone who treats you with respect and wants to take care of you."

"I'm not good at anything except sex." Vegas shrugged, lowering her body until she rubbed against him. Blade's body didn't react. "It seems I'm not good at that either."

"Oh, you are, but there's more to you than that. What did you want to be when you were growing up?"

"I won't play this game with you. I refuse to tell you personal things about myself to have you laugh at me behind my back. At the end of this *vacation*, you'll return to your perfect life, and I'll go back to reality. Last night, you said you wanted me for the rest of our time together. If you meant it, I'll be yours. But more than that? No. I'm not stupid."

Blade reached for her face. "Give me a chance when we leave here. You're a beautiful woman and your laugh makes me laugh. Since our first day here, you haven't stopped checking on the other women. You're protective of them." He brushed his mouth against hers. Not the way a man kissed a woman when paying for her time. But the way a man would kiss his lover. "What's your name?"

Vegas touched her mouth. Tears threatened to spill from her eyes.

"Please give me a chance to show you what life can be like." Blade pressed his lips to her wet cheeks. "You must have met someone good to know there are honourable people in this world. Forget about *how* we met. It doesn't matter."

"There is one good person I know. A social worker. I like her."

"Then I like her too. Okay, let's make a deal. When we leave, we can share our names. I'm not leaving you on this island. You might not trust me now, but you will. I promise."

Blade kissed Vegas again, long and slow.

He hoped she would realise how much was at stake.

Sunday, 12 December, 11:15 a.m.

Once the knife had sliced through the crime scene tape, Madison returned it to her pocket. She lifted the keys to the lock but couldn't control the shake of her hand to unlock the door.

Clay covered her hand with his, his other steady against her stomach, and helped her unlock the door. "I'm right here," he murmured.

Madison eased the door open. Her vision blurred. Emma's presence hit her from every direction. They had lived together for over three years. They'd been friends since their first day of school. A lifetime's friendship behind them and the years ahead had been ripped away.

She walked through their apartment, taking in the carnage that surrounded her.

The sofa they'd bought second-hand brought a smile to Madison's face until she stepped closer. Pieces of sponge protruded from the gashes in the material.

Madison jerked her head towards the refrigerator her parents had given them as it began its mechanical hum. Photos of her and Emma throughout the years held to its surface by magnetic letters they had used to leave each other notes for laughs or reminders.

Her heart ached to hear her friend's comforting voice. Madison steadied herself using the back of the couch.

Clay came closer and rubbed her back. "You can wait outside. I'll pack what you need."

The rhythmic movement of his hands grounded her. Madison turned around, burying her face in his shirt. "Emma wasn't drinking."

"I know. We will figure out what happened to her." Clay placed his fingers under her chin, easing Madison's head up. "Let me do this for you."

"No. I need to do this. Just wait right here."

Madison took a step towards her bedroom; Clay's fingers wrapped around her arm. "The message on your bedroom wall didn't say *Stop*." Madison froze. "It's a crude picture of a penis."

"It's a dildo. Let me guess, it's pink." She swallowed the bile rising in her throat.

"Let me pack your things. Maddie, you don't need to do this."

She yanked her arm from Clay's grasp and stormed to her room. Entering her room, Madison turned and stared at the pink drawing next to the door frame.

The bed broke her fall, yet her eyes remained glued to the drawing. "Noa should've killed him. *You* should've shot him. I should've killed him."

Madison leapt to her feet. Her fist connected with the

wooden door. "I. Will. Kill. Him." She kept punching until King's bark forced her to look at him.

Sunday, 12 December, 11:30 a.m.

Clay removed a pack of peas from the freezer and wrapped it in a dishcloth. "You should've waited outside." He removed three bottles of water from the fridge and handed one to Gina. Filling a bowl with water, Clay placed it on the floor. King lapped at it and returned to lie outside Madison's room.

"You met her when she was rescued?" Gina twisted the cap on the bottle.

"Yes."

"She's not your sister, Clay." Gina placed the half-empty bottle on the tabletop and peeked over her shoulder at Madison's bedroom door.

Clay shook his head. "I'm not even going to justify that comment with a reply. I expected more from you."

"Just because my sister broke up with you doesn't mean I stopped caring about you. Dammit, Clay, you're my boyfriend's teammate. By the way, congratulations on the job offer. When are you leaving?"

"I'm not." Clay tossed his empty bottle into the dustbin.

"She's too young for you, Clay. You *can't* turn down an opportunity like this. Not for this damaged girl. You feel protective of Madison because she's the age your sister was when she died."

Clay rolled his shoulders, turning his back on Gina. "If you can't remain objective with this investigation, you need to excuse yourself from the case. I won't allow you and your unfounded opinion of Madison to harm her, her deceased friend, or the missing women."

"You believe her stories?" Gina snorted. "By the way, my sister misses you."

Clay spun around. "What do you expect me to say to that?

Penelope left me. And I realise now it would never have worked between us. I wasn't in love with her."

"You dated for over a year, Clay. The problem was Penelope didn't *need* you, unlike this one who needs a big, strong hero."

Clay leaned closer to Gina. "You're right, your sister didn't need *me*. She just needed *a* boyfriend. *Someone* to stroke her ego, tell her she's beautiful, and worship the ground she walks on. It'll always be all about Penelope. Her rough day booking overseas holidays for rich people. Her hair that didn't fall the way she wanted it to. *Everything* was always about her. So much so, Penelope cheated on me."

"She cheated because you always put your job first. You were never around."

"Because I didn't want to be around her. I should've left her, or never even dated her. Dammit, Gina, she never even bothered to ask why my nickname is Slay."

A name the team had jumped on when their commander's then three-year-old hadn't been able to pronounce C and had ended up calling him Slay at a team Christmas party.

Clay ran his hands down his face. "If you can't do your job objectively, and to the best of your abilities, I'll ensure you're removed from this case."

Gina held his stare. "What is she going to do when she finds out you're moving to Marcel?"

"Nothing, because I'm not going."

Movement behind Gina caught Clay's eye.

Madison stood in her bedroom door, suitcases behind her. As Clay walked closer, he noticed her red eyes, even though Madison refused to look at him. He gave her the bag of peas and told her to place it on her hand.

Madison stepped out of the way for Clay to grab the suitcases and removed her phone from her back pocket. "We need to make a stop on the way." Madison pressed the bag of peas against her eyes instead.

Chapter 13

Underneath the table, Claire rubbed her hands together, trying not to pull on her cuticles. She grabbed her phone and read the message again, trying to calculate how long it would take Madison to get to the coffee shop. Calculating time had never been Claire's thing, she only had grade nine to her name. Counting money to make sure a john didn't stiff her, she learned on the street.

A bell chimed. Claire eased back into the chair as her friend stepped through the door. An unfamiliar man with a grey dog followed behind Madison. The man sat down at the table closest to the door. The dog stayed by his side.

Madison smiled and waved, making her way past the other tables. This was one of the reasons the girls loved Madison – she never acted as if she didn't know them. Any onlooker would think they were friends meeting for coffee. Madison always insisted on meeting in a coffee shop or a restaurant and didn't allow them to leave without finishing a meal, which she always paid for.

"Hello sweetie, I'm so glad you sent me a message. I've been meaning to talk to you since Friday, but I've been a little busy." Madison pulled the scarf from her neck, taking a seat next to Claire.

Claire gasped at the sight of the horrible red mark running across Madison's throat. "What happened?"

"Guess I'm finally asking the right questions or pissing off the right person. Which is a good thing." Madison hugged

Claire and kept her voice low. "I keep my promises."

Claire reached for the glass of water, but yanked her hand back. She lifted her head towards the man and the dog. "Personal protection?"

"Just a friend and my sister-in-law's dog. I'm watching him while they are away. But we're not here to talk about me. What's going on?" Madison placed a hand on Claire's.

"I'm worried about Natalie. I still haven't heard from her. And I got a job, not the kind you're hoping for. I'll be gone for a week or so, and I don't want you to worry when you don't see me around."

"You look nervous. What's wrong?"

"I can't tell you. It's part of the job requirement, discretion is everything." Claire stared at the table. "I'm sorry."

"Claire, please tell me what's going on. I can protect you."

"No, it's not that. It's … for this job, I had to pack for a week."

"Shit." Madison released Claire's hand and pushed her unruly hair behind her ears. "You can't go. I'm going to call the police and let them handle this."

"No, you can't. If he has them, he'll kill them if he suspects someone tipped off the police. I've been attending your brother's self-defence classes with you for a year now. I can take care of myself." Claire smiled with more confidence than she felt.

Madison shook her head. "I can't let you do this. We will find out what's going on. I promise."

"Madison, I didn't come here to ask for your permission. I bought a gun yesterday, and I know what I'm walking into. The money is good; enough to get me off the streets for at least three months." Claire shrugged. "If I'm wrong, we can laugh about it when I see you again."

"Is the gun legal?"

Claire couldn't look at her friend. Most nineteen-year-old girls didn't own a gun for the fun of it, least of all a registered one.

Madison reached into her pocket. "Here, take this, leave the gun. This is easier to conceal. Do you still have a second phone?"

Claire slipped the knife into the pocket of her jeans. "Yes, why?"

"Hide it in your luggage, or somewhere someone who might look can't find it. Send me a message when you get to your destination. Use our code words if you think you're in danger. And remember to include a place close to where you are." Madison wrapped her arms around Claire. "I don't like this. I told you I'd give you money to stay off the job until I've figured out what's going on."

"I can't take your money. You don't earn much, and don't even try to deny it. How many times have you bought stuff for us out of your own pocket and I'm not talking about meals?"

Madison smiled and cupped Claire's cheeks. "You're worth so much more. I'm really trying and I think maybe now the police will listen."

Claire smirked. "Guess how many of them are our clients? I can count my regulars on both hands. That's not to mention the others' regulars. I'll be safe, I promise." *I hope.*

She stood and walked past the man and the dog, wishing the men who paid her were half as attractive as Madison's friend. *Wouldn't need to fake it with him.*

Sunday, 12 December, 12:55 p.m.

Rows of vineyards streamed past, making way for trees and open fields with grazing cows and horses. The scenery remained blurred, no matter how many times Madison wiped her eyes. Neither she nor Clay had uttered a single word since leaving the coffee shop.

He reached for her hand and lifted it to his mouth. "I'm right here, Madison. Talk to me."

Madison pulled her hand back. "Please take me to my

parents. I can't deal with all this right now." Her eyes fixed on the passenger side window, blinded by tears.

"Not once in the past six months have you shut me out. Don't start now." Clay slowed the SUV and turned onto the dirt road leading to Luke and Noa's farm.

"Dammit, Clay, I asked you to take me to my parents."

"I will. As soon as we've talked."

Madison undid her seat belt and grabbed the door handle. "Stop. I'm getting out."

Clay slammed the brakes. A cloud of dust enveloped the SUV.

Madison jumped out and ran into the field, King right behind her. Noa's mare walked up to her, keeping an eye on King, who remained at a distance. Madison rubbed the thoroughbred's brown muzzle, before wrapping her arms around the horse's neck. She held onto the horse, listening to Clay's SUV continue the drive towards the house.

"Can I go back to last night?" she asked the horse, who nudged Madison's hand until she rubbed the mare's muzzle again. "Emma was alive. I hadn't yet admitted to Clay that I want him. Now Claire is walking into who knows what. And I can't do a damn thing to stop any of it."

Madison stared at the house. Clay stood next to the black SUV, watching her.

"I love him so much. I can't keep any of the women safe." She tried to control her breathing and sank to her knees. The mare stepped backwards. "He's going to kill me. He warned me in his letters. I knew this was coming. Detective Bitch is right – I'm damaged."

Chapter 14

Sunday, 12 December, 1:27 p.m.

Detective Larson placed her phone on the desk, mulling over her conversation with Detective Evans. He had relayed much of what Madison had told her. With Evans' caseload, Gina understood why he didn't have time to investigate the disappearances Madison had brought to his attention. Gina agreed that most of the women had probably moved on. But the circumstances of the bodies they'd found in Potters Park nagged at her.

Gina accessed the case files on her computer. No matter how long she'd been a homicide detective, there were still things that shocked her. The images in the photos were going to be lodged in her memory forever.

Five women had been brutally murdered; they remained unidentified. Gina reached for the Ziploc bag containing a hairbrush which lay on her desk. Madison had given it to her while Clay carried her suitcases to his SUV.

Gina leaned back in her chair and stared at the dark hair caught in the brush's bristles. It wasn't necessary for her to approve of Clay's infatuation with Madison. She didn't even need to like Madison as a person. But everyone in the department knew Madison Taylor played a big role in keeping the sex workers safe, as well as those who were forced into prostitution. Over the past two years, Madison had given them valuable information on drugs, arms and human traffickers.

It was a matter of time before someone came after her.

Foster Ericson. Not many details about the investigation and subsequent trial had been publicised. Gina accessed the case files. Six months earlier, Foster Ericson, aka Eric Foster, had murdered five people. He had tortured and murdered three women, as well as seducing a police officer to get information from her regarding the investigation. Then he'd killed her. Ericson's only male victim had been Madison's sister-in-law's therapist, Benjamin Clarke. After Clarke's death and Ericson's arrest, the police discovered Clarke had been a serial killer too. His total body count was higher than Ericson's.

So many unnecessary deaths, all because of Foster Ericson's decade-long infatuation with Noa Morgan, now Noa Taylor. He'd stalked her for years.

And then he had set his sights on Madison.

Foster Ericson would spend the rest of his life in prison. But Gina knew better than to assume his incarceration would protect Madison.

Sunday, 12 December, 1:52 p.m.

Sunlight danced on her. The wind tugged at her blonde hair and the scarf around her neck. Madison was the most beautiful creature he'd ever seen. Clay's heart ached for her. He knew the weight she carried because of her work. And what had been stripped from her since Madison had met Foster Ericson.

He never thought of her as the almost nude woman a serial killer had held captive in a wine cellar. In Madison, he saw beauty, strength, resilience, and his future. *I love her.*

King nudged Clay's arm and he petted the dog without taking his eyes off Madison.

When she opened the passenger side door, Clay stood up from the top step of the porch. He held his breath, waiting for her to face him. Madison didn't.

She removed her phone and stared at the screen. Clay felt his heartbeat in his throat and he clenched his fists. He closed the distance between them without her acknowledging his presence. Clay reached for her, but pulled his hands back.

"I call you *babe* because every time I see you, you take my breath away. You have no idea how beautiful you are. That makes you even more beautiful. Your heart is the most breathtaking part about you. I've wanted you since the first time we spoke here, in this house … I could smell you on my SWAT jacket."

Clay took a deep breath, and continued, "Do you remember when I met your parents? You were returning from a ride with your mother. You laughed even though your horse ran at full speed. In all my life, I'd never seen or heard anything so beautiful. I love that you share your work with me and cry about the women and young girls you can't save, but you still try. Madison, you're out on the streets every day, putting your life in danger for them. People have already forgotten about the bodies of the five women who were found in Potters Park, yet you keep talking about them and asking the police questions. You're everything I never thought I'd find in one person. When I look at you, I realise I've never been in love, because what I feel for you is so much more than my brain can comprehend."

He touched her shoulders, taking a step closer. Madison dropped her head forward as Clay pressed his lips to the exposed skin of her neck.

"Why are you telling me this?" Madison placed her hands on his.

"Because you need to know." He feathered kisses along the back of her neck.

"For months, I didn't allow myself to hope you'd want me, and now you're leaving. My best friend is dead. Emma died in *my* car. Claire is out there, probably with the others, and I'm powerless to protect them. And …" She sucked in her cheeks.

"I'm not going anywhere, Maddie." Clay wrapped his arms around her waist. "I'm never leaving you."

"You have to. It's your dream to go and work with the team

in Marcel again. I won't ask you to stay."

"Did you not hear when I told Gina that I'm not leaving?"

"You should go. This morning we spoke about how important your job is to you. It's one of the many reasons I ..."

Moisture dripped onto Clay's arms. "I thought about asking you to come with me, thinking a change of scenery might be good for you after what happened. But there's no way in hell I'm giving you up, Madison. Not for a job. Not for anything. At the end of the day, it's just a job. I want a life with you. I want to be at all the special family dinners, hold you every night, do the night feeds and nappy changes, all of it."

For years Clay had wondered whether he'd be a good father. His father had been the opposite of Madison's. *I have to tell her and let her decide if she still wants me.*

"Are you pregnant? Or did I get pregnant from kissing?" He didn't have to see Madison's face to know she asked it with a smile.

"The way Jamie and Spencer are together, and how they interact with the twins, even though they're not born yet, I want that with you. Not right now. Way too much other stuff I'd like to do with you first."

"This just got real." Madison turned in his arms, placing her hands on his cheeks. "You need to go and be the same superhero who saved me to other people."

"I'm not leaving. Luke offered me a job and it will give me the opportunity to have the life I want. What do you want, Maddie?"

"All my girls and young women off the streets. Emma to be alive. You. Everything you said – children, memories, all of it. But I can't let you take a job with Luke when you're capable of so much more."

Clay pressed his mouth to her forehead. "Do you trust me?"

"I'm not even going to justify that with an answer."

He took her hand, leading Madison into the house, and walked straight to the pantry. Clay opened the door and grabbed the lighter from the shelf. "Trust me."

He switched off the overhead light. Madison took his hand with both of hers.

Clay pulled her against him. "This is going to sound cheesy, but I need to explain something to you, so just wait before you laugh or say something funny." He kissed the top of her head.

Madison wrapped her arms around his waist and he could feel the tension ease from her body.

Darkness surrounded them.

"This was my life. I've told you about my father dying and my mother becoming an alcoholic. There were moments of light, such as the day I graduated, when I got accepted into the police academy and when I made SWAT." Three orange tongues became visible in the dark. "Every person we saved, bust we made, arrests, all of them are more flickers of light. But it was brief, and the darkness remained, suffocating me. Then one day, I carried *you* out of that cellar."

Clay flicked the lighter again, the flame visible longer than the previous ones.

"Then I heard you laugh long before I saw you riding your horse that day. Hold on." Clay stepped back, opened the pantry door, and reached for the light switch. They both blinked at the sudden brightness. "Every day since, this has been my life."

Madison glanced around. "Groceries? Life with me is tinned food, cereal, oh, at least a slab of chocolate and some other snacks."

She smirked when Clay pulled her into his arms. He lifted her until they were eye to eye.

"Yes. No. Madison Taylor, you're my light. Nothing I mentioned matters if you're not in my life to share it. Before meeting you, I celebrated the wins on my own, or had a quick drink with the team, but now I celebrate all of it with you. And sharing it with you makes everything more real."

Madison closed her eyes. "I'm damaged, Clay. You deserve better."

"I'm going to strangle Gina. You're not damaged. I've never seen you as damaged, and I never will. You're mine, Maddie. If you get cracks, because life happens, I'll glue you back together by loving you every single day, and ordering pizza as often as you want."

"The pizza is important. Without it, this won't work. I want extra cheese, and—"

"Pepperoni. Or avocado if it's chicken. And enough garlic to kill a village of vampires."

"You don't have to decide today about working with Luke or going to Marcel. If you choose to go to Marcel, I'll go with you as soon as I know what happened to the women."

"Marcel isn't an option. I can't leave my mom here, and moving her isn't the best thing for her. Our lives are here, Maddie. I can always work part-time with the team in Shadow Bay. Are you my girl?"

Madison wrapped her legs around his waist. "Are we in the eighth grade?"

"I need *you* to know that you're mine. If it means asking you to be my girlfriend, then so be it."

Madison brushed her mouth against his, but didn't smile. "I feel selfish to have this with you when death and destruction surround us."

"You deserve a moment of light amid all the darkness. I promise, soon you'll only see light. We'll find out what happened to the women."

"I've always been your girl, Clay Davis. I kissed a bunch of frogs to get to you and I have no intention of letting you go. However, we need to talk about the narcissistic chameleon."

Chapter 15

Claire loaded her suitcase into the back of the black sedan and patted her back pocket. Her second phone was hidden inside her suitcase. Claire hoped she wouldn't need it.

When other little girls dreamt about being princesses, mermaids or fairies, Claire had already known she'd have to resort to selling her body to survive. Girls like her didn't have other options, not when faced with the cruelty of life from birth.

The man sitting in the driver's seat was one of her regulars. Adam. That's what he called himself. Despite hiding his real name, he never hid his true nature. All the girls hated him. Adam left marks on their bodies and scars on their souls.

You can't charge full price when you're a bruised and broken whore.

Claire reached for the seatbelt, realising the odds of dying at this man's hands were greater than getting into a car crash. She tried to remember the word her English teacher had called situations like this. *Iron-something.*

Adam placed a hand on her knee, dragging it along her thigh. Claire bit back the scream when his pinkie touched her. She wondered how it would feel to be touched by a man when you wanted him to touch you, when the brush of a pinkie brought anticipation, not dread. Claire had never experienced anticipation, lust, or love.

"It's a pity we don't have time for a quickie. Once we reach our destination, you'll have to pay me for being your personal driver." Adam fired up the engine and stepped on the accelerator, keeping within the speed limit.

Claire shifted in her seat. "Where are we going? You didn't say much when you called." She chewed on a cuticle.

"Don't do that, baby. You need to be perfect for them," Adam said without taking his eyes from the road.

"Them?" The taste of copper filled her mouth. Claire stared at her finger. A red spot appeared at the corner of her thumbnail.

"Did you think I paid you this much for one guy? No baby, you're going to have the time of your life."

Claire wiped the blood on the passenger seat.

Adam brought the car to a halt and stepped out. "Hurry, you don't want to be late."

"I've never been on a boat." Claire wondered which of the boats would take her to hell. "Adam, I need to use the bathroom. Is there one around here?"

Adam marched around the back of the car, scanning the parking lot. He grabbed a fist full of her hair, yanking her out of the car. "We don't have time for this." He pushed his tongue into her mouth. "Go. Before I deliver you to them, you better thank me for allowing you to pee. And you, my sweet girl, know what I like."

Claire grabbed his crotch and tried to calm the disgust raging inside her. "Thank you. I'll do that thing you *love*, the one with my teeth." She nipped at his mouth.

"Hurry." Adam pushed her away so hard she stumbled backwards.

Claire rushed to the bathroom, next to the vacant space, which had once been a seafood restaurant. She locked herself in a cubicle, yanked her phone from her pocket, and sent a text message to Madison. *I shouldn't have come.*

Before walking out of the bathroom Claire took a deep breath, despite the foul smell that hung in the small space.

Adam waited with her suitcase by his feet. "Give me your phone."

Claire held it out to him with a steady hand.

He snatched it from her and checked the call log and messages. "Good girl. I'm going to hang onto this. You don't need it where you're going."

Sunday, 12 December, 2:30 p.m.

Madison forced her mouth from Clay's. He had carried her out of the pantry to the forbidden couch. She trailed her fingers over the stubble on his jaw. Kissing Clay was her new favourite thing.

"What are you thinking about?" Clay gazed down at her with a satisfied grin on his face.

"What it will be like to be naked with you." Madison swivelled her hips, pressing her groin against his. She heard a moan and realised it had come from her.

Clay pressed his mouth to her neck and whispered, "I think it's time we—" Madison's phone rang. He turned his head and glared at the phone laying on the coffee table. "Whatever it is, it can wait a few hours."

"Hours? My, my, aren't you full of yourself?"

Clay rubbed himself against her. "You're going to be."

Again, Madison heard a moan. This time, it came from Clay. She loved Clay's directness. The weight of his body on hers. *Too many clothes.* She drew a deep breath. "It's from one of my friends. I have a specific alert tone for them."

Clay pressed his mouth to hers for a quick kiss and eased himself off her.

Madison stared at the bulge in his jeans, drawing her bottom lip between her teeth. "I want him." She pointed at Clay's crotch.

"Oh, he wants you too." Clay walked to the kitchen and leaned his head against the refrigerator.

Madison dragged her eyes from his butt and reached for her phone.

Claire: Hello, are we having coffee soon? Found a stunning little café at the marina. xoxo

"Call Detective Larson. She needs to send officers to the marina. Claire is in danger." Madison dialled Claire's number. Her call was rejected. On the second try, it went straight to voicemail.

Sunday, 12 December, 2:38 p.m.

Adam cursed as her left foot snagged on a fishing net. The roar of an engine made him jerk his head up. He turned and ran towards the car, keeping his head down and his body as low to the ground as possible.

As the car sped through the gates, he removed the bitch's phone from his pocket. Keeping one eye on the road, he read the message again. *Fuck*. The phone rang for the second time. *Madison*.

He pulled into the emergency lane and switched on the hazards. From the glove compartment, Adam retrieved a voice changer. It had served its purpose in gold.

The phone rang again. He held the device to the speaker. "Hello, Madison. Another whore is dead because of you. Poor, sweet, innocent Claire. Tsk, tsk, tsk. I warned you, but did you listen? Foster will be happy to hear that you kept his letters. I guess you really love him. See you soon, *Madison*." He ended the call without giving her a chance to speak.

Adam lowered his window, removed the battery from the phone, used his shirt to wipe his prints and then tossed it into the tall grass.

He eased the car back into the lane and sped up. His knuckles turned white as he held onto the steering wheel.

Adam couldn't risk having more detectives looking into the disappearances of his girls.

Madison Taylor had to die.

Chapter 16

Sunday, 12 December, 2:43 p.m.

Madison slumped down on the couch, gripping the phone tight. *Claire's dead.*

Clay sat on the coffee table and eased the phone out of Madison's death grip. "I spoke to Gina. Officers were dispatched to the marina. She'll contact me as soon as she knows anything." He sighed. "What did he imply with Foster's letters?"

Madison dropped her head. No way around it. The cat was out of the bag and coughing up a decomposing fur ball. "He sent letters addressed to Emma. After she read the first one, she realised it was meant for me. Foster isn't allowed to contact me and the corrections officers read all of his outgoing mail. The letters were very cryptic, but I knew it was him, and what he was implying."

"Where are the letters now?" Clay knelt in front of Madison.

"The man on the phone broke into my apartment and took the letters. I looked for them when I was busy packing my things. They're gone." Madison pushed her fingers through her hair and stared at the hardwood floor. "I think he attacked me. He killed Claire."

Sunday, 12 December, 3:00 p.m.

A woman's foot, caught in a discarded fishing net, was all

Detective Larson could see as she walked along the pier closer to where two uniformed officers stood.

What the hell is Madison involved in?

Gina stopped walking.

The red hair of a young woman drifted on the water. The body gently swayed like an upside-down slow dance.

Footsteps on the wooden planks became louder. "Detective Larson," said a familiar voice.

Gina remained focused on the victim. *You're so young.* "Doctor Seymour." She turned to the officers who had arrived at the scene first. Water dripped from the younger officer's hair and his uniform stuck to his body. "Did you check her pulse?"

"Yes. We got here, saw her foot, I jumped in, checked her pulse, but there wasn't one. I then swam to the ladder down there to get out." He pointed towards the end of the pier.

"When can we bring her up and check for identification?" Gina asked, looking at her wristwatch.

"It's going to take a while. My team should arrive any minute. Go do your thing, Detective. I'll call you as soon as we're ready to move her." Doctor Seymour shook her head. Gina had noticed her doing this whenever the victims were young.

"Thank you. Where is Doctor O'Reilly? I need to speak to him about the remains found in Potters Park."

"He's on vacation and won't be back until early January. I can access the files and run you through his notes."

"Thanks. I'll still call him as he was at the scene and did the autopsies. Hate to intrude while Doctor O'Reilly is on a much-needed vacation, but this can't wait."

Doctor Seymour stepped aside when her team arrived, allowing them to start processing the scene. "He can't be reached."

"What do you mean?" Gina scratched the back of her neck.

"Wherever he is, there's no reception."

In this day and age people were only unreachable when they chose to be. Gina headed back to her car and gave instructions to the junior officers. She scanned the parking lot and the few surrounding buildings.

Underneath the weather-beaten bathroom sign, a surveillance camera pointed towards her.

Sunday, 12 December, 5:05 p.m.

The horses were back in the stable and taken care of, as per Luke's strict instructions. King ran around in the garden. Clay sat on the porch swing, trying to gather the strength to face Madison. Gina had called him while he was alone in the stables.

Madison walked out the front door and stopped when Clay's eyes met hers. "Did they find Claire?"

"Gina asked that you go to Shadow Bay tomorrow morning to identify the body. Why did Claire ask you to meet for coffee?"

Madison's legs failed. She sank down on the porch, pressing her palms to her eyes. "Hello means help. Breakfast is for another girl. The sender will include her name to tell me *who* is in trouble. Lunch is for an average john. Dinner for someone we have spoken about, like a pimp or someone else who has been giving them problems. Coffee is the word we use for a police officer."

"You're saying a police officer murdered Claire?" Clay stood and helped Madison to her feet.

"Yes." Madison rubbed her temples. "We need to find out who has had contact with Foster."

Clay pressed his lips to her hair. "Gina is looking into it."

Madison turned and stared towards her parents' farm, wrapping her arms around her waist. "Clay, I need to do something. I can't just sit here and wait for another message. I don't know what to do. For more than a week, I haven't been able to reach five of the women I'm trying to get out of this line of work, this life. Claire was desperate to find her friend

Natalie. I suspect one of the bodies found in Potters Park might be Angie – Claire's sister. Gina has Angie's hairbrush. The crime lab can compare it to the DNA from the bodies." Madison covered her face with her hands. "Why didn't Claire listen to me?"

Chapter 17

Sunday, 12 December, 6:17 p.m.

Archer slapped Jersey's butt before pulling her down on his lap. "You're someone else's tonight. Sorry sweety, but I haven't played Vegas yet."

Jersey pouted, pressing her chest to his face. "Are you sure? She hasn't been out of Blade's room since after lunch."

"What the heck, you're good enough for another night." Archer lifted her and licked at Jersey's nipple through her bikini top.

"You know how to make a girl feel wanted."

"This isn't about you, remember? You're here for us. You open your legs and mouth, get paid a lot of money for your skills, and you get to be here." He extended his arms at shoulder height.

Jersey reached for her gin and tonic, emptying the glass in one gulp. Archer was right. The money was great, and she had never seen a house this big, let alone slept in one. She could go skinny dipping and sunbathe nude. No one was around to complain when they earned their keep on the beach. Here, no one heard you scream. The rooms had to be soundproof.

Blade and Vegas strolled past, hand in hand. Jersey wished she could spend the night with him. Blade was an enigma. *A unicorn.*

Their first night on the island, she'd been confused when all he'd wanted to do was talk. Jersey knew what she was being paid for and had touched him first. Blade hadn't wanted to have sex with her, no matter what she'd tried. It brought her to tears when he'd continued talking to her as if she was an actual human being and not a whore. Blade's embrace had been warm when she reached for the bedroom door, and then he touched her and focused on *her* pleasure. He kept telling her she was a beautiful woman who deserved more. Sure, Jersey might've had the occasional orgasm with a john, but that was sheer luck. Luck which left her feeling dirty and emptier than she had become accustomed to. Being with Blade hadn't left her feeling like week-old garbage.

Archer moved her bikini bottom to the side and touched her bare skin with a calloused finger.

This is the last game. Next year, I'm going to find a proper job.

Jersey opened her legs.

Sunday, 12 December, 6:30 p.m.

The garage door opened. He drove in, closing the door before switching the engine off. This was the house they'd always dreamed of owning, but on Adam's salary they wouldn't have been able to afford it. Not even with his wife's income as a nurse could they have considered buying it. Many people worked second jobs. He saw his side business as a means to an end. Soon, they'd leave it all behind and retire on a tropical island. As long as there was sun, sea, sand, and sluts, he'd be a happy man.

His wife stood in the doorway, connecting the garage to the scullery. "You're back early?"

"I didn't get to take her to the island." Adam kissed his wife's cheek, walking past her.

"What happened?"

"The dumb whore sent a message to that bitch, Madison Taylor. Her last message was deleted, but Claire didn't realise her phone would show *who* her last message was sent to. I killed her just to be safe and as an extra warning to the nosy little social worker." Adam removed a glass from the shelf and poured himself a brandy.

"You can't go around killing girls at the drop of a hat. You messed up big time with the ones you buried in Potters Park. What did you do with this one?" She took the bottle from him and poured her own drink.

Adam stared at the marble countertop. "Let's forget about it. I noticed you didn't have the car's bumper fixed. Are you losing your touch with Johnny?"

"He's out of town for the weekend. I left a message asking him to come over on Monday. You better be anywhere but home when Johnny gets here."

"Ah, honey, really? I love watching other men get you off." Adam smirked.

"Last time he heard you move around the house and you know we can't afford to lose him. He does good work."

"I'm sure he does. You moaned like a whore. Fake it much?"

"No, that's how I sound when I'm not faking it. Not that you would know. You treat me like one of your whores. It's always about you. I think I'm going out tonight to scout for talent, maybe hold an audition or two of my own."

Adam spun around; the glass barely missed his wife's face. She didn't flinch. "You only get Johnny, and only when we need him to fix something. A wife must be devoted and faithful to her husband."

Her forced laughter filled the house. "Don't you dare forget who runs our side hustle. Now be a good boy and stroke your bruised ego tonight. I know how much you wanted to go play with the *big boys* on that pretty island. I'm heading out. Don't wait up, baby."

He waited until he heard the garage door close and reached for the bottle of brandy. The liquid burned his throat. Adam didn't care. The idea of another man touching *his* wife drove him to murder.

"Sorry, Eva. Johnny isn't coming back."

Chapter 18

Clay held a plate towards Madison. "You need to eat."

Madison glanced at the pizza. "I'm not hungry." She rubbed his arm, moving her hand up to the roundness of his shoulder. Her nails dug into the material of his light blue t-shirt. The colour matched Clay's eyes. "Everything has gone to shit."

"He was caught on the surveillance tape at the marina, but they can't see his face because he wore a baseball cap. The car is a black BMW sedan. The number plate came back as stolen." Clay placed the plates on the coffee table and gave King a stern look. King returned to his bed and sighed, resting his head on his paws. "I love this dog."

Madison snuggled into Clay's arms and breathed in his scent. She wanted to cry, but her tears were spent. Not even after being rescued had she cried this much in a single day. In less than twenty-four hours, she had lost two friends. Dead. Murdered.

"When we move in together, we're getting a dog like King. Doesn't have to be a blue-nosed pit bull, but definitely one like him." Clay pressed his lips to Madison's temple.

"People are dying and you're thinking about our future?" She eased away and turned to face him. "How do you do it?"

"We can't change anything about those who have died. But if we focus on the future, we can gather the strength to get over the mountain in front of us. I'm not minimising Emma, Jenna or Claire's deaths, but you need a break from the darkness."

79

Clay ran his thumb along her jaw.

"Make love to me." Madison lifted his hand to her mouth, kissed his thumb, and sucked on it.

Clay held his breath as her tongue circled his thumb. "Not like this," he whispered. "I don't want you to think about our first time and remember it's the day Claire was murdered."

"I just want to forget about all of this. Even for a little while."

"Let's go for a run. Or we can go shoot at the indoor range. I'll bring my HK416."

Madison wiped her eyes. "I don't have the strength to get off this couch, never mind going for a run."

"Wait, you thought I'm going to do all the work, Miss Let's-Make-Love?" Clay hugged her.

"I'll summon all of my energy for you, Officer Davis." Madison's fingers trailed up his inner thigh. "Besides, sex is revitalising. People write songs, poems, even books about it."

"I have a question." Clay took her distracting hand in his and intertwined their fingers. "Claire mentioned it being *good* money. Would they have left for a week or two without getting some form of upfront payment?"

"No. They're all smart about how they run their business. I've heard some of the older women telling the younger ones how to ensure they always get paid. A lot of men come to Shadow Bay for a couple of nights on business. They like paying a woman to keep them company after hours. The women always request a deposit, and believe me, the men don't mind paying, especially if they're regulars."

Clay nodded. "Then we need to follow the money. If the missing women were all paid by the same person, we can figure out who killed Claire. *If* it's the same person."

Clay reached for his phone and dialled Gina's number. She answered on the fourth ring. "You're a pain in my ass, Davis."

"Are you at the morgue?"

"No, I just got back from there. The victim's neck was broken. Madison needs to come in tomorrow morning to identify the body. I assume she's still with you. Where are you staying?"

"It's on a need-to-know basis and *you* don't need to know."

Gina snorted a laugh. "Pain. In. My. Ass."

Clay ignored her. "Can you access the bank accounts of the missing women?"

"You know I can't. Unless they're dead, we can't just access their bank accounts without probable cause. You SWAT boys are all about busting down doors, but us detectives have rules to follow."

In the background, Clay heard a man's voice. "Tell Duke I said hello. Okay, well, start with Claire's then. We think whoever took them – *abducted* might be the correct word – paid them an advance. Madison says it's how the women operate, with clients who didn't just pull them in off the street. Most of the missing women aren't on street corners. I'll talk to Maddie about where they find their clients. Perhaps there's a link."

"Foster Ericson hasn't had any visitors and hasn't handed in any letters to be posted. Clay, are you sure she isn't fabricating this?"

Clay pushed to his feet and walked out onto the porch, closing the door behind him. "Have you read the file? Do you know what that monster did? How dare you say Madison fabricated the letters? What about the dildo painted on her wall? The attack on the street? You saw the mark on Maddie's neck. Someone smuggled those letters out for him."

"Everything you mentioned, she could've done herself. How is Madison's overall mental health if she's still seeing a psychiatrist months after nothing happened to her, apart from being abducted? From what I read in the file, Foster cared about her and didn't hurt her physically. No record of him raping her. She spent about forty-eight hours with him, and not once did he hurt her. Except for the spiders, but even they weren't venomous. Is Madison taking any anti-depressants or sleeping pills?"

Clay ended the call and pressed the decline button every

time Gina tried to reach him. Again, his phone rang. This time Duke's name appeared on the caller ID.

"Clever to phone me from my friend's phone, Gina. I never expected you to sink this low."

"Slay, Gina's heading to Madison's parents' house. She wants to apologise to you. You better call Gina before she causes trouble for Madison with her parents. I assume they don't know what's going on," Duke said.

Clay had known Duke long enough to know when he was pissed off and one had to stay out of his way.

"What is it with Gina? She needs to do her job."

"She received a call just before you called. Her former partner was gunned down outside his house. Remember our last drug bust? It appears someone came looking for revenge."

Clay pressed a palm to his forehead. "I'm sorry to hear that, but it doesn't excuse her behaviour."

"I know. Call Gina and stop her. I'll talk to her when she gets back and I promise to get her to back off from Madison. I remember, Slay. I was also there *that* day."

"Thank you, Duke. I appreciate the heads up."

Clay ended the call and dialled Gina's number. He gave her directions to Luke and Noa's place. After Clay ended the call, he went back into the house.

Madison leaned against the staircase. The SWAT jacket he'd given her months earlier covered parts of her. The zipper pulled down low, barely covering her modesty.

Chapter 19

The monitors came to life. She swivelled the chair, glancing from screen to screen. A predatory sneer spread across Eva's face. *Good little puppets.*

"We might have a problem with Blade and Vegas," Charlie said.

"Why? They look pretty happy to me."

"That's the problem. They haven't had sex and they've been touchy-feely the whole day." Charlie reached past her and clicked on a video recorded earlier in the day.

Eva rested her elbows on the desk and leaned closer to the screen, watching and listening.

Blade touched Vegas' arms and lifted her hands to his chest. "I meant every word I said in the pool. To show you how serious I am, we won't have sex again until you *want* to. If and when you want me. But I am going to kiss you, because I can't get enough of your mouth."

Blade kissed the whore. He ended the kiss by slowly pressing his mouth against hers again. Vegas smiled with her eyes closed.

Eva slammed her fists on the desk. "Shit. If he wants her, he will have to pay full price for lost revenue and income. Not even he has that kind of money. Pretty sure he'll lose interest the second I tell him how much money we're talking about."

Charlie touched Eva's shoulders and used her thumbs to work on the knots in Eva's neck. "Wait for it, my love. What happens next will bring you more money than you thought possible. Blade is such a caring puppet. I like him."

Eva leaned into the hands on her neck and closed her eyes until she heard the unmistakable sounds. "Beautiful, rugged Blade. Such a caring lover. Those gifted hands. Thank you for keeping your head out of the shot. Perhaps I'll charge you half price for her." Eva turned her attention to Charlie. "I wonder what the others think about him keeping Vegas to himself."

"They're taking it pretty well. Seems the boys play well together. I, on the other hand, hate sharing you with your dick of a husband."

"Do you hate him or his dick?" Eva spun the chair around, grabbing onto Charlie's hips.

"How much longer before you leave him?"

"As soon as I've dotted the last i's setting him up for *all* of it. And ensure you and I are long gone before he goes down. Enlighten me, my brilliant Charlie. Where am I tonight?"

"Right where you belong – with me." Charlie stared down at Eva. "Idiot thought we wouldn't find the tracker he'd installed under your car. *Dickhead* knows exactly where you'll be spending the night. You are staying, aren't you?"

"Of course, my love. Adam has no reason to suspect I'm doing anything other than venting about the state of our marriage to my best friend."

"He killed Johnny. I followed Adam and recorded him entering and exiting Johnny's house. Additional evidence to sink the sadistic bastard."

"I wanted him to kill Johnny." Charlie dropped to her knees, pulled Eva's top over her head and unclasped her bra. "I love you, *my* Evie."

Eva arched her back. "I know."

Sunday, 12 December, 7:45 p.m.

Madison held her breath, waiting for Clay to run, speak or grab her. His expression became unreadable. Silence hung between them, broken sporadically by the deafening beat of her heart.

She pulled the zipper up to her neck and ran up the stairs. He claimed to want her, but each time Madison tried to take things further, Clay talked her out of it using logic or by staring at her.

Madison tried to close the bedroom door, but it didn't slam shut.

Clay's palm rested against the door. "Are you naked under my jacket?" he asked, running a finger down the zipper.

"It's a crucial part of what I have in mind for you." Madison grabbed a fist full of his shirt and pulled him into the room.

"You're beautiful, Madison." Clay reached for her face, dipping his head until their lips touched. The restraint he'd held for the past six months snapped as he unzipped the jacket and pushed it off her shoulders.

Madison placed her hands on his chest, trying to catch her breath. "I don't want to be the woman who slept with a serial killer any more. I want you, inside me, and to know what it feels like to make love."

Clay stepped back and smiled. "You're mine."

"I've always been yours." Under her palms, Clay's laboured breathing matched hers. Madison sank to her knees and undid his jeans. She glanced up at him, his eyes closed. His belt clanked on the wooden floor.

Madison yanked down his boxers, trailing his length with her tongue, and heard him draw in a deep breath.

Clay released his breath. "Are you sure you want to do this after everything that happened today?"

"I'm still the same person I was this morning when you came into the room. You're still the only man I ever want to do this to." She took him in her mouth and twirled her tongue over his tip.

Clay threw his head back and ran his fingers through her hair. "Gina's coming."

Madison tilted her head and stared up at him. "Is your name Gina?"

Clay smiled, pulling Madison to her feet. "I've always loved your mouth for your wit. Now I love it for its mind-blowing abilities." He pushed her towards the bed. "I want to take my time with you."

"I don't want slow. Clay, I need you. Inside me. You said you'd show me *deep*." Madison nipped at his mouth as he eased her down on the bed. Clay toed off his shoes, stepped out of his jeans and boxers, and yanked his shirt over his head. Madison could only stare at him in wonder. "You have no idea how gorgeous you are, Clay Davis."

"Madison, look at me." She did. "*I* want *you*. *I* love *you*."

She bent down and kissed him. A kiss of surrender and letting go of the self-hate she had carried for six months. In that moment, nothing mattered except Clay, and being one with the first man she had ever loved. "Good, because I love you too."

Sunday, 12 December, 8:24 p.m.

They cleared the table, carrying the plates and cutlery to the kitchen. Tiffany washed the glasses, Vegas loaded the dishwasher, Kayla cleaned out the pots and pans, and Jersey prepared dessert. Dakota packed away the salt, pepper and salad dressing before wiping down the white marble countertops.

"I'm jealous of you," Tiffany said to Vegas. "Blade is a catch, even outside of this house."

Vegas smiled without joy, keeping her face hidden from the other women by focusing on loading the last plates in the dishwasher. "It doesn't matter. We'll go back to Shadow Bay and I'll never see him again. This is their fantasy, not ours."

Jersey wiped her hands on a paper towel. "I'm done with this life. When Archer groped me earlier, something inside me snapped. I can't do this anymore."

"We don't have a choice," Dakota said, jumping onto the countertop. She swung her legs, careful not to bump her heels against the cabinets.

"We do. Waiting tables doesn't pay as much, but at least you won't be selling your soul. I'm going to talk to Maddie, maybe get into one of the classes she's always telling us about." Kayla placed a hand on Dakota's knee. "You're still young enough to get out in time. You're not yet as broken as the rest of us."

A week earlier, Dakota had turned eighteen. She felt decades older. Kayla was wrong. She was every bit as broken as the rest of them. Adam had seen to it.

Jersey drizzled chocolate over the cheesecake. She licked the chocolate from her fingertip. "I want to be a chef." They all turned their attention to her. "What? I enjoy baking and maybe I can make a living from it."

Vegas wrapped an arm around Jersey. "We can all get out of this life and become whatever we want. It might be hard at first, but we can find a house and move in together. That way, we can take care of and support each other. We need to get out of this life … before it kills us."

Kayla wiped her eyes, careful not to smudge her mascara. "We're not getting off this island. I knew that the moment Adam brought me here and saw the four of you. We're as good as dead. Just like the five bodies the police found in Potters Park. Five of them. Five of us."

Vegas fought the urge to tell her friends what she knew. Madison had told her about five women who'd gone missing two years earlier. The December before, ten women had disappeared. So far, they had found five unidentified female bodies. *Where are the others?*

Lightning cracked overhead. They all jumped and laughed. Together, they walked out of the house, back to the men who saw them as nothing but playthings.

They didn't matter. Not as women. Not as human beings.

In many ways, they didn't exist.

They didn't live with dreams of a better future. They survived, day by day.

Their deaths? Silent.

Chapter 20

The gate intercom sounded. Clay checked the security camera before opening the gate. Even before Clay opened the door wide enough, King wiggled through and ran onto the porch. King gave a low growl, his full attention on the visitor who'd interrupted his nap.

Rain pounded the earth. Stepping out of the car, Gina opened a black umbrella.

Again, King growled. Clay patted his back. "I feel the same, but neither of us can bite her."

He thought about the woman drying her hair upstairs. *My Madison.* Their love making had been rushed and hungry. As they'd showered, Clay had taken a moment to appreciate the sight of her naked body, her perfect curves, and the sexy birth mark next to her belly-button. This wasn't how he'd wanted it to happen, but Clay didn't regret it. They had the rest of their lives for slow and sweet. He knew what it had meant to Madison to take control of the act itself and regain control of her sexuality. *I have to tell her.*

Gina shook the umbrella as she stepped under the roof. King inspected her with his nose, gave a sigh, and strolled into the house.

"I'm sorry, Clay. What I said was uncalled for and cruel. Madison didn't ask to be abducted, and I can't imagine how hard it must be for her to move on from it all. I still don't approve of her being in your life, but it's because of your past with my sister. As for the work Madison does with the prostitutes, and the information she's given us about what happens on the streets, she's remarkable and fearless. I heard about how she stepped in and stabbed a pimp who beat one of his girls."

Clay shrugged, crossing his arms over his chest. "That pimp now keeps an eye on Madison when she's on the streets. He claims it's out of respect, but I think he's shit scared of her."

Gina nodded. "Life is stranger than fiction. Anyway, I wanted to apologise to you in person. And I promise to give my full and unbiased attention to this investigation. The murdered and missing girls deserve justice, irrelevant of their life choices."

Madison cleared her throat. "*Women*. Stop calling them girls and prostitutes. As a woman and a detective you should understand the difference. The women I work with aren't victims of trafficking or drug addicts. They made the worst decision imaginable to survive. Sure, they could've become waitresses and live in a single bedroom apartment with six other people. It's not our place to judge them. My job is to show them a way out, or at least to try."

Madison invited Gina inside, asking her to take a seat in the living room. She walked to the kitchen and made coffee.

Clay poured and handed both women a mug.

Madison rolled the mug between her hands. "A woman I work with – let's call her Vegas, that's her street name – is a medical student. She wants to save lives, and getting paid for sex is how Vegas puts herself through medical school. It covers the expensive fees, textbooks, and she has food on her table and a roof over her head."

Madison blew on her coffee, savouring the aroma. "*Dakota* turned eighteen last week. Three years ago, she ran away from home, after her mother stopped trying to keep her boyfriends from going into Dakota's room. She doesn't have any other family. Do you think Dakota should've stayed in her mother's house, to be raped by which ever man her mother brought home that week? At the age of seven, *Dakota* realised her mother always had extra money after she was raped. Imagine your own mother selling you to paedophiles …"

Madison walked to the fireplace and leaned against the wall. "These women aren't statistics. They aren't drug addicts desperate for their next fix. They're actual human beings who are hurting every day because they don't realise life could be better for them. They carry the weight of their choices with them, and will do for the rest of their lives. Gina, please help me uncover what happened to the women found in Potters Park, and the others who are still missing. Claire died trying to find her sister. And her friend, Vegas, is still out there. I can't reach Vegas, Dakota, Tiffany, Kayla or Jersey."

Gina reached into the bag she had placed at her feet. "You never saw any of this. I'll leave it with you, but burn it after you're done." She held a big file out to Madison. "I need to warn you, it's not pretty. There are images you can never get out of your head."

Madison took the binder and pressed it against her chest. "I'm sorry to hear about your partner."

"Thank you. He transferred to Narcotics a few years ago, after his niece ran away from home. He believed she'd come to Shadow Bay, and working on street level gave him the opportunity to search for her. Paul always suspected she was one of the women who'd gone missing. That file has all the information he uncovered. He was frustrated and angry that the identification of the bodies found in Potters Park wasn't given priority."

Madison walked to the dining room and switched on the light. After moving the chairs away from the table, she opened the file.

From the living room, Clay stood and watched her. He wanted to look through the file for her, but he knew how stubborn and determined she could be. More than that, Madison loved every woman she met through her work.

Gently, Madison removed the photos from the file, spreading them out on the table.

The sound of her restrained sobs forced Clay's legs to move. He stopped far away enough to give Madison space, but close enough that she knew he was there.

Madison braced her hands on the table, leaning her head forward. A puddle formed on the mahogany surface. She took a deep breath, wiped her eyes and the moisture from the wooden surface. "I read through the medical examiner's autopsy report. Did I read it right – the cause of death is undetermined, but the victims' bodies were *butchered* post-mortem?"

Gina joined Madison and touched her shoulder. "Yes. Post-mortem injuries showed one victim was burned. Another cut in half. One was bludgeoned. And one had an arrow embedded in the back of her neck. Jane Doe number five had a bullet hole in her skull with no exit wound."

"Low calibre bullet, one with controlled expansion, or a hollow-point round could've done that," Clay offered.

Madison rummaged through the papers to her left. She frowned, tracing her finger down the page. "They all had severe damage to their sternums."

"Yes, looks like their chests were cracked." Gina shook her head.

"Like doctors used to do during open heart surgery. Still do, in some cases." Madison bit down on her fist. "Why would he kill them and *then* mutilate their bodies? In five different, yet very distinct ways." Madison rubbed her throbbing temples. "I studied criminology as part of my degree. I remember repeat killers often have a signature. His might be opening the victims' chests, but why?" She scanned the autopsy reports and paged back to the first page, which held hand-written notes. "Are these case numbers?" Her pointer finger tapped on the paper.

Gina nodded when Madison turned towards her. "I brought copies of those two unsolved homicide cases. I want to discuss them with the medical examiner, Doctor O'Reilly. He conducted the autopsies on these two cases and the Potters Park Five."

"Call him now," Clay said as Gina pulled two smaller files out of her bag.

"I've been trying to reach him, but his phone is switched off. He's on leave until the new year. I spoke to Doctor Seymour, but she isn't familiar with these cases. She was at a symposium in November when the Potters Park Five were found. And when the other two murders occurred, she was on maternity leave." Gina handed Madison the files.

Madison read as fast as her stomach allowed. "This is sick. It doesn't make sense." She stared at her reflection in the mirror on the opposite wall. "What if we're not looking for one killer, but five? Each with a unique signature."

Sunday, 12 December, 8:59 p.m.

Vegas watched Blade sitting in the hot tub. The back of his head rested on the wooden edge. She couldn't see whether his eyes were open. Blade had a thing for the stars. She didn't understand his fascination. Vegas never thought of looking upwards. She was too focused on the goals, or job, in front of her. She slipped into the water next to him.

Blade smiled. "I can't wait to get off this island. Do you want to spend Christmas with me?"

"The fantasy ends when you leave." Her focus remained on his mouth. *Too good to be true.* The clench in her heart became unbearable.

"Tell me your dreams." Blade reached for her hand, pressing his lips to each of her fingers.

"*A* dream. It's what gets me through each day. But you know the rules. We're not allowed to discuss who we are away from here." She didn't see anything other than Blade's mouth. Something so beautiful could easily break what remained of her heart.

"If you want to kiss me, kiss me. You don't have to wait for me to make all the moves." Blade cupped her cheek, her lips pressed against his palm. "See, it's not that difficult."

"I'm here to create your fantasy, not mine." *How long will it take me to forget you? Until the day I'm murdered?*

"Why can't we both have what we want?" Blade pulled her closer, pressing her head against his big shoulder and angled her head up.

Darkness surrounded the stars; the moon was a mere sliver.

"What's your fantasy?" He kissed the top of her head. "I like your hair in a messy bun, or whatever it is you women call it."

Again, she felt a spasm in her heart. *Vegas* had never been called a woman. Whore, slut, baby, thing and trash she heard almost daily. But never a word that didn't make her feel filthy.

Blade kept his voice gentle. "It's only us out here. You can tell me."

Vegas shut her eyes. Tears rolled down her cheeks. "For the next two years to go by in the blink of an eye."

"What's going to happen two years from now?"

"Life."

"I hope that you'll trust me enough to tell me. Soon. I think you should be in a profession where you take care of people. I've said this before, but there's something comforting about you, the way you are with the other women. Do you have siblings?"

"No. Let's do something. I'm here for you, and it's not to play therapist. Unless that's what you want."

Blade eased her head from his shoulder and asked her to look at him. "There is nothing boring about you. Are you forgetting how much fun we had this afternoon? I haven't laughed that much in ... never. You have a wicked sense of humour, and your poker face is one of the best I've ever seen."

You have no idea.

Vegas trailed a finger along the fine lines at the corners of his eyes and then ran her hands through his dark hair, which had greyed at his temples. Gently, she touched his mouth.

Blade kept his eyes on her face and his hands off the parts

of her body she'd started to hate. "I have no expectations, but you're killing me. Please kiss me."

Vegas stared at his lips; her heart shattered. She decided to give him whatever he wanted and remember their time together for as long as she remained alive.

If her heart hadn't been sold along with her soul, she could've fallen in love with him. If Blade was real and she wasn't a whore.

Just two more years … if I can survive that long.

Chapter 21

Madison sank to the floor, rocking back and forth. Anguish clawed at her. She pressed her palms to her eyes, but kept seeing the photos of the victims' bodies. The Potters Park Five. The words written in the autopsy report echoed in her brain. Even though none of the bodies had been identified, Madison felt guilty. *I failed to protect them.*

Clay sat down behind Madison, drawing her into his arms. The sound of thunder broke the suffocating silence which filled the room.

Dread spread throughout the house.

Gina shifted her weight and stared at the files laying on the table. "I'm going to go," she said, her voice filled with less venom than before.

Gina told Clay she'd see herself out. King raised his head, watching the visitor's every move. When the front door closed, his blue eyes focused on Madison.

She turned, leaning her head against Clay's chest. Madison opened her mouth, but no words or sound came out. The crime scene photos replayed in her mind. "We have to find Vegas and the other missing women before they end up like them." She pointed at the table. *Even in death, you weren't spared from the cruelty of this world.*

"I know. We all need to get some sleep. Tomorrow is going to be a rough day. The identification is scheduled for nine. Gina asked to speak to us afterwards."

95

"Where are they, Clay? Where are they being held? Why hasn't anyone found the bodies of the other ten women? I should've kept them safe."

"Don't do this, Maddie. You have done more for them than most people ever did. The sad truth is — you can't save them all. Focus on the ones you have saved and the ones you will save in the future. Come, let's go to bed." Clay stood, holding a hand towards her.

"Some women have opened their hearts and souls to me. They wish they could have an actual relationship with a man. They wonder what it's like to be held, wake up next to someone, and go on a real date with no expectation of sex. Men pay for their smiles, access to their bodies, and a piece of their dignity. By the time they resort to sex work, life has already destroyed and ripped them apart. The closest they get to any form of affection is when I, or one of the other women, hug them. Can you imagine living like that?" Madison placed her hand in his.

Clay pulled her up and hugged her hard. "As I've told you, your heart is the most beautiful thing about you, Madison Taylor. Thank you for allowing me into your life. We will find out what happened to the women who disappeared. And figure out a way to save Vegas and the other four missing women. Are you hungry?"

"Not after seeing the photos, but thank you for always taking care of me." Madison kissed his chin. "You keep me grounded. I don't deserve you."

"Do I not deserve you?" Clay tilted her head up and brushed his mouth against hers.

"You deserve the best there is in this life. And so do my friends."

"You're the best thing for me, Maddie. There isn't anything or anyone better than you. And the women know you care about them. You give so much of yourself to everyone around you."

Clay led her up the stairs, switching off lights as they made their way to the guest bedroom. He squirted toothpaste onto her toothbrush and handed it to her. Side by side, they brushed their teeth and smiled at their reflections in the mirror. Their domestic rituals were expanding beyond heating pizza and watching television together.

Madison wished the darkness would leave them to live their lives. And for every woman, or any person forced into the most horrific life, to find their own light.

She snuggled into Clay's shoulder after he switched off the bedside lamp. His warmth and scent calmed her.

Sunday, 12 December, 11:01 p.m.

The fragility of what they were stepping into slammed into Clay. He had to tell Madison the truth and allow her to decide whether she wanted to be with him. The real Clay Davis.

"What's wrong?" Madison pressed her lips to his chest.

Man up, she deserves to know.

The duvet rustled as Clay pulled her head back to his shoulder. He ran his fingers through her curls and tried to find the perfect opening line. There wasn't one, not for what he was about to tell her.

"Madison, I love you more than I ever thought I could love anyone. You deserve to hear the truth about me. I won't blame you if you no longer want a future with me."

Madison hugged him with the arm across his waist. "Nothing you tell me will change how I feel about you."

Clay closed his eyes. "I don't know if I'm able to have children."

"We can always adopt. For obvious reasons, I'm open to the idea."

"No, that's not what I meant." Clay took a deep breath. Fear and revulsion collided in his stomach. He exhaled, and said, "My father was a paedophile."

Madison placed a hand on his heart. "You're not one and never will be. Clay Davis, you are a good man and an amazing person. You will never hurt an innocent person, let alone a child."

Madison's kind words broke his heart. "I should've done more to protect my sister."

Madison pushed up on her elbow and touched his cheek. "How old were you when he was arrested?"

"He wasn't arrested. He never paid for his crimes. My sister wasn't his only victim." Clay would never forget the faces of the little girls in the photos he had found when he cleaned out his father's belongings.

"Other victims?" Madison traced small circles over his heart.

The gentleness in her touch and voice gave Clay the courage to tell her the whole story.

Except for those who had been in the house that night, no one else knew.

"He was the head of international sales for a vehicle manufacturer and travelled a lot. After he died, I found the photos hidden in his office. My mother was there with me. That's the day she started drinking."

"And you? How did you cope after learning the truth?"

Clay placed a hand over hers and brought it to his lips. He willed the words from his mouth, but failed.

"How did he die, Clay?" Madison whispered.

She deserves to know what I am.

"One night I snuck out of the house to go to a party, as sixteen-year-olds do. Later that night when I came back, I heard a noise coming from my sister's bedroom." Clay released her hand and wiped the moisture from his eyes. "I walked in on him raping her. My sister was nine years old."

Madison's breath caught; her body stiffened. "I'm sorry your sister had to live through it, and for you to see it." She pressed her mouth to his chest and returned her head to his shoulder. "What did you do?"

"I stormed into the room and beat him to death with my sister's field hockey stick. It stood next to her bedroom door.

Even back then, I was big for my age. The same size as him. I couldn't stop."

"Fair fight then. I'm glad you didn't stop."

Clay's heart clenched at Madison's words. He'd been sure his actions would have repulsed her.

"You don't have to tell me the rest. I'm not going anywhere. I don't love you less. In fact, I love you even more." Madison lifted her head and asked Clay to look at her. "I always knew you're a superhero. You did what you had to. You protected your sister and countless other children."

"I need to tell you the rest." Clay nudged her head back to his shoulder. Not looking into her eyes made telling her easier.

Madison laid an arm across his waist and placed a leg over his, moving as close as possible. *She's still here.*

"The struggle woke my mother and brother. My mother became hysterical until she saw my sister's face. Then she knew. My brother grabbed the stick from my hand and beat his lifeless body until he couldn't lift the stick anymore."

Clay told Madison how they had cleaned the room, burned the bedding, carpet and everything else covered in blood in the downstairs fireplace. That night, his sister started sleeping in his bedroom. He moved into his brother's room. They shared until Clay moved out after finishing high school. They'd placed his father's body in the boot of his car and driven it into a bad part of town, where they set the car on fire. The police had suspected he got on the wrong side of a pimp, as a few other men had turned up in the boots of burnt-out cars with their skulls bashed in. Even then, Clay had followed the news, keeping to his boyhood dream of becoming a police officer.

"You're mine to protect now," Madison said. "What you did proves you're nothing like him. Any child would be lucky to have you as a father."

Clay pressed his lips to the top of her head, hugging her tight. "Thank you for not running."

"Where am I going to run? Besides, I'll keep running circles, right back to you. You're my future."

Chapter 22

The previous night's storm had caused havoc across the city. Numerous homes were flooded. Streets remained blocked off and a few landslides had occurred at beachfront properties.

Gina parked behind the crime scene investigator's van, pulling the hood of the raincoat up. She climbed out of the car and pressed her hands into the pockets.

An officer walked with her towards the beach. Neither said a word.

Closer to the shoreline, people scurried over the sand. Some took photos, others set up a perimeter. Those waiting to do their jobs stood hunched over against the unrelenting rain. The homeowners huddled together under an umbrella, talking to another officer.

Gina found Doctor Seymour and was grateful for the cup the doctor held out to her. There was no time for her morning shot of caffeine, having only been woken up an hour before. Getting to the scene had taken longer than normal. Traffic was a nightmare. People forgot how to drive as soon as the first raindrops fell and, in this downpour, the streets were filled with idiots behind steering wheels.

"What do we have?" Gina asked the officer standing to her right.

"The homeowners came down here earlier to check on the damage. The man stumbled and fell next to a stick. As he pushed himself up, he realised it wasn't a stick, but a bone. He's a vet. After inspecting the bone, he realised it wasn't from an animal. His wife then called us."

"How long before we can start digging?"

"In this rain? Your guess is as good as mine. The CSIs are busy putting up a tarpaulin over the cordoned off area. Preliminary excavation has produced a human skull. It's why you're here, Detective." Doctor Seymour drank the last of her coffee. "I examined the skull when I arrived. It appears the victim was shot. Finding the bullet is going to be a mammoth task."

"No more saying a needle in a haystack. From now on, it's a bullet in a landslide." Gina shook her head.

With the tarp erected, Gina watched from a distance as the excavation started. Without anything to do for the time being, she played with the car keys in her pocket while thinking about her other cases. The sound of her phone ringing broke her train of thought. "Larson."

"Good morning to you, sunshine. We examined the car retrieved from the bottom of the cliff at Perry Bay. Was the owner involved in a bumper bashing recently?"

"Not to my knowledge. Why?"

"The car's bumpers are colour coded; blue, like the rest of the car. The rear bumper has black paint on it."

Gina kept the phone pressed to her ear, using the hood to protect it from the rain. "Is it possible that someone ran the car off the road?"

"Yes. I read the report. No skid marks at the scene."

"Thank you." Gina ended the call and turned to Doctor Seymour. "Do you have the results of the blood alcohol level for Emma Thompson?"

"Yes. Zero. Ms Thompson didn't have a drop of alcohol in her system."

Gina sent a text message to Clay.

Gina: Was Madison in a bumper bashing recently? Or did she maybe notice that someone bumped her car while parked somewhere?

Clay: No. Why?

Gina: I don't think her friend's death was an accident.

Monday, 13 December, 7:40 a.m.

Adam finished the bowl of muesli and placed it in the dishwasher. He reached for a banana. Last night had left him hungry but satisfied. He had sent the girls home at around three o'clock, giving him four hours of sleep.

His wife hadn't come home. It never bothered him when Eva spent the night with her friend Charlotte. She often did after they'd had a fight.

As he finished his second cup of coffee, the garage door opened.

He waited.

Eva glanced at him and walked to the coffee machine.

"You look like shit." Adam ran a finger along the rim of the mug and leaned back in the chair, studying her. "You girls stay up late doing each other's nails and hair? You clearly didn't get your *much* needed beauty sleep, darling."

"Something like that." Eva kept her back to him. "Did you hear about the landslides at Paradise Beach? I've always said they built those houses too quickly. Money, money, money." She turned to face him, lifting the mug into the air in a mock toast.

"No, I haven't." *Shit.* "I'm heading out, I need to take provisions to the island. What are you doing today?"

"I'm working the night shift. Remember to buy enough alcohol and condoms. Our supplier will meet you at the marina with the party drugs."

"Thanks." He stood and pressed his lips to her cheek on his way to the garage.

"Adam, I'm not touching our bed sheets. Wash them and put clean sheets on before you leave. You know how I feel about your whores in *my* bed."

"Sorry, darling, I got lonely without you. Hope you have fun with Johnny later."

Gina sipped her coffee. "I'm not a necrophiliac."

Adam's hand froze on the door handle. "Then you better find a new mechanic to fix our cars and service you."

Two houses down the street, he pulled the car to the kerb and slammed his fists against the steering wheel. Disposing of the bodies on vacant land earmarked for residential development had been risky. At the time, Adam had reasoned, it would take years before the development got approved. Strings were pulled, bribes paid, and a month later the land had been sold.

Chapter 23

Doctor Seymour pulled the white sheet back, exposing the victim's face.

Madison nodded. "Her name is Claire Wallis." Madison stepped away from the table and turned to Clay, waiting for Doctor Seymour to cover Claire's face. "Did she suffer?"

"No. Her neck was broken. Death would've been almost instantaneous."

Madison drew a deep breath. The smell of chemicals and death suffocated her. She stepped closer to the table, touching the top of Claire's head through the sheet. "I'm so sorry. I should've kept you safe."

Clay reached for Madison's shoulder. "Why is it so quiet in here today?" he asked Doctor Seymour

"Most of the team are at Paradise Beach."

Madison lifted her head. "What happened?"

"Landslide. The owner discovered a body. I can't divulge details, but *that* information will be in the papers." Doctor Seymour shrugged.

"Is Detective Gina Larson there? We were supposed to meet her here for the identification."

"Yes, but she should arrive soon. Not much she can do until we've completed the excavation of the bodies."

Madison frowned. "Bodies?"

Doctor Seymour pulled the latex gloves from her hands and threw them into a bin. "Just one body. I meant all the bones.

This has been a busy weekend. I haven't slept much. Sorry."

Madison looked at Clay, noticing he also picked up on the pathologist's back-pedalling.

The double steel doors opened and Gina stepped into the autopsy room. Her fringe stuck to her forehead. When Gina and Doctor Seymour's eyes met, Gina nodded, then shook her head. Dark circles were visible under Gina's eyes.

"What happened?" Clay asked.

Madison hoped they'd remember Clay was also an officer of the law and therefore on their side.

"Can't talk about it. Sorry." Gina wiped her fringe from her forehead, drying her hand on her pants.

"You found five, didn't you?" Madison asked and reached for Clay's hand.

"I can't confirm or deny that we've found skulls. The investigation is ongoing."

Madison's hand lifted to her mouth.

Gina met her stare and gave a slow blink. "Let's go talk in my office. Have you identified the body?"

"Yes, it's Claire," Clay answered.

Madison stared at the young woman, her friend, laying on the steel table. She shut her eyes, forcing herself not to dwell on the cruelty of life. Not now, that could wait until Vegas and the other women were safe.

Another piece of Madison's heart broke. A wound which would never heal.

Monday, 13 December, 9:10 a.m.

Madison and Clay followed Gina to her office. They thanked Gina for the coffee she handed to them in disposable cups. A raincoat hung off the corner of a steel filing cabinet.

Madison noticed the files stacked on Gina's desk. Most days she loved her work, but Madison didn't want to deal with the horrors the police dealt with daily. Thanks to Foster Ericson, she had survived a nightmare and saw the harsh reality of life etched into the faces of the women she worked with.

Clay cleared his throat. "Gina, it's just us. What's going on at Paradise Beach?"

"They aren't done processing the scene. Doctor Seymour should be on her way back there, and I'll be too, after we're done."

"We can do this later." Madison placed her cup on the edge of the desk.

"No, we can't. You were right. Emma wasn't drinking." Gina held up a hand as Madison opened her mouth to say, *I told you so.* "I know. We're going to treat their deaths as suspicious until we find evidence proving it was an accident."

Clay leaned forward in his chair. "You found paint from another vehicle on the bumper?"

"Yes. A black vehicle. The paint will be analysed. Hopefully, we can get a make and model, depending on the paint used."

"Emma's cousin, Jenna, looks like me. We're the same height, our hair is the same colour and style, when I don't straighten my curls. What if I'm the person who was supposed to be killed?" Madison increased her hold on Clay's hand. "Have you figured out how Foster Ericson managed to send me letters?"

Gina ruffled her damp hair. "No. Foster hasn't had any visitors since his sentencing. The judge prohibited him from speaking to journalists and people who may want to write a book about him. A criminal psychologist has requested access to Foster to interview him. The judge hasn't decided on it yet. I spoke to him yesterday."

Clay angled his body around Gina's desk and tossed the disposable cup into the dustbin. "He's in contact with guards and other prisoners. Maybe he paid someone to smuggle the letters out."

"Plausible. I'm looking into it. But Foster isn't very popular with the other prisoners. They have attacked him a few times."

"Good, I hope next time they kill him." Madison leaned

back, crossing her arms over her chest. "Noa, her father, and all the families of his victims deserve to have final closure. As long as he's breathing, the chapter remains unfinished."

"For you as well, I assume?" Gina asked without malice.

"I just want closure for everybody else." Madison turned to the man sitting next to her. "No, I don't need Foster to die to move on with my life. As long as he remains locked up, I can live."

Clay's smile morphed into concern. "On Friday, Maddie was attacked, and her apartment broken into and ransacked. Saturday night, Emma and Jenna were *possibly* murdered. And yesterday, Claire was *definitely* murdered. Maybe this is linked to Madison pushing for an investigation into the disappearances of fifteen women and not orchestrated by Foster Ericson. Have you identified the man in the video taken at the marina?"

"No, but we suspect he might've worn a disguise. He wore a long-sleeved shirt, despite yesterday being one of the hottest days we've had so far."

Madison rubbed her temples. "He was hiding a scar or a tattoo. I know he's a police officer. Claire wouldn't have made a mistake about that."

Gina sighed. "Do you know how many police officers we have in Shadow Bay and the surrounding towns? Close to a thousand. Not to mention, reservists called in during the holiday season to patrol the beaches."

"It has to be someone who knows I'm pushing for further investigations into the Potters Park Five. And the fifteen missing women I'm aware of. Not even considering the five who I'm unable to get hold of." Madison stopped rubbing her temples. In her bag, she found painkillers and swallowed two capsules with the last of her coffee. "Are you sure your former partner was murdered because of a drug bust and not because he searched for his niece?"

"The investigation into his murder is still open. He was shot in a drive-by. The gangs in Shadow Bay prefer it to hands-on killings, especially when the victim is a police officer. Paul isn't the first officer we've lost in such a cowardly manner."

"A fellow police officer would know that." Madison shook her head. "Perhaps Paul asked too many questions about his niece or confided in the wrong person."

Chapter 24

Monday, 13 December, 10:30 a.m.

Blade gripped Vegas' hand as they watched the boat dock. Rushed footsteps behind them; Dakota ran into the house. Archer walked past, pushing a cart towards the jetty. Everyone else joined them and made comments regarding the provisions they were hoping for. The party drugs had run out two nights ago.

Adam followed Archer, who pushed the cart up the steep wooden walkway. Crush headed to the boat and returned with a couple of grocery bags.

With a beer in hand, Adam returned to take in the beautiful scenery, or so he said. He turned to Vegas. "Well, hello my gorgeous girl. Your tan is coming along, but leave the top. The tan lines are ugly."

She moved closer to Blade, her arm pressing against his.

"How about you and I go find ourselves a spot to, you know, talk?" Adam's tongue circled the rim of the beer bottle.

Blade stepped in front of Vegas, clutching her hand, his arm bent behind his back. "Sorry, Adam, Vegas and I have plans today."

"Can't fault you, man. She's a fine piece of ass." Adam glanced at the house. "I'll go see who has time for a *chat*."

Blade released Vegas' hand and walked up to Adam, staring him straight in the eye. "We paid for them. You don't get to touch them. I think it's best if you get back on your little boat and leave."

Adam sneered at Blade, placing his hands against his chest. "Whatever dude. There are way hotter girls than these worn-out whores back in Shadow Bay. Besides, as soon as you leave, they'll be mine again." He grinned at Vegas over Blade's shoulder. "There's a birthday gift I'd like to give to Dakota."

Blade grabbed Adam's wrists. One eyebrow raised as a flash of pain crossed Adam's face. "Dakota is ours."

Glass shards scattered as the beer bottle smashed onto the wooden deck. Adam marched back to the boat.

Resting her forehead against Blade's back, Vegas whispered, "Thank you."

He turned around with an expression on his face that she hadn't seen before. "What did he do to you?"

Vegas looked at her feet, shaking her head.

"Hey." Blade placed his fingers under her chin, easing her head up. Fear and shame filled her eyes. "Let's go down to the beach."

Monday, 13 December, 11:08 a.m.

Blade pulled two sunloungers under the gazebo and waited for Vegas to sit. "Talk to me. I can help."

"No one can protect us from him."

He reached for her hands. "I will."

"Why are you here? A man like you doesn't need to pay for sex." Vegas yanked her hands back and walked towards the ocean.

Blade followed her. The cool water offered a welcome relief after the sand burned the soles of his feet. "I'm not here for sex. Something else is going on and I'm going to find out what it is."

Through the strands of her dark hair, Vegas stared at him. He ached to push it away from her beautiful eyes, but didn't.

"What are you, a detective?"

"No. I'm a medical examiner. Why are you here?"

"I'm getting paid to be here." She blinked, sending tears down her cheeks. "My friend went missing last December, after getting a two-week job. She never came home."

Blade pushed his fingers through his hair and exhaled out loud. "I was there last year. I had no idea the women were paid to be there. Adam sold it as a *singles holiday*. Last month I got called to a scene where the remains of five females were discovered—"

"In Potters Park." She finished for him.

"Yes. It didn't take long before I realised the five victims were the ones I had met in December."

Vegas reached for his hands. "How did she die?"

"I couldn't determine the cause of death."

Vegas' eyes narrowed. "You don't have to spare me the details."

"I'm not. I can't – couldn't – determine the cause of death." To give her details about her friend's death would be cruel. Against his better judgement, he continued, "There are distinct marks on their bodies. The marks made me realise it wasn't a holiday for single people. I'm here to conduct my own investigation." He lifted her hands to his mouth. "And I found you."

"Are you real?" Vegas frowned.

Blade laughed, stepping closer. He cupped her face and touched his forehead to hers. "Yes, I'm real. I want to help you get away from this place and this life. When we get back to Shadow Bay, I want to keep seeing you. It doesn't matter how we met. I like you and promise to keep you safe."

"You can't keep me safe from him. He's a police officer."

Anger exploded in Blade's veins. "What? Adam is a police officer?"

Vegas nodded.

"What did he do to you and the other women?" Vegas lifted her head to meet his eyes but didn't answer. "No matter what you tell me, I won't turn my back on you. I realise it's going to take time to trust me, but I care about you."

She stepped backwards and stared up at the darkening clouds. "He forced us to *audition* to come here."

"He raped you?" Blade asked through clenched teeth.

She nodded, then shrugged, wiping raindrops from her face. "Can a whore say no?"

Across the dark grey waters, Shadow Bay drew her focus. The streaks of water falling from the sky obscured their view of the city in the distance.

"Of course! I'm going to kill him."

Vegas grabbed his hand. "You can't. If he murdered the others, Adam won't hesitate to kill you. No matter who you are. My friends and I are already as good as dead." She pushed her fingers through her hair and twirled it behind her head. "Adam lets the men go. And then kills the women. Don't do anything. Go home and then get the right people involved."

Blade grabbed her shoulders, pulling her against his chest, and wrapped his arms around her. "I won't let him hurt you or anyone else. I'll get us away from here. Look at me." She did. "I *will* keep you safe." He kissed her forehead.

Vegas beamed up at him with a glimmer of hope in her eyes. *I want her.*

Chapter 25

Monday, 13 December, 11:50 a.m.

The laptop bag weighed heavy on her shoulder, but it was nothing compared to the weight of the two boys growing inside her. Jamie scratched her sides and remembered that the book had said not to do it. An itch needs to be scratched, she thought, hoping she wouldn't find her baby sister and Clay scratching each other's.

Madison wasn't a baby anymore. The devil, Foster Ericson, had forced her to grow up and re-evaluate her life choices, not only when it came to men. Not a day had gone by that Jamie didn't wish Foster had been killed during his arrest. But with two hostages in a small dark cellar, the risk had been too high.

Despite Foster's incarceration, Jamie kept tabs on him. She hoped the next time another inmate attacked him would be the last. Foster Ericson deserved to die a slow and painful death. For what he did to Noa, Madison, and all his other victims. And for threatening the life of her unborn sons.

The back door opened as Jamie reached for the handle. She smiled. *Clay*.

"Good morning, Jamie. May I say you look beautiful and radiant today?" Clay eased the bag from her shoulder.

"Flattering me won't make me worry less about Maddie." She stepped past Clay, grateful for the glass of cold water he held out to her.

"Where do you want to sit?"

"The forbidden couch. I need to get my feet up. And Luke

isn't here to worry about my water breaking on their damn special couch." Jamie waddled towards the living room, waiting for King to try to knock her off her feet. "Where's King?"

Jamie glanced into the dining room and noticed the stack of papers on the table. Years as a detective had ingrained the image of case files in her memory.

"Madison took him for a run." Clay held out his hand to help her sit.

Jamie slapped it away. "I'm not an invalid."

"I know, just trying to help. Haven't been around a pregnant woman before, so I don't know what you need."

"What I *need* is the truth about that stack of case files on the dining room table. This might be the house of a former detective, but the man house-sitting has no reason to have case files in his possession. Not to mention the woman staying with him, who has a very nasty bruise on her throat." Jamie drained the contents of the glass and handed it to Clay. "Spill it, Slay. What's going on?"

He placed the glass on a coaster. "I'm taking care of it."

"What is *it*?" Jamie didn't decline Clay's offer to help get her legs onto the couch. She waited as he arranged pillows under her aching and swollen feet.

Clay sat down on the carpet. "Have you kept tabs on Foster Ericson?"

"Maybe. Why? Is Maddie in danger? I'll kill Foster if he even thinks about Maddie." Jamie didn't doubt with Foster being locked up, Maddie and Noa were probably all he ever thought about.

"He's still in prison. Calm down mommy-bear, it's not good for the boys."

Jamie flinched and touched her left side.

"What's wrong?" Clay came to his knees.

"Sit down, Davis. The baby just kicked or stretched. I'm not sure anymore. They're getting too big."

Clay's eyes sparkled. "May I? I've never felt a baby kick before. I had to help deliver a baby once, but it's not the same."

Jamie took his hand, placing it on her stomach. "You can talk to them. They've been able to hear for a couple of weeks now. It was the biggest mistake of my life telling Luke."

Clay moved his hand over Jamie's stomach and laughed when the tiny human pressed under his palm. "What is that? A foot? A hand?"

"I think it's a foot. Luke is teaching them about rugby and Spencer isn't helping at all with his nightly sing-songs. They love the sound of their father's voice." She laid her hand on Clay's. "What happened to Maddie?"

Clay refused to look Jamie in the eye. "Sorry, but I can't tell you. The stress won't be good for you or Lucas and Davis." He grinned.

"We're not naming one of our boys after you. Not unless you make an honest woman of my sister before they're born."

"If I ask Maddie to marry me will that count?" He leaned closer to Jamie's belly. "I'm going to be your favourite uncle, not Luke. I'll teach you about ice hockey and make pizza whenever you come to visit."

"Seriously, what is with you and Luke trying to convince the boys who their favourite family member will be?" Jamie wiped the tears streaming down her face. "Thank you for being you, Slay."

Clay jerked his hand away from Jamie's stomach. "I didn't mean to make you cry. I'm sorry, Jamie. The idea of life growing inside of you? It's beautiful and miraculous. I never wanted to have children, but now with Maddie ..."

He shook his head. "Maybe I'm getting broody." Clay cleared his throat. "I need a beer or to go shoot something. Your hormones are affecting me."

Jamie grabbed his forearm. "You can talk to the boys whenever you want. And because you are a part of our family, you're allowed to touch my belly. Hold up – you're considering asking Maddie to marry you? Slay, you better tell me what happened to her neck. Last thing, please help me get up. I'm going to have a look at those files, seeing as you refuse to tell me what the hell is going on." Jamie released her death grip on Clay's arm and scooted to the edge of the couch.

Clay helped Jamie to her feet. "I like you too, *Detective Hard-ass*. Yes, I'm going to propose to Maddie when we're both ready. Of course, I'll ask your parents and Luke for their blessing. Luke will be upset if I don't ask him as well. As for the bruise around Maddie's neck, she was attacked on Friday night. Her attacker strangled and threatened her. We believe the attack might be linked to her work with the sex workers. That's the reason for the files on the table. No evidence yet, but we're considering all possibilities."

Jamie placed her hands on her lower back. "Who gave a civilian access to active case files?"

"Detective Gina Larson is working the case now."

"I know her." Jamie frowned. "Can't say I care for her as a person, but I've heard good things about Larson."

Clay laughed. "Gina isn't everyone's cup of tea, but she's good at her job. Gina is better with the dead than she is with the living."

"The files are on the Potters Park Five, aren't they?"

"Yes, how did you know?"

"I know my sister. Madison mentioned the disappearances of the women she is working with. It's understandable she'd consider any unsolved murders to be linked when the victims are female. Are they hers?"

"We don't know yet. DNA will prove if one of the remains is the sister of a woman who was murdered yesterday. Jamie, I beg you, don't worry about this. I'm not letting Maddie out of my sight, and Gina is good at her job."

Jamie pressed her palms to her eyes, trying her best not to let fear overrule logic. She'd already come too close to losing Madison six months earlier. "Not letting her out of your sight? Where is my sister?"

"Right behind you," Madison said.

Chapter 26

Monday, 13 December, 1:09 p.m.

The bed in the infirmary was much more comfortable than the cot in his cell. Here, the noise levels were at least tolerable. Long before she opened the door, he knew she was on her way. Her smell sickened him. He'd rather die than taste her. Ironic that *she* was the gatekeeper out of this hell.

He didn't deserve to be locked up with only the memories of Emily and Madison's taste. Emily wasn't Emily anymore, but Noa. Both deserved to die excruciating deaths for deserting him. If they'd appreciated his love and everything he'd done for them to be together, he wouldn't be here.

The electric doors glided open. Her repulsive scent assaulted his nostrils. He steeled his expression, keeping the endgame in mind.

"Baby, you need to stop getting into fights. I love having you to myself, but I'm worried the next one will be your last. You keep on pissing off the wrong people." Her putrid fingertips touched his arm. The shackle clinked against the steel bed frame.

"You know I'll do anything to be alone with you. It's a price I'm willing to pay for you, my love."

She bent her head down and brushed her mouth against his, licking her lips as she pulled away. "I missed you."

"I know. How is our plan coming along?" He reached for her face with his free hand, wishing he could wrap it around her throat and squeeze the life out of her.

"It's taking longer than I expected because of the risks involved. I don't want you to die."

"Imagine what it will be like when I can make love to you, taking my time to explore every part of you. It's the one thought keeping me sane while I'm left to rot in this place."

"Soon, my love. I promise." She removed his file and scanned through it. "You've been lucky, again. You're like a damn cat."

"A cat who can't wait to lick you." He forced a smile.

She stared at the blanket covering his groin and frowned. "I thought you'd be happy to see me."

"It's the pain medication, baby, not you. You know how eager I am to do *things* to you. Tell me what's happening on the outside."

She told him about the attack on Madison, knowing that's what he wanted to hear. As she spoke about Madison, the pain medication proved to have no effect.

She stared down at him. "You will always want her. Here I am, risking everything for you, and you get hard hearing her name."

"Not her name, baby. Your voice. The glee on your face, telling me how badly she was hurt. But Madison is mine to kill. Who attacked her, and why?"

"Your *precious* Madison is poking around in something she shouldn't. Poor little mouse, thinking she can play with the cats. If you don't get out of here soon, someone else is going to kill her long before you can."

First order of business once Foster escaped – find whoever had dared to hurt his Madison and rip him apart. Then, hunt down Emily and Madison, and kill them.

Monday, 13 December, 1:15 p.m.

Five women missing for close to two years. Ten for almost a year. A month after being discovered in Potters Park, five female bodies remained unidentified. *Poor child, if only you had held the scavenger map the right way around.*

Emma and Jenna were both dead. The investigation was ongoing.

Claire.

Another five women hadn't been heard from in days. Assumed missing.

In the middle of all this carnage? Madison Taylor.

Jamie's palms slammed on the dining room table. "Madison Taylor, what the hell have you stumbled on?"

"We don't know yet, but we will get to the bottom of this and I'll protect Maddie. She's safe here." Clay draped an arm over Madison's shoulder.

Jamie pointed at the mirror behind her. "Take a hard look at yourself. The mark around your neck. This is not staying safe. Dammit, Madison." She reached for the closest chair and sat down hard.

"This is why we didn't want to tell any of you. You can't handle the stress. Mom and Dad are still recovering from what happened to Noa and me in June. Luke is going to go ballistic, and Spencer is going to be angry with me for upsetting you." Madison pressed her face into Clay's chest.

"The police found more bodies this morning, after a landslide at Paradise Beach. We hope the medical examiner and the forensics lab will find evidence which will lead to the arrests of the people involved." Clay rubbed Madison's back.

"People? Arrests?" Jamie asked.

"Yes, we suspect more than one person is involved, based on the evidence from the Potters Park murders."

Jamie reached for the glass of water and pressed it to her left cheek.

"Please keep this to yourself. I'm safe here." Madison walked around the table, dropping to her knees by Jamie's side. "I'm safe. Nobody knows where I am, except detective Larson." Madison reached for her sister's hands.

"You suspect a police officer is involved? Yesterday, he

murdered Claire. And now you're saying Emma's death wasn't an accident. Dammit, Maddie, I can't go through this again. When Foster had you, I couldn't breathe. I've never been so scared in my life."

Madison pushed to her feet and cradled Jamie's head to her chest. "This is not the same as what happened with Foster. He's in prison."

"Has he been sending you letters, too?" Jamie wrapped her arms around Madison's waist.

"What do you mean, *too*?" Clay asked.

"He's been sending Noa letters. We didn't want to tell you because we didn't want to scare you."

Dread settled over Madison. Her soul crushed under the weight.

Death, his death, would be their only way to be free of him. Forever they'd be bound to him, as Foster wanted her and Noa to be.

Madison realised Foster was a secondary threat. *If he is second, who is first?*

Monday, 13 December, 1:30 p.m.

An hour earlier, the sky had cleared, making way for the heat of the sun.

It would take days to reconstruct each body. Four skulls, ten femurs, five pelvic bones, eleven clavicles and many smaller bones lay waiting to be identified.

The crime scene investigators continued excavating in areas where the ground-penetrating radar showed possible remains were buried beneath the sand. They wouldn't stop searching until they were sure they'd found every bone and any other piece of evidence that could lead them to the murderer.

Doctor Seymour studied the scene and shook her head. For a moment, she closed her eyes, breathed in the salty air and appreciated the caress of the light breeze on her face. Some crime scenes forced her to take multiple moments to clear her head. The horrific things humans inflicted on others never ceased to amaze her. It kept her coming back to the job. Year after year. Not everyone could handle working with the dead. To her it was an honour to speak for the victims. No matter what stage of decomposition the bodies were in, she treated them all with the same respect she showed the living.

She opened her eyes and inspected the skulls, lifting each in a gloved hand. Her voice remained a whisper as she asked them for answers.

In awe, Gina watched Doctor Seymour. This wasn't the first case they'd worked together on, and it wouldn't be the last. Not with the city's high murder rate. She kept out of the way of those working the scene. This was their domain. She had to wait her turn.

Gina stepped underneath the tarp. "Anything you can tell me so far?" she asked after Doctor Seymour returned the fourth skull to the table.

"Five females. Three are Caucasian, and one Asian based on the morphology of the skulls. One had given birth, based on these shotgun pellet-sized pockmarks on the pelvic bone." Doctor Seymour showed Gina the bone impressions. "I'll contact a forensic anthropologist to confirm my findings. From the length of the femurs, I estimate early twenties, maybe late teens. Two of the jaws still have wisdom teeth present." She removed the gloves and tossed them into a waste basket. "One victim suffered a gunshot wound to the cranium. Won't be sure about the others until we've reconstructed their skeletons."

"Found something!" A voice came from the excavation area. Gina and Doctor Seymour walked to the man, waving his hand in the air. "What's this?" he asked.

Gina hunched down and stared at the item embedded in the sand. "The tip of an arrow. This is a dump site. The same as the Potters Park Five." She pushed to her feet, pulling the phone from her pocket. "How long do you estimate these bodies have been out here?" she asked Doctor Seymour.

Gina tried to hide the tremble in her hand by clutching the phone harder.

"My best guess? Two years."

Chapter 27

Adam stared at the activity on the beach. Even at a distance, Detective Larson appeared more solemn than she tended to look at crime scenes. He wondered why. Walking over and asking about the case was too risky. He didn't have a reason to be at the scene.

Another round with Dakota might help ease the tension in his shoulders, but for now she was someone else's to play with. The men had paid a lot of money for the girls, and he still had others to break. A well-broken-in girl offered a much better ride in the long run.

Adam's phone rang. He answered without looking at the screen. "Hello, darling. Do you want me to hurry home before you leave for your shift?"

"What's going on at Paradise Beach?"

"Not sure yet. Don't worry, my love. It's been two years."

Eva cursed until she ran out of words. "You keep screwing up. I told you to dump them in the ocean, but no, you buried them where they were bound to be discovered. Where are the others?"

Adam sighed. "Where they'll never be found."

"You are a dumb and cocky sonofabitch."

"Calm down, darling. Nothing traces back to either of us."

"This is bad for business. *My* business."

"*Your* business? *I* started this. Have you forgotten how I got the money for your perky tits?"

"I made it an enterprise. And don't you dare tell me it was your idea when I was the one who planted the seed."

Adam turned away from the scene, making his way back to his car along the shore.

"Do you remember our wedding anniversary three years ago? After we sent the whore home, I said she had beautiful eyes and wondered how much money people would pay for eyes like hers? I even said no one cares when whores go missing." Eva's voice cracked as she tried not to laugh. "I made you, Adam. Clean up *your* mess. I'll deal with you tomorrow."

Monday, 13 December, 2:18 p.m.

Blade stepped onto the deck and scanned the surroundings. This was his best chance of speaking to Torch alone. The others had paired up for the afternoon.

Vegas was busy tending to Dakota. He didn't know what had happened, but the way Dakota had rushed off when Adam arrived spoke volumes. The last time he saw Dakota, pain radiated off her in waves. Her eyes were vacant.

He hated it.

Blade lowered the sunglasses over his eyes and took the chair next to Torch. He knew Torch's name outside of this house, and the dire consequences if people were to find out how Torch spent two weeks of his year.

"Did you know Adam rapes the women?" he asked, twisting in the chair to face the man next to him.

Torch kept his eyes closed with his face lifted towards the sun. "What Adam does to them is between him and them."

"So, you're aware that they are sex workers?" Blade asked.

Torch yawned, extending his arms into the air. "I guessed, based on the amount of money we pay to be here."

"The Potters Park Five are five of the women we spent last December with. I found evidence they were murdered around the time we left the house."

"In their line of work, it doesn't surprise me. Why are you telling me this?"

Despite wanting to scream and pulverise Torch's face, Blade kept his voice low and controlled. "You don't know the details of their murders. One victim was shot. One had the tip of an arrow embedded between two of her neck vertebras. Another had been cut in half at the waist with a very sharp blade, like a katana. The fourth woman was bludgeoned, and the fifth's skeleton showed burn wounds."

Torch turned to face him. "Where are the other five?"

"Buried somewhere." Blade shrugged. "The sternums of all five had been cut open. I found evidence linking the Potters Park Five to two unsolved murders from two and a half years ago. The bodies were found within days of the murders. Their sternums had been cut open and their organs removed. Something is going on and we need to find out what it is … before it's too late."

Crush stepped out of the house and pulled up a chair. "I know what's going on." Blade and Torch stared at him. "We're being recorded having sex with the girls and the footage is uploaded on the internet."

Torch leaned forward in his chair. "How do you know this?"

"I stumbled on it when I was looking for porn. Remember Sabrina, from two years ago? Well, maybe you won't, seeing as you only joined our little group last year. I found a video in which Sabrina was the star. The longer I watched, the more things I recognised in the background. When the camera angle changed, I saw my tattoo." Crush laughed, stuck a cigarette between his lips and lit it. He took a deep drag, sending a cloud of grey smoke into the air. "I'm a porn star. My mom will be so proud."

Torch grabbed the chair's armrests. "I can't have my face in a porn video. Do you have any idea what this will do to my career?"

"Calm down, the videos never show our faces. The girls are

at the centre of the show. Different angles, but always the girl. And maybe your dick, depending on what's happening."

"There are more videos?" Blade asked. The hair on the back of his neck stood up.

"Yes, after the video I found of myself and Sabrina, I started digging and found a crapload on different sites. Last year's threesomes were spectacular. It got me through after I left my girlfriend in February and inspired some of my best work this past year."

Torch fumed. "This is ludicrous. What if they didn't cut out our faces in every video? I didn't sign up for this. Shit." He pushed to his feet and stormed to the poolside bar. He returned with three tumblers filled to the brim with a golden-brown liquid. Blade and Torch both cleared the contents in one gulp.

Monday, 13 December, 3:01 p.m.

The taillights of Jamie's car disappeared between the row of oak trees. Madison leaned into Clay's embrace, resting the back of her head against his chest. Jamie had agreed to keep the information they'd discussed to herself, but Madison couldn't help but worry about what the burden would do to her. Jamie and Spencer were living with their parents so that Spencer could tend to the business of the wine estate over the holiday period, and it was easier for Jamie to be at the shooting range when necessary to meet clients.

"I miss Noa," Madison said.

"I know." Clay hugged her tighter. "You two have grown close over the past couple of months and not because of your shared love of music and performing on stage."

"Why didn't she tell me about the letters?"

"Why didn't *you* tell her about *your* letters?"

Madison smacked his triceps. "No fair, Davis. It's not the same." She sighed. "It is."

"You both wanted to carry on with your lives and wanted the same for each other. Families protect each other. It's why Jamie wants to protect you now. But this time around, you have me to keep you safe."

"I can't believe there was a time you weren't part of my life. Thank you for being the one who carried me out."

"When I rushed into the cellar, I noticed nothing but you. There was this primal urge inside me to get you out of there. When I stepped through the door, I noticed Noa and her dad, but rage consumed me when I glimpsed the shackle around your ankle. The only thing I could think about was getting you as far away from *him* as possible."

"You've never told me this." Madison dropped her mouth to his forearm.

"Couldn't say this to my friend. Not without you realising I'd thought you were the most beautiful woman in the world the first time I saw you, despite a killer having held you captive."

"You wouldn't have thought so if I wasn't half-naked," she said, her mouth against his skin.

Clay pressed his lips to the back of her neck. "It was your eyes, not your boobs."

They moved to the porch swing and rocked, watching King move closer to the horses. He walked backwards when the stallion and mare lifted their heads. The mare's sides were filling out.

"How long before you think Noa will be pregnant? Her horse is," Clay asked.

"I hope Foster is in the ground before that happens. I hope he dies within the next hour. Scratch that, minute."

"I know, babe. Gina called while you walked with Jamie to her car."

"It's them, isn't it?" Madison drew her legs to her chest, resting her arms on her knees.

"That's the assumption until they have DNA evidence. Same as the Potters Park Five."

"Why are they doing this?"

"Why do any criminals do what they do? Because they can."

"Why not take women from the streets? Or homeless people? All the women I work with are free agents, if I can call them that. They're very specific regarding their clientele. Are they being held somewhere? For how long? And where? By who? Who is the police officer in the middle of all of this?"

"We will find answers to all your questions. Gina said they've looked at security camera footage from outside the bar where Emma was last seen. A black sedan pulled away from the curb minutes after Emma and Jenna walked down the street. But the sedan in yesterday's video, from the marina, didn't have a scratch on the bumper or a dent."

"Maybe he has more than one car, or had it fixed? Perhaps he fixed it himself. Where are Vegas and the other four? Do we still have time to save them? Sitting around and waiting is driving me insane. I should start making arrangements for Claire's funeral."

Madison leaned into Clay's arms. She thought about Claire and how far she'd come since they met. Claire had considered better options to earn a living and wanted to finish her high school education.

On the other side of the row of oak trees lay her parents' wine farm – Lamont Estate. For the umpteenth time, Madison wondered how her life would've turned out had she been born into a different family. It didn't feel natural not to tell her parents about what was going on. Aaron Taylor had been a detective. Laura was the reason Madison had decided to become a social worker. It was through her mother's work she had Luke for a brother. Most of the women Madison worked with either didn't have siblings or their siblings ended up on a similar path or worse … Dead.

"I'm going to ask my parents if we can bury Claire in the family graveyard. My maternal grandparents would have a fit. They never accepted Luke as part of the family. That's why I've hated them for as long as I can remember. But Claire deserves to rest in a place filled with peace and love."

"Just when I think I can't fall more in love with you, I do. I swear, Maddie, you have the most beautiful heart." Clay placed a hand over her left breast. The corners of his mouth lifted.

Chapter 28

According to Crush, inside each room there were multiple cameras; all positioned towards the bed. If Crush had told them the truth. Blade wondered if there were also cameras throughout the house and the rest of the property. This wasn't the only house on the island. Each property was fenced off down to the beach, giving occupants complete privacy. The only way to reach the island was by boat. *Too far to swim.*

Blade reached for Vegas. "Let's go to the beach."

"Are you sure? We could play poker, but let's up the stakes and play strip poker."

He rolled onto his side, placing a hand on her stomach. Above his thumb, Vegas' ribs jutted out. None of the women ate much. It bothered him. They were either not used to having so much food around or wanted to keep their bodies in shape.

Vegas liked to run. They'd gone for a run first thing in the morning. If he wanted to keep up with her in the future, he'd need to start training regularly. He hadn't asked – a gentleman never does – but he guessed Vegas to be around twenty-five. Fifteen years his junior. Enough of a difference to raise eyebrows, but not enough for a relationship not to work. No matter what, he'd get her safely off the island and pursue a relationship with her. The real her and not the fake name she'd used for too long.

Vegas turned her head, her back remaining flat on the mattress. "What are you thinking?"

"How incredible you are. You're beautiful. Let's go to the beach. I want you so much, but I'm exhausted after our run. I'm getting too old for this."

She smiled, her eyes squinting. "Would you rather go to the beach than have your way with me?"

"Who said I won't have my way with you on the beach? But you need to do all the work. My legs are still shaking from trying to keep up with you this morning."

"It's never *work* with you. Only immense pleasure."

Blade closed his eyes and fought the urge to take her, remembering the cameras. He rolled off the bed and walked to the wardrobe. With his back to the room, he grabbed two beach towels and stuffed them into Vegas' oversized bag. He slipped another item in between the towels and grabbed a pair of swim shorts, undressing in front of her. It seemed best to keep whoever was watching them, believing they were oblivious to the cameras.

Vegas moved closer, wrapping her arms around his waist and pressing her cheek against his back. Her fingernails trailed up his legs and stopped short of where his reaction to her jutted towards the wardrobe.

"He wants me," she murmured. Her breath a whisper on his skin.

"I want you more."

Once they reached the beach, they settled on the beach towels. Vegas handed Blade a bottle of water.

"I know you said we won't have sex until I want to, but back there in the room, I wanted to. Wasn't I clear on that?" She lifted the bottle to her mouth.

Blade reached for Vegas' hand and moved closer. "You were. Believe me, not making love to you was one of the hardest things I've ever done."

Vegas placed her fingers against his mouth. "Don't call it that. Please."

He kissed her fingers and held her hand. "I like you. I'm

interested in you. In every way a man should be interested in you. We won't have sex because there are feelings involved here. Or am I the only one who feels this way?"

Vegas shook her head. "No. I wasn't sure you felt the way I do. It's been a very long time since I was last involved with someone. Never dreamt I would be again."

Blade sighed. "I haven't been in a relationship since my divorce. Seven years. The main reason I didn't want to do anything – there are cameras inside the rooms. Someone is recording footage of all of us having sex and posting it online."

She opened her mouth and froze. "Not only do they kill us, but they make money from us having sex. What's really going on here?"

After looking around to ensure no one else was close by, Blade reached inside Vegas' beach bag. "Can you please give me that?" He stared at her wide-brimmed sun hat.

She handed it to him without question.

"Thank you. Please keep an eye out for anyone coming down to the beach. I need to make a phone call and we can't risk being caught."

Vegas pushed her hair behind her ears. "There's no reception here."

"I borrowed a satellite phone from a friend." Blade smiled. "We're getting off this island tonight."

Vegas stood, positioning her feet on either side of Blade's hips. He leaned back and placed his hands next to his head, the phone pressed to his right ear. The wide brim of the hat covered his face and hands.

Vegas' hips swayed to a song only she heard. Blade contacted his friend and within seconds, relayed the message. He came upright and pressed his mouth to her inner thighs as he returned the satellite phone to the beach bag.

Vegas sank down on top of him and removed her hat, placing it on her head.

"May I please request you do that again when we are far, far away from here?" he asked.

"Do what?" She rested her arms on his shoulders.

Blade pulled her closer, pressing his mouth to her throat. "My friend will come get us tonight. Be ready. We'll figure out where to go as soon as we're away from here."

"I know who we can ask for help. While we wait, do you mind dancing for me?"

Blade laughed, easing his hands up her back. He pulled Vegas' shoulders forward and pressed his mouth against hers for a brief kiss. "Anything for you."

Never in his life had he danced for a woman, but Vegas wasn't just any woman.

Chapter 29

Gina stared at the crime scene photos she'd stuck to the board in her office. "Where are you?" she asked Doctor O'Reilly. Gina lost count of how many times she had dialled his number. He'd either switched off his phone, or wherever Doctor O'Reilly vacationed, there wasn't any reception.

After spending most of the day on her feet, Gina's back and neck ached. By the time she'd left the scene at Paradise Beach, they had found a fifth skull. Doctor Seymour was certain that all five of the skulls were female.

A knock on the door pulled her attention away from the board. "Come in."

"Word is Doctor Seymour and her team found the remains of at least five females at Paradise Beach." Detective Evans sat down, anticipating the creak of the leather. This wasn't his first time in Gina's office. "Larson, do you think the remains are that of the women Madison Taylor is nagging my department about?"

Gina reached for a pen and twirled it between her fingers. "We'll have to work this case together. Do you have any leads on the five women Madison reported missing on Friday?"

"Nothing new. They might've left the city or they're in a hotel room with a tourist. The city is teeming with tourists this time of year. And many men, women, even couples, come to Shadow Bay for the booming sex industry and not the scenery."

A sad fact about many tourist destinations. "The women

134

Madison works with don't work with pimps or out of brothels, so I understand your reasoning. But you agree that five going missing two years ago, ten last year and five again this year, can't be a coincidence. The numbers speak for themselves."

"I agree with you. But I have nothing belonging to the missing girls with DNA on, to compare to the remains found."

"What about the hairbrush Madison gave you?" Gina leaned forward, resting her elbows on the desk. She locked stares with Evans.

"I handed it to the lab. With the current backlog, we're looking at a minimum of twenty-one days before we'll get the results. I spoke to the head of the lab and explained the urgency of this case. He said they need to prioritise their work." Evans shrugged. "As soon as I have results, I'll contact you. But that might identify one body. What about the others?"

"I don't know, Evans. This is a mess." Gina pushed her fingers through her hair and tied it at the back with a hairband she found in the desk's top drawer. "*If* we have a serial killer on our hands, one who kills during the festive season, how long will it take before tourists start going elsewhere? You know how the public forms their opinions. I'm expecting the mayor to call any minute and put pressure on us to solve this. The media have already reported on the discovery this morning. Paradise Beach is prime real estate for investors. And tourists from across the world flock to that beach, and this city, to escape the colder weather in the northern hemisphere."

Evans rubbed the stubble on his chin. "You think this is the work of a serial killer?"

"Until we find evidence proving otherwise, it's a reasonable assumption. It could be gang initiations, or a pimp trying to get rid of the competition." Gina massaged the back of her neck.

"I tell you what, I'm going to wait a few more days. *If* the girls Madison claims are missing haven't shown up by then, I'll approach the captain and discuss our options. We might be allowed access to the girls' apartments. That's all I can do at this stage. We better hope and pray that when the girls turn up in a few weeks, they don't sue the city and police department for searching their homes."

Gina thanked Evans and waited for him to leave before opening the desk's bottom drawer. The hairbrush Madison had given her lay on top of a stack of cold case files. Seeing as Evans had handed in the one Madison gave him, there was no need for Gina to waste the lab's valuable time and limited resources.

Monday, 13 December, 10:40 p.m.

Of all the women he'd had sex with, she came the closest to being his equal. He'd made a mistake; Emily wasn't anything like him. The long and ugly scar on his once magnificent abdomen was a constant reminder of her treachery. His Emily belonged to another man. Luke Taylor. The muscle monkey. The Neanderthal. Foster should've shot him in the head and not aimed for the heart. *Fucking Kevlar.*

She eased off him, holding onto the side of the bed for support. Her legs were unsteady after riding him like only she could. Foster liked this one. She was a taker, just like him.

With her there were no pretences. No need to stroke her ego. No sweet words to keep her inline.

"When I get out of here, I expect this every day." Foster grabbed between her legs and rubbed his palm against her, watching her mouth open and her head fall back.

"I'm all out of orgasms. Think I had two." She placed a hand over his. "Maybe we can try for more later. I'm on shift until tomorrow morning." A predatory sneer spread across her face.

Not the most beautiful woman he'd ever had on top of him, but she made up for it in other ways.

"How is the plan coming along to get you out of here?" She stepped away from the bed, pulling down her skirt.

"The bitch is stalling, but I'm working on her."

She smirked. "I bet you are. Did your stitches hold?"

Foster lifted his shirt and stared at the gauze. "Looks fine. You held back tonight. Who tired you out?"

"The bitch did. Tried to make up for a week's worth of not tasting me in a few hours. I had to think about you to get off." She laughed. The sound wasn't pretty.

"You lie so well. If you'd been my lawyer, I wouldn't be in here."

"If you had spent time planning your actions, you wouldn't be here. It's all about planning, the details, and the execution." She patted his shoulder as if consoling an enemy.

"Touché. I've learned from my mistakes. This time, I won't make any." Foster wouldn't admit he'd made a mistake to anyone else. In her, he'd found a mirror image of himself. "Can you please bring me some water? I'm not allowed to walk too much. Doctor's orders."

"Your doctor isn't very intelligent. She still has no clue what's going on. Her primary focus is on Adam and getting him out of my life. Weird, because she thinks the two of you will ride off into the sunset."

"Let the puppet do her dance. We know what *our* end goal is."

She pouted and pressed her breasts together. Foster ran his finger along the groove. "Oh Evie, please love me. Oh Foster, please love me. Fucking idiot. But Charlie serves her purpose. She's making me a tonne of money and one of her contacts came through. A week from now, I'm putting this city behind me and moving my enterprise."

"Oh Evie, but what about me?" Foster pouted.

They both laughed.

Emily/Noa and Madison were going to die. Then Foster would be free to reinvent himself.

Chameleons – that's what Foster and Evie were.

Chapter 30

Tuesday, 14 December, 3:55 a.m.

Blade hugged the warm body lying next to him. Vegas had fallen asleep a few hours earlier. He couldn't sleep. The pressure of the gun shoved down the front of his pants was a constant reminder of the danger they were in. He couldn't relax. Not until Vegas was safe, and he'd found a way to rescue the women they'd leave behind.

"Honey, wake up," he whispered against her ear. Vegas stiffened and held her breath. "I want to have sex on the beach. Right now. I want to come as the sun rises," Blade said, louder than necessary.

Vegas pushed out of his arms and walked to the wardrobe. "Good thing we didn't unpack the towels yesterday. I don't like sand getting into my hard-to-reach places. Let's go. I've been waiting to have you inside me."

He touched her shoulder as Vegas reached for the door. "Okay, but we need to be quiet. I don't want an audience. Nobody gets to see you naked except me."

She turned and kissed him. "Hurry, I want you."

Hand in hand, they tiptoed through the quiet and dark house. When they reached the wooden walkway, they increased their pace.

The sound of an approaching helicopter replaced the symphony of crickets and frogs.

The sand slowed them down. Using their hands, they shielded their eyes against the blast of sand the rotors whisked into the air.

Blade glanced back at the house, noticing light in the entertainment room's windows. "Run!" He lifted Vegas into the helicopter. "Go." Blade slapped the pilot's shoulder and reached to close the door.

The helicopter lifted into the air, heading over the black water. Vegas looked past him and saw the others standing on the deck.

He turned to her and touched her knee. "We will save them. I promise. Call your friend. I hope she can help us."

Vegas dug inside the bag for the satellite phone and punched in the numbers. The day she'd met Madison Taylor, she had recited Madison's number until it became a rhyme she'd never forget.

Tuesday, 14 December, 4:05 a.m.

The music became louder. It took Madison a few seconds to realise the noise came from her phone. In the darkness, she reached for the illuminated screen and answered, despite the caller ID showing a combination of numbers she hadn't seen before. "Hello?"

"Maddie, it's Vegas. I need your help."

Adrenaline spiked in Madison's veins. She reached for the lamp on the bedside table.

Clay blinked at the sudden light. In an instant, he sat with his back against the headboard, on full alert. Receiving a call in the middle of the night wasn't uncommon for either of them.

Madison clutched the phone to her ear. "Where are you? I've been worried sick. What's going on? What's that noise?"

"I'm in a helicopter. I'll explain later. Madison, we need your help. Where can I meet you?"

Madison glanced at the curtains. She could explain to her parents later. "Ask the pilot to land on the farm to the east of Lamont Estate. I'll switch on the floodlights. How far away are you?"

Vegas confirmed with the pilot. "About twenty minutes. Tiffany, Kayla, Jersey, and Dakota are still there. We have to save them. Please."

"We'll talk as soon as you get here." Madison ended the call and reached for her clothes.

Clay did the same, shrugging on his jeans and pulling a shirt over his head. "I'll call Jamie and inform her about the helicopter. And ask her to keep your parents calm until we can explain this to them."

"Thank you." Madison's hands shook as she tried to fasten her bra.

Clay walked around the bed to help. "Never put one *on* a woman before."

Madison smiled despite the anxiety pulsing inside her.

Clay called Jamie while Madison ran downstairs to switch on the floodlights. She paced the length of the porch, wringing her hands.

Tuesday, 14 December, 4:27 a.m.

Clay glanced up at the helicopter as it lifted off the ground. The pilot saluted him. *Commander Voight?* How was his commanding officer involved?

Noticing a man walking next to Madison's friend, Clay reached for his gun.

Madison ran into the field and threw her arms around the dark-haired woman, sending the poor woman stumbling backwards. The man grabbed both of them before they fell.

Clay released his grip on the gun, extending his right hand. "Doctor O'Reilly, we've been looking for you."

"Clay." Blade shook Clay's hand, but kept an arm around the woman's shoulders. "Considering the circumstances, call me Declan."

The woman stared up at him. "You weren't lying. You are a medical examiner?"

"Yes. My name is Declan O'Reilly." He stepped to the side and held a hand towards her.

"I'm Natalie King, a medical student." A hint of a smile tugged at the corners of her mouth. "*Former* sex worker."

Declan reached for Natalie's face, dropping his mouth to hers. "And now, you're mine."

Madison and Clay shot each other a questioning glance. King brushed against Natalie and Declan's legs. Natalie stiffened and stared at him.

"Oh, don't mind him. King thought you called him when you said your surname. He's just a big lovable puppy even at almost three years old. Don't be surprised if he sticks to your side. King loves women." Madison turned towards the house. "Let's go inside. I'll make coffee. We need to talk."

Natalie rubbed King's head and jerked upright. "We need to save the others. They're still on the island."

"Seal Island?" Clay asked.

Declan nodded. "Yes, please call it in. However, discretion is of the utmost importance. One man is a very prominent figure in our city."

Madison placed an arm around Natalie. "I don't care if he is the president. Clay, call Gina. We have to save my friends. Too many women have died."

Tuesday, 14 December, 4:39 a.m.

Gina grabbed her badge and gun as she ran out the door; Duke right behind her. After Clay had woken them up, Gina contacted Captain Wilson while Duke called the SWAT team's commander.

"I still think it's weird that Voight was already awake and not his usual grumpy self," Duke said to Gina.

"We have to make it in time." She buckled her seatbelt as Duke pulled the car out of the driveway. The neighbours had made peace long ago with the occasional squeal of tyres, no matter the time. In fact, most of them appreciated having members of law enforcement living on their street.

"We will be. I still can't believe Doctor O'Reilly is involved in this." Duke shifted gears, steering the Mustang into the sharp turn.

Gina's heart sat in her throat. Not because of the speed Duke was driving, she was used to it. "You can't say anything to anyone about his involvement. As for the other men on the island, Clay said one is a prominent figure in Shadow Bay. Our primary objective is getting the women to the safe house. Captain Johnson, in River Valley, is making his house available to them. His property is at the foot of the mountain and there's only one road leading up to the house. I've got officers on the way there now to access the property and identify any weak spots. Knowing Captain Johnson, he probably has landmines on the perimeter, an arsenal instead of a pantry and attack dogs." Gina leaned back in the passenger seat.

"He served in the military. What did you expect?" Duke brought the Mustang to a screeching halt at the gate of SWAT's headquarters. He grabbed the back of Gina's neck and brought her mouth to his for a hard kiss. "Be safe, baby."

"You too." Gina kissed him again before jumping out of the car.

They ran towards the awaiting helicopters. Gina climbed in and blew Duke a kiss as he took a seat in the other helicopter. *Please, don't die.*

Chapter 31

The glare of the monitors was too much for her sleep deprived eyes. *Never a good time for screen time.* She rubbed her eyes and refocused on the screens. The bedrooms were empty.

With a click of the mouse, she switched on the cameras that were positioned throughout the rest of the house. It reminded Charlotte of all the nights she spent watching reality television. Alone.

Despite their guests' life choices, they kept their indulgences to the bedrooms, the bathrooms or the swimming pool.

"Why the hell are you all awake so early?"

In the living room, four of the girls sat huddled together on a couch. Tiffany handed the youngest girl tissues.

Torch puffed on a cigar, a tumbler in his other hand, pacing outside on the deck.

Trigger and Archer threw darts.

Crush stood in the kitchen, arms crossed, watching the kettle.

"Four girls. Torch. Trigger. Archer. Crush. That's eight." She clicked through the other live feeds. "Where are Blade and Vegas?"

Her fists slammed on the desk. "Dammit, Evie. I told you we should've installed cameras on the beach, but no, *too expensive.* We could've had great footage to sell."

A muscle in her jaw twitched as Charlotte watched footage recorded earlier in Blade's room. "Okay, Blade and Vegas went

143

to have sex on the beach. Why is everyone else awake? And why is the little bitch crying?"

Charlotte grabbed her phone.

Evie answered on the third ring. "Do you know what time it is?"

"Send Adam to the island. Now. Something happened and I can't find Blade or Vegas on any of the feeds."

Evie sighed. "Maybe they're having fun on the beach or watching the sunrise."

"That doesn't explain why Dakota is crying and the girls are huddled around her. Vegas is the mother-figure in the group. No way in hell she wouldn't be there to take care of Dakota."

Evie yawned. "Maybe she has PMS, or a guy got rough. Who knows with these sluts."

"Evie, you're not listening to me. Everyone is awake. They've never been up this early and the men appear on edge. Torch is already drinking and smoking a cigar. And I know they all went to bed and slept. You're not here to play with me, so I watched them play."

"Okay, I'll send Adam. Calm down, you're getting worked up over nothing." Evie ended the call.

Charlotte tapped a finger to her lips and grinned. "Goodbye, Adam. She is mine now."

Tuesday, 14 December, 4:40 a.m.

The coffee burned her mouth, but the pain didn't register, her mind occupied by what she was hearing. Madison touched Clay's knee as she leaned forward to place the empty mug on the coffee table.

"You had no idea the women were paid to be there to have sex with you?" Clay asked Declan before turning to Natalie. "No offence."

"None taken." She ran a hand along King's head. He'd made himself comfortable on Natalie's lap the moment she'd sat down on the couch.

Declan rubbed Natalie's back. "No. I didn't. My understanding was everyone was there out of their own free will. Like I said, a vacation for single people."

Natalie kept her eyes on King. "We weren't forced to be there, but he made it impossible to say no to the money we'd get paid. We realised we were in trouble when Adam picked us up to take us to the island. The moment we saw his face, we all knew it wouldn't end well. The reason I didn't try to run away before getting on the boat – Angie. My friend." She turned to Declan. "I gave Madison Angie's hairbrush. The crime lab can compare Angie's DNA to the women found in Potters Park."

Declan tucked Natalie's hair behind her ear. "As soon as I get the results, I will tell you."

"Adam?" Madison asked.

"He's a police officer. I guess he told us as a warning. It worked. He became a regular client for all of us. Adam has a sadistic streak. He unleashes it whenever he's in the mood to draw blood and leave bruises. We have to find Dakota."

"What happened to her?" Madison stepped around the coffee table, taking a seat next to Natalie.

"Adam happened. He raped her again, after the *audition*. Dakota didn't say anything, but the way she reacted when he arrived yesterday, said it all."

Clay leaned forward, placing his elbows on his knees. "Do you know Adam's surname?"

"No, just that he's a police officer. He wanted me, but Blade – sorry Declan – wouldn't let him take me." She turned to Declan. "You should've let him. Adam's going to take his anger out on someone else."

Declan pulled her closer. "You also had a physical reaction to his presence. He spoke to you and you moved close enough that your arm pressed against mine. No way in hell I'd allow him to breathe the same air as you, never mind lay a finger on you. I saw the way he stared, and the things he said."

"Adam wore a disguise when he picked me up at my

apartment before taking us to the island. He didn't wear it whenever he came for his *visits*." Natalie shuddered. "If you can arrange a sketch artist, I can describe Adam's real face."

"I'll ask Detective Larson to set it up," Clay said.

"Who's the man you want to protect, Declan?" Madison glared at him.

"It's not that I *want* to protect him. There will be a shitload of repercussions when his involvement and what happened on these *vacations* are made public. He will see to it that I lose my job, but I don't care." Declan reached for Natalie's hand. "He's the mayor of Shadow Bay."

Madison's and Clay's jaws dropped to the floor. Madison shook her head and sighed. "Did he know the women are sex workers?"

"Yes. But he wasn't aware of the hidden cameras."

"What hidden cameras?" Clay asked.

"One of the other men told us that Adam, and whoever else is involved, records what happens in the bedrooms. The footage is available on various porn sites."

Natalie cursed. "Adam mentioned we'd get performance bonuses. Now I understand what he meant, but he wasn't planning to pay us. We were going to die there."

"If the mayor is in these videos, how has none of this come to light?" Madison asked.

"The men's faces aren't visible. The footage only shows bodies." Declan pushed his fingers through his hair and sighed. "The women's identities aren't protected, unlike the men."

Natalie covered her face with her hands. "So much for a career as a doctor. No one wants *Doctor Porn Star* as their surgeon."

"We didn't do anything." Declan removed her hands from her face. When Natalie looked at him, he smiled. "You're going to be fine."

"No, I'm not. I didn't spend the first night with you, remember?" Tears streamed down her face and she pushed to her feet, walking towards the kitchen.

Madison followed and held Natalie as she cried until they both sank to the floor. "It's going to work out. We will find out who is behind this and stop the videos." Madison stroked Natalie's hair, ignoring the moisture seeping through the back of her shirt.

"Once it's on the internet, there's no way to erase it."

"Then we will say it was revenge porn posted by an ex-boyfriend."

Natalie moved away from Madison and wiped her face with the back of her hand. "You always have an answer for everything." She leaned back and rested her head against the cupboard. "How is Claire? I need to call her. May I use your phone?"

Madison reached for Natalie's shoulders. "I'm sorry, Nat. Adam killed Claire yesterday. She was trying to get to you, and he must've figured out that Claire contacted me."

Natalie drew her knees to her chest, dropping her head forward. "*Coffee.*"

Chapter 32

Commander Voight gave the signal. Gina rushed into the house.

In the living room, four women sat on a couch. Despite holding onto each other, their bodies trembled.

Gina stepped further into the room, holstering her gun. "I'm Detective Gina Larson. Madison Taylor sent me."

Tiffany clutched Dakota to her side. "He took Vegas."

"Vegas being Natalie King?" Gina asked.

"I think I heard Madison call her *Nat* once, but we only know each other's work names," Kayla said. "He abducted her."

"Your friend is safe. The man saved her. *He* is the reason that we, the police, are here."

Dakota lifted her head from Tiffany's shoulder. "You need to find Adam."

"Who is Adam? One of the men?" Gina asked, taking another step closer.

Tiffany laid a hand on Dakota's back. "Do you want to tell her, or can I?"

The small nod of Dakota's head made Gina sink into the nearest chair.

"He raped me the day he brought me here. You can go to my apartment. There's a used condom in the bin in the bathroom. Adam raped all of us." Dakota buried her face in a pillow. "He sodomised me."

Gina steeled her face. "Thank you for telling me."

A SWAT officer cleared his throat from the doorway and nodded. Gina returned her focus to the women. "The four of you are going to stay at a safe house until this case is closed." She stood. "Come. A helicopter is waiting to take us there."

"Will Vegas be joining us?" Jersey asked as they all rose.

"I don't know. I need to speak to her and will have to talk to all of you to get your statements."

Kayla grabbed the arms of the women beside her. "We were going to be the next Potters Park Five."

Gina shook her head. "All I know, whatever was going on here, it wasn't meant to end well."

They walked out of the house to the awaiting helicopter. As they lifted towards the sky, the women took one last look at the house.

"We are *all* done with that life," Tiffany said.

Tuesday, 14 December, 5:25 a.m.

Being prepared for any and every situation imaginable was how she had managed to survive her entire life. Nothing surprised her. Nothing phased her.

She glanced at the clock positioned high on the wall. *Time to go.* After she'd ended the call with Charlie, she used her phone to monitor the activity on the island. *Technology is a girl's best friend.*

Charlie had demanded that she call Adam. She didn't.

Eva stopped once she reached the parking lot, taking a moment to herself. The bright new day and all the possibilities it held made her smile like a Cheshire cat.

After all this time, the burner phone underneath the driver's seat of her car was finally going to be used. Eva emailed the video and address to the police. That done, Eva dialled the last number she ever expected to.

"Good morning, Shadow Bay Police Department. How may I direct your call?"

A free app she'd downloaded months earlier, disguised her voice. "The man who murdered the Potters Park Five lives at 159 Ocean View Drive. He's also responsible for the disappearances of several prostitutes and homeless people over the past few years. I've emailed you a video of him killing Johnny Reed. Ensure the forensics people dig around in the man's backyard. He calls himself Adam. That's his second name. It's not the name he uses in his official capacity with you."

Eva ended the call and lit a cigarette, savouring the taste of victory.

Tuesday, 14 December, 5:30 a.m.

Clay leaned his forehead against the back of Madison's head as they stood waiting for the kettle to boil. She rubbed his arms which were wrapped around her waist.

"They're safe, Maddie. We'll go see them once they've settled in and Gina has talked to Declan and Natalie."

"This will only be over when those involved are in the ground. You need to be part of the arrest. Promise me you'll use deadly force."

"I can't. Unless we get a direct order. And with a case like this, we might not get it. Too many questions need to be answered."

Madison spooned instant coffee into the mugs. Clay poured water and milk. They carried the mugs into the living room.

"The other women should arrive at the safe house any minute." Clay handed Declan and Natalie each a mug.

"What's going to happen to us? Prostitution is illegal." Natalie blew on her coffee.

Clay gave Natalie a warm smile. "You won't be prosecuted. Not in a case like this. But you'll all need to give your statements to Detective Larson. She'll be here later to talk to both of you."

"Will Declan lose his job over this?" Natalie asked.

Declan lifted her hand to his mouth. "I don't care about my job. You're safe, the others are safe and hopefully, we'll uncover who is behind this. I can practise medicine anywhere and there's no reason I'd lose my licence. When I made the payment last year, I didn't know the truth. This year, I did but didn't engage in intercourse. Natalie and I didn't spend the first night together. However, stuff happened on my end, not sure about her. Not that I care."

Natalie lowered her head. "*Stuff* happened on my end, too. And stuff happened between you and me. You didn't get your money's worth with me, but we did some serious *fluffing*." She smiled, pursing her lips.

"Fluffing? You make it sound like porn. Again, I don't care what you did before the night we watched our first movie together. All I care about is you." He brushed his lips against Natalie's palm. "Nothing that comes out during the investigation matters, as long as whoever is responsible is caught and locked up."

Madison rolled the mug between her hands. "Tell me about the other cases you referenced in your report on the Potters Park Five's files."

"A few years ago, I performed autopsies on two women." Declan sighed. "Natalie doesn't need to hear this."

"I'm not leaving." She called King, patting the couch.

Declan pressed a palm to his forehead. "Your guard dog won't make me change my mind. What I'm about to say isn't something I want you to have stuck in your mind."

King glanced up at Declan before pushing his head under Natalie's arm.

"Continue, Doctor O'Reilly. I'm not leaving."

Declan stared at the coffee table. "Both victims' hearts, kidneys, livers, spleens and corneas were removed. Whoever performed the *procedure* tried to remove the second victim's uterus."

"In your professional opinion, are we looking for a killer who keeps the organs as trophies or a cannibal?" Clay asked.

"Based on the precision and location of the severing – organ harvesting. The first two victims died during the *procedure*. I can't pinpoint the exact cause of death. The decomposition of the Potters Park Five is too advanced for me to conclude whether their organs had been removed. But their sternums were cut open with what I believe was a Stryker saw. The same as the previous two victims."

Clay decided to share what Gina had told him. "Yesterday, the CSIs found numerous human bones at Paradise Beach. They aren't done at the scene, but they believe they've found at least five victims so far." He needed a moment to structure his next sentence. "The rib cages aren't held together. Doctor Seymour said it looks as if the victims' chests were cut open."

"The same as the remains found in Potters Park and the two unidentified victims," Declan said.

Clay nodded. "That's not the only consistency. Gunshot. Arrow tip. Fragments of a skull were found. One victim's remains show signs of burn trauma. They're not sure about the other victim yet, as they're still reconstructing the skeletons."

Declan rubbed his hands over his face. "They were setting us up. We weren't allowed to use our names. Adam gave us names, based on 'our occupations or hobbies'. Archer is an artist whose work I've seen at exhibitions, but calling him *Painter* or *Brush Stroke* doesn't sound as dangerous or mysterious. He is an avid hunter, but doesn't believe in guns. I'm Blade because I own a collection of swords and cut up dead people for a living."

Natalie shifted her entire body on the couch to face him, placing a hand on the back of Declan's neck when he leaned forward. "You don't cut up dead people. You find answers from the dead to make those who killed them, or hurt them, pay for what they've done. Who said you cut up dead people?"

"They found me on an online dating site. Angel befriended me and after a few weeks of talking, she invited me on a retreat. She told me it was a singles vacation and sold me on the idea. At the time, I thought I was paying for accommodation, food, those sorts of things, but never the women." He glanced at Natalie. "You have to believe me."

Madison's heart clenched at the misery in Declan's eyes. She grabbed Clay's hand.

"Hey, I'm never going to judge you. But why does a man who looks like you, as educated as you are, and treats women as well as you do, need to resort to online dating?" Natalie didn't move.

"My ex-wife left me because the idea of me touching dead bodies all day and then coming home to touch her made her *physically ill*. I *repulsed* her for choosing to become a medical examiner and not a plastic surgeon. She would've forgiven me if I'd become a gynaecologist, but no sane person chooses to see the things I do every day."

"Bitch. I'll rip her throat out for hurting you like this." Natalie returned Declan's smile.

"I like you more every single day." He pressed his mouth to hers, pulling away before the kiss deepened.

Madison and Clay shot each other another questioning glance.

Declan continued, "I tried to date. Women were either repulsed by my work or had a morbid fascination, which is a red flag. Online dating gave me the opportunity to be someone else and interact with people. I never went on any dates, except with Angel." He glanced at Natalie. "I slept with her. With your friend. I'm sorry."

"No judgement from me, but this big puppy dog might disagree with me." Natalie laughed. "Besides, you slept with Angel, not Angie. The person she was when working couldn't be further from who she was at home. Angie was my best friend. Angel was a colleague."

Chapter 33

Tuesday, 14 December, 6:18 a.m.

The house teemed with activity. The crime scene investigators arrived five minutes after the helicopter took off with the women.

Exactly what did you stumble onto, Madison?

Gina understood the fear, shame, and hopelessness she'd seen in the eyes of the four women. No one deserves to be raped, degraded or treated as an object – Gina's therapist had helped her come to that realisation years ago.

The rooms remained as they had been left. She waited outside the door of the first room as the CSIs collected evidence. Adam must've left a part of himself in the house. As soon as the team arrived, Gina asked an investigator to collect the garbage and fingerprint all the surfaces Adam might've touched, including the groceries and bottles of liquor. She gave clear instructions to search for a broken beer bottle.

Dakota had locked herself in an upstairs bedroom when Adam arrived. The other women kept an eye on him as he moved around the house. They had remained together, sitting on the first step of the staircase leading to the second floor.

"Detective Larson, I've found motion detection cameras in all the rooms. They are Wi-Fi enabled, and set up for live streaming." The investigator Gina had christened *Blitz* called out from down the passage. No one found crucial evidence at a scene as fast as Blitz. Gina had to toss a coin to decide on a nickname for him – Blitz had won instead of Hound.

"We should also search the rest of the house," Gina said, walking towards the room Blitz was in.

"The team is already searching downstairs. What do you think went on here?" he asked.

Gina stared at the bed, wondering whose blood remained on the white sheets. "I don't know. Not yet. I'm heading back to go and interview our witnesses, the ones who alerted us to this."

Gina asked a female officer to pack the women's belongings, which she'd deliver when she went to interview them. She walked through the other bedrooms and adjoining bathrooms. For the second time, she wondered why the men paid for sex. Did they not have wives, girlfriends or someone they could booty call? Were they unsatisfied with their current relationships? Did their partners not meet their expectations or want to play out their fantasies?

Every piece of furnishing, inside and outside of the house, screamed luxury and comfort. Considering not only the location, but the food, alcohol, Viagra and the women, it must've cost the men a small fortune to spend two weeks here.

Gina dreaded the idea of calling her captain and informing him that the mayor was smack in the middle of this. Whatever *this* turned out to be.

She stepped back into the hallway and reached for her ringing phone. "Detective Larson."

"Detective, we received a weird call from a woman earlier this morning. She gave us the address of a man, who she claims murdered the Potters Park Five. She said his name is Adam. He is, according to her, responsible for the disappearances of numerous prostitutes and homeless people. I dispatched officers to the address. You're not going to believe who Adam is. This has got to be a prank."

"Who is Adam?" she asked. The penny dropped when she heard his name.

Gina ran, taking the stairs two at a time, through the sliding doors and onto the deck. She kept running down to the beach where a helicopter waited to take her to River Valley.

Tuesday, 14 December, 6:18 a.m.

The door slammed shut. Adam didn't care if she woke up to an empty bed. A whore in the daylight was as unsightly as his wife's face, any time of the day.

He got into his car and retrieved his work phone from the glove compartment. There were no missed calls from his superior officer.

Eva thought she owned his ass, but Adam wouldn't dream of giving anyone the power. He enjoyed holding it too much.

Leaning back in the seat he stared up at the window of his latest acquisition. This one he'd decided to call Rose. She had bloomed under his touch. A perfect addition to the girls he'd already auditioned for next year's retreat.

Within the next two months, the island property would pay for itself. He had customers and whores lined up; money rolled in like an avalanche.

Life is great.

The sound of his personal phone ringing drowned out the sound of the money streaming in.

"Good morning, my darling Eva. How are you on this beautiful morning?" He reached for the key in the ignition and transferred the call to the car's Bluetooth system.

Her shrill voice came through too loud. Adam adjusted the volume. "Where are you?"

"I did some scouting last night. You're going to love the newest addition to our line-up. I'm on my way home. I'll see you in fifteen minutes."

"Hurry and get your ass over here. I'll explain when you get here, but we have a big problem. Blade and Vegas left the island."

"What the actual fuck? How?" Adam slammed his fists against the steering wheel.

"I'm not sure. Just get home so that we can discuss doing damage control."

Adam exhaled hard. "How do you know they left?"

"No time for explanations. Just get here. Now." Eva ended the call as Adam shifted into drive.

The tyres left a black streak on the road. Smoke and dust obscured his view in the rear-view mirror.

Tuesday, 14 December, 6:30 a.m.

The smell of bacon filled her nostrils as she opened the front door. King pushed past and ran towards the kitchen. Madison sent Clay a text message to say she arrived at her parents' house. Not that he didn't have access to the cameras on her parents' property. Luke's study looked more like a cybercrime unit than an actual office.

Madison: I'm here.

Clay: I know, because you're not here. Would kiss you if you were.

Madison: This will be over soon. Then I can kiss you whenever you want. I had a different kind of wake-up call in mind for you.

Clay: If it's you naked in the shower, then we have the same idea.

Madison placed a hand over her mouth, as her stomach did a slow roll. *Why did we wait this long?*

"Why are you standing like that?" Laura asked.

Without thinking, Madison lowered her hand, before containing the grin.

"Nothing, just a text message." She kissed her mother's cheek and headed to the living room.

Her father was set in his morning routine – coffee in his favourite chair while reading the newspaper. Over the years, it had gone from a printed copy to an electronic one on his tablet.

"From Clay?" Laura pushed.

"Yes, Mother."

"I take it you two have finally admitted you're not friends, and you never were." Aaron placed the tablet on the side table.

Madison walked over and pecked his cheek. Aaron grabbed her arm. "Out with it, young lady. Big smile on your face. A helicopter landing on Luke's property in the early hours. Not forgetting the fact that you're now, all of a sudden, wearing scarves. Your mother and I aren't dumb enough to believe you're trying out a new style."

Madison excused herself and went to the kitchen. Caffeine was needed to get her through the discussion she was about to have with her parents. And a lot more of it for the rest of the day.

She returned to the living room, a big mug of very strong coffee in hand, to find her parents on the two-seater leather couch. They held hands, as they often did.

Madison sat down, facing them, and drew her legs under her. "Where do you want me to start?" she asked and savoured the taste of her mother's favourite blend. Madison rolled the mug between her hands and noticed her parents' intent stares.

"You roll a mug like that when you're anxious. Think you started doing it with your sippy cup as a toddler," Laura said.

"Let's start with the good news, because the bad news is horrific." Madison pressed her palms tight against the mug. "Yes, Clay and I admitted we were never friends, and it's better than I ever dreamed it would be. Even under the current circumstances." She used her right thumb and pointer finger to press the soft flesh between her eyes. Madison shook her head, fighting the tears burning behind her closed eyelids.

Jamie walked into the living room and eased down on the couch next to Madison. She touched Madison's shoulder and whispered, "I'm here. We can talk them through it. Together."

Madison nodded and told her parents about the fifteen missing women, the bodies which had been discovered in Potters Park and Paradise Beach. She cleared the contents of the mug and told them of Natalie's call and what had happened on Seal Island.

Her parents remained quiet throughout her monologue. She couldn't meet their eyes. When Madison looked up, she noticed her mother had pulled her legs under her bum. *Some things are hereditary.*

"What can we do to help, baby?" Aaron asked.

"Can two people stay in the bridal cottage? It's crucial that no one knows they are here."

Laura nodded. "Of course. I'll go prepare everything for them. Don't worry about meals. I'll stock the fridge with some basics and either Dad or I will take them meals."

"Thank you, Mom. Another thing, can we bury Claire in the family graveyard? She didn't have any family. Claire was murdered because she tried to uncover what happened to her sister and to find Natalie. When Angie's body is identified, can she be buried here as well? Please. They deserve to be in a place of peace and love, even if it is in death." Madison wiped her eyes.

The rest of the family did the same.

"I'm so proud of you, Madison," Aaron said, clearing his throat. "You have a beautiful heart."

She grinned. "That's what Clay says."

"Well, the man is crazy in love with you and he has good reason to be." Jamie patted Madison's leg.

Laura and Aaron agreed to bury Claire and Angie in the family graveyard. And the remains of any victims who weren't claimed or identified.

Laura lowered her feet to the carpet and leaned forward. "Sweetie, how much danger are you in? You were attacked, threatened and your apartment broken into. I agree, Emma dying in your car wasn't a coincidence."

"I'm safe here. Clay's watching me like a hawk. King is always with me, and I carry my gun." She pressed a hand to the weapon between her breasts.

Aaron and Laura walked around the coffee table and hugged

their daughters, reminding them they were proud of all six of their children. But they loved their two grandsons the most.

In typical Taylor style, Clay was inducted into the family without even being in the room, or having a say in the matter.

Chapter 34

Police cars blocked off Ocean View Drive on both ends. Adam climbed out of his car and considered walking up to an officer he hadn't met in person before to ask what was going on.

The hairs on the back of Adam's neck stood up when he noticed Detectives Carmichael and Jones. Carmichael's eyes locked onto his, a flash of recognition flaring as he reached for his service pistol.

Adam ran back to his car, speeding away.

Sirens wailed behind him. Blue lights flashed in the rear-view mirror.

"Fuck!" He dialled Eva's number. The call went to voicemail.

Adam sped up, exiting onto the highway. "You better be at Charlotte's. Bitch. I'll make you pay for this."

The wailing sound became louder. He focused on the road, swerving through the early morning traffic. Dying in an accident wasn't an option; Eva had to die first. *Till death do us part.*

Motorists slammed their horns as Adam's car passed them. Without using the indicator, he crossed all the lanes to take the turnoff. The sound of the sirens grew fainter.

A glance in the rear-view mirror relaxed his grip on the steering wheel. When Adam turned onto Charlotte's street, he used the indicator. No need to draw further attention to himself.

He parked in front of Charlotte's garage. The grass spat up

water as Adam's shoes pounded down, running towards the front door.

An invisible force knocked him off his feet.

Time stopped.

He flew.

The last thing Adam saw was smoke, glass, and bricks hurling towards him.

Tuesday, 14 December, 7:00 a.m.

Madison stood in the doorway of Luke's house, her senses teased by the smell of bacon. She held the door open for King and took a moment to appreciate the view from Luke's property.

To the west, oak trees obscured the view of Lamont Estate. North, the mountain remained a physical reminder of the earth's powerful forces. To the south lay Shadow Bay and the ocean. And somewhere out there lay the remains of the women who were still missing. Madison didn't dare to hope that any of them would be found alive.

Arms wrapped around her waist. If not for the familiar smell, she would've reached for her weapon.

Clay turned her towards him and cupped her face. "Good morning, my beautiful Maddie." He brought her lips to his, the kiss slow, numbing her senses. "New thing for us, a kiss like that every morning."

"Yes, please." Madison rested her cheek against his chest. "And bacon. I'll do anything for you if you make me bacon and eggs every morning."

To them, talking about breakfast wasn't a strange thing. They'd shared most of their meals over the previous months. Whenever their jobs allowed, they had eaten together, done grocery shopping together and went to kickboxing and the shooting range. Clay tried to attend every gig her band played. Out of the three she'd played since getting back the nerve to go on stage, he'd missed one, due to work.

She had shared her fears, tears, and anger with him, and Clay had told her about his parents. For every fear Madison had, Clay taught her how to protect herself. Almost every tear he had wiped, and he took the brunt of her anger when they sparred.

Madison shook her head.

"What's wrong apart from you being hungry? I can hear your stomach growling."

"We were never friends." Madison increased her hold on him.

"No, but we tried. We've been *us* since you called me the morning after I came to fetch my jacket. Which, for the record, you look incredibly sexy in. And out." Clay's chin rested on her head. "I'm crazy about you, Madison Taylor."

"I thought you love me or were they just meaningless words to get inside me?"

"I love you, but it doesn't mean I can't be crazy about you and feel this whenever I see you." Clay removed her right arm from around his waist, lifting her hand to his chest. Madison smiled up at him, feeling the rapid beat against her palm. She placed his other hand over her heart. Clay returned her smile.

"We can bury Claire, Angie, and any of the other women who aren't claimed in the family graveyard. My mom will take care of Natalie and Declan. She and my dad understand how important it is for their location to remain a secret. We can take them to the honeymoon cottage later. Where are they?"

"In the kitchen preparing breakfast. I'll go take care of the horses." Clay pressed his mouth to hers and called out to King. The dog came around the corner with a guilty look on his face. "Natalie gave you bacon, didn't she?"

"He smiled at me. How could I say no to that face?" Natalie called from the kitchen.

Madison wondered how long it would take her to call Natalie by her real name and not her work name. For Clay it was easier because he didn't know Vegas. Just as he had never known the person Madison was before she'd met Foster Ericson.

"You realise it isn't an actual smile he's giving you?" Madison watched Clay walk towards the stables. King ran ahead of him.

Natalie's laughter carried from the kitchen. "I've never owned a dog. You can't fault me for not knowing anything about them. Besides, King is adorable."

Madison found Natalie and Declan standing shoulder to shoulder at the stove. Natalie speared the bacon with a fork while Declan cracked eggs into a pan.

She jumped onto the kitchen island, staring at their backs. "When did *this* happen?" Madison asked.

They twisted their necks to look at her, then focused on each other. "Second night on the island," Natalie answered with a girlish smile.

"Something clicked when I found her watching a movie alone."

"Liar. You saw me crying, and being a doctor, you couldn't miss an opportunity to help someone. Someone who you thought might give you answers about what was going on there."

"No. A woman cried while watching a comedy. And I wanted to enjoy her company, instead of sitting through another movie by myself. It really is one of my favourites." Declan bumped his hip against Natalie.

Madison realised light had pierced through the darkness she'd seen in Natalie, or rather the darkness Vegas had carried like a shield.

"Declan, why didn't you approach the police after doing the autopsies on the Potters Park Five?" Madison asked. She filled the four glasses standing next to her with fresh orange juice.

"I couldn't go to them and admit that I inadvertently paid for sex with the very women I suspected to be the Potters Park Five. By my preliminary estimate, they'd died within days after I had sex with some of them. The detectives would've arrested me. But if I went to them with evidence, I reckoned my chances were better of not having charges brought against me. I spoke to the detectives in Missing Persons and Homicide, asking them to keep me up to date on their investigations. It's not like I had DNA samples to compare to that of the bodies." Declan removed the pan from the stove and lifted the eggs onto the plates. He caught Madison watching him. "Is it something I said, or am I dishing the eggs wrong?"

Madison shook her head. "No, I'm just thinking. I gave Detective Evans one of Angie's hairbrushes, which I got from Claire." She glanced at Natalie. "Would it be possible to arrange for the bodies and all other evidence to be sent to Richard Davenport's laboratory? Doctor Davenport is my sister-in-law's father and I have it on good authority that he has helped the police before."

How Madison had met Richard didn't matter. Neither did the secret they shared.

"Depending on how my interview with Detective Larson goes, I could make a few calls. While you were out, I reviewed the case files on the dining room table. You should burn them or we can say I requested the copies. Again, it all depends on how my meeting goes with Detective Larson." Declan returned the pan to the stove before facing Madison. "There's nothing I can add, except I believe there are more people involved. Adam doesn't strike me as the mastermind behind an organ trafficking organisation. Sex trafficking? Yes. But organ trafficking is much more complex. Higher stakes equal more players. And someone with extensive medical training."

Clay walked into the kitchen; his expression dark. "Gina called. The women are safe, and the men are also in a safe house. Adam is in custody."

Madison's jaw dropped. "That's too easy."

"No, it isn't. Adam's house and the house he was running towards both exploded. At the same time."

"Any officers hurt or worse?" Declan asked.

Clay nodded. "Yes, two officers at Adam's house. Only Adam was injured at the other house, but the bastard isn't dead. An ambulance is taking him to Shadow Bay Hospital. With any luck, he'll be discharged later today. According to the paramedics who treated him at the scene, he has a broken arm, a concussion, and a few lacerations."

Tuesday, 14 December, 7:10 a.m.

Everything was gone. Destroyed. Who could've done this to her? One person came to mind – Adam.

Adam with his movie star good looks, insatiable sexual needs and the scars left on every woman he touched. Hate wasn't a strong enough word to describe what she felt towards him. *Fucking Adam.*

Charlotte had asked the warden for a personal day. He didn't question her. In the four-and-a-half years she'd worked with him, she had never asked for anything. Today she had more work to do than taking care of sick prisoners who deserved to die. None of them deserved to breathe. Except one.

Where would she sleep tonight? What would she wear tomorrow? Charlotte hated shopping.

Stepping through the prison gates, she called the one person who cared. The person who would always be there for her. The first person who had loved her.

Soon, she'd be with Foster. *Forever.* Now wasn't the time to set their plan in motion.

Charlotte called the last person who'd contacted her and waited for the call to connect. Most days, her phone didn't ring at all. Not even a spam call.

"The number you have dialled is no longer in service."

Dialling the number again, she lit a cigarette and waited. The same automated voice answered. Questions raged in Charlotte's mind.

"Where are you, Evie?"

***

Tuesday, 14 December, 9:15 a.m.

Gina returned downstairs and nodded at Captain Johnson, who handed her a mug of steaming coffee. He invited her to have breakfast with them. His wife had gone all out for their guests. Nervous laughter came from the dining room.

"Captain, thank you for opening your home to them."

Sincere laughter filled the entire house. Captain Johnson's smile reached his eyes. "That's my wife. She has an uncanny ability to make people feel comfortable. If you have trouble getting straight answers from the women, just ask her to talk to them. Darla would've made a prolific interrogator or a hostage negotiator." He still loved watching her calm animals – the best vet in the district.

"I'll remember that. The officers stationed around your farm will keep you updated when their shifts change, but we don't foresee any abrupt changes. Everyone's committed to finding out what happened on that island, and those responsible."

He showed Gina into his office and closed the door. "Do you think we have another serial killer on our hands, or what? Your captain briefed me on the investigation. My heart stopped when I heard Madison Taylor's name. That young woman and her family have suffered enough. Her father and I worked together for years. The Taylors are salt of the earth people. Darla and I attended their son's wedding this past weekend."

Gina sipped the coffee, realising the mistake she had made when she first met Madison. Whether she approved of Clay's relationship with her, Gina remained on the fence, but all four women had asked to speak to Madison the moment they'd arrived at the farm. Gina had watched them closely as they spoke with Madison on the phone. The dread which had filled the women's faces before was replaced with sincere smiles.

"We're not sure what this is. I'll be heading to Shadow Bay Hospital later to question the suspect. Do you mind if I use your office to speak to the women individually?"

"Not at all. Who do you want me to send in first?"

Darla Johnson knocked on the door, opening it at the same time. "I know how this part works, *Detective*." She smirked, looking at her husband.

Her expression changed to stern and maternal when Darla turned her attention to Gina. "At least let them shower before you talk to them. While they get cleaned up, you, young lady, *will* sit down and eat breakfast. Don't think I haven't seen that same exhaustion and hunger on my husband's face."

Gina agreed in order to fill her empty stomach, but also because she understood what the women were going through in the aftermath. Buried deep inside her was a scared young girl. Thanks to her therapist, as an adult, Gina understood empathy. No longer did she consider fear as a weakness, but a by-product of the reality of life. The women deserved a hot shower and time to process what had and could've happened to them.

If not for Gina's aunt and uncle taking them in, she might've ended up sitting in the dining room. *One of the women missing.*

Chapter 35

Tuesday, 14 December, 11:00 a.m.

Laura unlocked the door to the honeymoon cottage. "Welcome to your temporary home. I stocked the fridge with a few basic items. Either my husband, Aaron or I will bring you lunch and dinner. Breakfast you can make whenever you drag yourselves out of bed." She winked at Declan and Natalie.

"Mother." Madison rolled her eyes.

"I don't care what other people's children get up to. In my eyes, my children will forever remain wholesome." Laura stepped inside and pointed towards the wardrobe.

"Maddie said you're the same height and build as Jamie and Spencer. They've offered to lend you some of their clothes until I can go to town and buy whatever you need."

Madison laughed. "Correction. Jamie's size *before* she fell pregnant."

"Don't let your sister hear you say that. She can still kick your ..." Clay glanced at Laura, "... behind."

Natalie wiped her eyes. "This isn't necessary, but thank you." She reached for Declan's hand.

"Thank you, Mrs Taylor. We appreciate your hospitality and will reimburse you for all expenses, including meals and accommodation."

Laura lunged forward, throwing her arms around them. "You will do no such thing. The only thing that matters is that you're safe."

She gave them a quick tour of the cottage and pointed out where the panic buttons were located, explaining that they were linked to Luke's main security system.

Clay handed a phone to Declan. "Our numbers are in the contact list. If you need anything, call. It goes without saying, but don't call anyone else. To the rest of the world, you're still out of reach."

Natalie shook her head. "You don't have to worry about us endangering this investigation or any of your lives. Declan risked his life, and perhaps his career. I won't throw it all away with a stupid phone call. Besides, I don't have anyone to call."

After Madison, Laura, and Clay left, Declan headed to the bathroom to shower. Natalie sat on the four-poster bed and took in the cottage's ambiance. Laura had handpicked every item. Of this, she had no doubt. Each object resonated with the caring and nurturing woman she'd met.

Laura's warmth reminded Natalie of her parents. Every night she went to bed missing them, and wondering what they would've said about how she earned a living, had they been around. She was done selling her body and soul for money. Even if it meant she had to spend the rest of her life paying off a student loan.

Declan returned with a towel wrapped around his waist. Natalie bit her bottom lip. "Why are you crying?"

"I want to be a neurologist. Both my parents had strokes eight years apart. My mom had spent her last few months in a care facility. It bankrupted my dad. If other people can fight in their line of work, so can I."

Declan dropped to his knees in front of her. His hands were warm against her cheeks. "Your wish is my command, Natalie. I'll help you in any way possible. I suspect you won't allow me to pay for your studies. What about an interest-free loan? You can stay with me. I live within walking distance of the medical campus. You can have your own room. If that's what you want. In no way am I putting any kind of pressure on you. Whatever you decide is up to you, and I'll respect your decision. Promise me we will always be open and honest with each other?"

Natalie closed her eyes. "Are you real, Declan O'Reilly?" When she opened her eyes, his lips touched her forehead.

"What do you want, Natalie King?"

"Hold me."

Declan did until Laura returned with a three-course lunch.

Tuesday, 14 December, 11:30 a.m.

Kayla closed the door on her way out of the office. Gina leaned forward, lifting her arms and covering her head. It was dangerous to put yourself in a victim's shoes, but she couldn't help it. Their stories could've been hers, or that of her sisters. Gina wiped the moisture from her cheeks and breathed a deep, calming breath. It was time for the last woman's statement. Gina walked to the door and asked Dakota to join her.

Dakota didn't look a day older than sixteen. As the young woman took a seat next to her, Gina remembered what Madison had told her about how Dakota ended up on her radar.

"Do you want a glass of water or anything before we start?" Gina smiled.

"No, thank you. Mrs Johnson practically force-fed us breakfast. Don't think I need to eat for a week." Dakota rubbed her stomach. Through the white tank top, her ribs were visible.

"If you want to stop and take a break, just tell me. I'm not here because of how you earned a living. I'm here because of Adam and everything that's coming to light as this investigation progresses. How did you meet Adam?"

Dakota shut her eyes. A single tear trickled down her face.

Gina hated feeling this powerless. This was the very reason she had worked her butt off to get into Homicide. She couldn't deal with the emotions of the living, without making their pain her own, and seeking retribution for what happened to them. Only Duke knew how often she danced on the fine line between right and wrong.

"Dakota, did any of the men on the island rape you?"

Dakota shook her head. "A whore can't say no."

Gina's fists clenched. "Of course, they can say no, sweetie. No person has the right to your body, no matter what."

Dakota looked at Gina, more tears spilled down her young face. "I met Adam when I went to the station to report a rape. I waited to talk to a detective in that unit for rapes and stuff. He just walked over to me and sat down. Adam said he'd take my statement, as he could see I was uncomfortable being there." Her bony shoulders moved up, then down. "I thought he was trying to help me."

"Were you reporting your rape?"

"No. One night, a friend came home, she was beaten so badly her eyes were swollen shut. The next morning, she told me a john wouldn't stop and the more she begged him to, the more he hit her."

"Was the john arrested?"

Dakota smirked. "Adam never did a thing with my statement. After my friend died, I went back to the station. They had no record of the statement I gave to Adam. *Adam* didn't work there. I described him to the officer at the front desk. She said it sounded like a bunch of officers. And handed me a pamphlet for Narcotics Anonymous. The bitch thought I did drugs. Sorry."

Dakota continued to tell Gina about the paramedics she had to contact to remove her friend's body. The officer at the front desk hadn't believed her and refused to send anyone to the apartment.

"Did you speak to anyone else about this?" Gina fought against the outrage burning in her core.

"No one cares. We're invisible. Our lives. Our deaths. Sometimes wonder if I even exist."

Against all her training, Gina reached for Dakota's arm. "I care. Madison cares. Adam was arrested. He will *never* hurt you again."

Dakota grabbed a tissue from the box on the desk and wiped her eyes. "I have proof he raped me the day he took me to the island. Go to my apartment. I hid the phone inside the panda-teddy-bear on my dresser."

To hide her shock, Gina took a deep breath. Dakota's resilience and bravery knocked the wind out of her. "I'll send an officer."

"No. *You* go. I don't trust the police."

Gina nodded. "I'll go. Dakota, if you knew Adam wasn't to be trusted, exactly how did he end up being one of your regulars?"

Dakota stood and turned towards the window. She gazed at the mountain. "The man who had raped and beaten my friend – viciously enough that the paramedics said she'd probably died from bleeding somewhere inside her body – wasn't arrested. Adam killed him."

"How do you know Adam killed him?" Gina forced herself to remain on the couch and not hug Dakota.

"A couple of days after my friend died, Adam knocked on my door. He asked me to take a drive with him. He wanted a chance to 'make everything right'. Adam apologised for *forgetting* to file my statement." Dakota pulled her hair back and tied it in a high ponytail. "The thing is, I knew the man who had killed Bethany. His face was always on TV. Some big lawyer who helps the bad guys. Adam drove straight to this guy's house, and we waited. Adam didn't say a word, and that made me even more afraid of him. Next moment the motherfu—sorry, the douchebag walked out of his house. Adam started the car and shot him as we drove past."

Dakota turned to Gina, wrapping her arms around her tiny waist. "When we stopped back at my place, Adam turned to me and said, 'This happens to anyone who touches my girls. You're my girl now. Show me how grateful you are to have my protection.'"

Gina's nails pressed into her palms. She remembered the drive-by shooting of the defence attorney. "How old were you when this happened?"

"I'll never forget the day. My sixteenth birthday."

Chapter 36

Despair radiated off the unexpected guest. Madison considered hugging her, but thought better of it. She stepped to the side. "Please come in. Do you want tea, coffee, water?"

"No, thank you." Gina walked straight to the dining room table and stared down at the files.

Madison stood motionless in the foyer, studying Gina and the exhaustion surrounding her – a suffocating cloud. She said nothing. Instead, she fetched a bottle of water from the fridge and placed it on the table.

Tentatively, she touched Gina's shoulder. "It's hard to hear their stories."

"How do you do it? Day after day, knowing what they're going through? Not knowing when one of them will get a disease, assaulted, or murdered?"

Madison shrugged. "Kickboxing. Hours at the shooting range. Evenings spent in silence with Clay." She removed her hand from Gina's shoulder. "I fight for the ones who decide to get out of this life. If I can save one, it's one safe."

Gina turned to her. "You've saved five women. They've decided to get out."

King rushed into the dining room and rolled onto his back at Gina's feet. She bent down and scratched his belly. "Madison, if you hurt Clay, you'll answer to me. Keep in mind, I'm dating one of his teammates. I will find out. If you get yourself killed, because you stepped into something far bigger

174

than we realise, you will still answer to me." She stared up at Madison.

No matter how hard she tried, even biting her tongue, Madison refused to not speak her mind. "Gina, why are you threatening me? Your sister cheated on him. She left Clay. She hurt him."

Gina looked at King. "Clay was never even in love with Penelope. Madison, he didn't look at my sister the way he looks at you. He was never protective of her or stood up for her. Believe me, Penelope has a gift for pissing people off. Clay is my friend. Therefore, it's my duty to warn you – hurt him, or get yourself killed, and you'll have me to answer to."

"It's going to be hard answering to you if I'm dead." Madison grinned, then realised Gina wasn't joking. *The woman has no sense of humour.* "Detective Larson, if you wish to write this down, please do. I, Madison Taylor, love Clay Davis and won't put his, or my, life in danger. I know what losing his sister did to him. But I wouldn't be the person he loves if I step away from this now. At least eighteen people have been murdered, including the two homeless people and Claire. Those responsible need to be brought to justice."

Gina sank into the nearest chair. "He raped her. She's still a child."

"He raped all of them." Madison sighed and straightened her spine. *It's time.* "I can prove it."

Lines appeared between Gina's eyebrows. "Dakota told me about the video recording she made. I'm on my way to her apartment to retrieve it." She held a hand up. "Officers are outside her apartment door to ensure whoever else is involved in this isn't cleaning up after Adam. Or waiting for the women to return home, seeing as they're no longer on the island."

Gina leaned back in the chair, opened the bottle of water and drank half the contents before returning her focus to Madison. "Did the other women also make videos?"

Madison shook her head, rubbing her hands together. "I have DNA evidence."

"Maddie, what did you do?" Clay stood in the doorway, arms crossed over his chest.

Gina's phone rang.

Tuesday, 14 December, 1:43 p.m.

Behind Madison's chair, Clay leaned against the wall, shaking his head. Fear gnawed at his stomach. He faced danger on an almost daily basis, but the idea of Madison putting herself in danger ... He took a deep breath.

She's here, she's safe. Foster's in prison. Adam's in hospital under police guard.

He covered Madison's shoulders with his hands, rubbing his thumbs along the back of her neck.

Gina paced the length of the dining room, listening to whoever was on the other end of the line. Before she'd taken the call, she instructed Madison to keep quiet.

The call ended.

Gina sat down and drank the rest of the water in the bottle. "The men gave their statements to Detective Shepherd, who is working with me on this case. They'll remain at the safe house until we have proof that they didn't know what happened to the women after the *vacation* ended. Doctor O'Reilly and Natalie will stay here for the time being. It's impossible for one person to be responsible for organ trafficking, sex trafficking, and the manufacturing and distribution of pornography. There are more people involved than Detective Evans."

Madison's hand lifted to her mouth. "Detective *Evans* is Adam?"

Gina nodded.

Madison fidgeted with a cuticle on her thumb. "I met with him on Friday. I gave him Angie's hairbrush." Leaning forward, she massaged her forehead with her fingertips. "He destroyed it, didn't he?"

"No, Evans signed in evidence on Friday."

Clay sighed. "Why are we avoiding the fact that Madison somehow has DNA evidence proving Evans raped the women rescued from the island? Do you have evidence of him committing more rapes?" Madison didn't look at him. "Gina, why are you not like a hound on the hunt for the DNA?"

"Because, Clay, maybe I don't want to hear how Madison came to be in possession of it. Perhaps I don't want her to implicate herself in something which could affect this investigation." The corners of Gina's mouth lifted. "I'm not in the mood to arrest her."

"The women and I knew the risk when I approached them with my plan. However, I'll tell you everything. And handover the evidence, *if* you guarantee, in writing from your superior officer, that none of the women or the other person I got involved in this will be charged with anything. I take full responsibility and will accept any repercussions."

Clay reached for Madison's hand, intertwining their fingers. With his other hand on her cheek, Clay waited for her to look at him. "Am I going to think you're brave or stupid?"

Madison smiled, pressing her lips to his wrist. "I hope for one of those, but probably both."

Gina asked to be excused to call her captain and ensure no ramifications for Madison, although it would've been easier to request if she knew exactly what Madison had done. She returned and stroked King's head, who sat sentinel next to her chair.

Madison chewed her bottom lip. Clay pressed his lips to her head and whispered, "If this impacts the investigation, then talk. If not, keep quiet."

"I have access to DNA samples of the other nine women who went missing last December. As for what Detec—no, he doesn't deserve to be called Detective. I have DNA evidence proving Adam raped the missing woman – his semen and their blood."

Madison listened to Clay's advice and didn't disclose anything that didn't seem pertinent to the investigation.

"Okay." Gina gave a slow nod. "Where is it?"

"Not here. It's being kept safe under the correct conditions for DNA preservation."

Clay smiled and walked to the kitchen, returning with three bottles of water and King's water bowl. "The person keeping it safe. I met him the day I met you."

"Yes."

Gina glanced between them. "Who?" She shrugged. "Not that it matters, because we agreed to keep *him* out of this. Madison, explain to me *how* you got your hands on all this DNA."

Madison untwisted the cap on the bottle. She sucked in her cheeks and began with the part that was legal. "While studying towards my degree, I started working with the prostitutes in Shadow Bay. It wasn't a requirement for my degree."

"You wanted to help." Every day, Clay found another reason to love her. Not only because of Madison's caring nature, but also the bravery she'd shown the day the pimp tried to attack her.

It occurred to him that helping was part and parcel of being a Taylor. Luke's arrest and conviction record remained one of the highest in the country. Jamie would've reached the same heights in her career, had she not taken a position in the small town of River Valley. Clay would never have dared to say that to Jamie's face, not after the she'd brought down a truck hijacking syndicate on her own.

"On the streets, you see and hear a lot of things. People trust me because I'm not a police officer. No offence to either of you." Madison offered them a sincere smile.

"None taken," Clay and Gina said.

"In early October of last year, I started meeting with Tiffany for coffee. Her real name is Samantha. She had turned twenty-five that September and, on the streets, that's like being a grandma. Someone had approached her with an offer to get off the streets and cater – for a lack of a better word – to a more sophisticated market than the average john pulling up to the kerb."

"Did Adam approach her?"

Madison shook her head. "No, Angie told her about it. Wait, Angie approached Declan with the two-week vacation story. Was she working for Adam? Why the hell did she get involved with him? He's a sadist. The women are petrified of him. Had he threatened her into working for him?"

"It's on my list when I interview him tomorrow." Gina rubbed her red eyes. Her stomach grumbled loud enough that Clay and Madison heard it from the other side of the table.

Madison pushed to her feet. "My mom brought lunch. There's an extra plate. She keeps forgetting Clay doesn't eat as much as Luke."

Clay shook his head, his mouth forming a crooked smile. "I don't have to maintain the muscle mass Luke has to. I can't chase a suspect down, rappel from a helicopter, or do my work being all muscles and no stamina."

Madison pushed her fingers through his hair. "I've always liked your body more than his."

"I'd hope so. He's your brother. Biology aside." Clay smacked her bum as she walked past him.

Madison returned from the kitchen with a plate of food for Gina and a treat for King.

Gina dug into the chicken wrap. In between taking bites, she said, "Okay, Slay, I approve of her. When this investigation is over, the four of us are going on a double date. Perhaps to the shooting range. I want to see for myself if Madison's aim is as good as Duke claims. By the way, he adores you."

Madison's smile reached her eyes. "The feeling is mutual." She frowned and tilted her head to the right. "When the women gave their statements, did they tell you how they met Adam?"

Gina nodded, wiping her mouth with the napkin. She swallowed, shaking her head, and reached for her phone. She held up a hand when Madison opened her mouth. "Sir, I need access to the ballistics report from Paul Wallace's murder case.

The lab needs to compare it to the ballistics report from the drive-by shooting of Jeffrey Baker two years ago. Do you remember the one who was gunned down in his front yard?" She nodded. "Just like Paul. Sir, the thing is, Baker wasn't working on a gang-related case at the time. He was the lead defence attorney on that big pyramid scheme investigation."

Gina ended the call. Clay and Madison both stared at her in silence. "Annabelle Wallace was your former partner's niece?" Madison asked, knowing the answer.

Gina's lips quivered. "Paul got too close. I'm going to ensure Ben *Adam* Evans never breathes free air again."

Acid burned in Clay's stomach. Adam had murdered a decorated and well-respected detective. *Why did he warn Madison?*

Tuesday, 14 December, 3:29 p.m.

"The number you have dialled is no longer in service." Charlotte wondered if the voice automated notification grew irate at her incessant calls. It didn't sound like it did.

A knock on the door startled her. She peered through the peephole and opened the door for the waiter carting the room service she'd ordered. She thanked him, handing him a tip.

Making herself comfortable on the bed, she wondered what it would be like if Foster was with her. Would he hold her? Would he do all the things he'd promised? She had never been with a man before Foster, or anyone else, except Evie. A thirty-three-year-old virgin when she'd fallen in love with Evie. If she didn't consider what Adam had done to her. She refused to.

Charlotte was homeless, staying in the penthouse suite of a hotel Eric Foster had designed. Back when he'd killed some people and before everyone had heard the name Foster Ericson. She grinned.

It's important to have similar interests to have a long and happy relationship.

On the tablet lying next to her, Charlotte read the news

while she ate. Nothing newsworthy had happened, except for two houses exploding. Her home. Even if her name wasn't on the title deed, it would always be her first home. The one thing her father had taught her – never leave a paper trail. He'd be proud of the lessons his little Charlie remembered.

Chapter 37

Tuesday, 14 December, 6:07 p.m.

The SUV rounded the corner, passing the family graveyard. In the coming weeks and months, more tombstones would join those of the generations of Lamont's buried on the farm. A visual reminder of those who some would forget, but not Madison. She smiled despite the moisture dripping onto her black shirt.

Clay placed a hand on her thigh. "What are you thinking about?"

Madison intertwined their fingers. Instead of looking at Clay, she stared at nothing in particular near the foot of the mountain. "Their deaths are not silent. I know. You know. Everyone needs to hear or read their names when those responsible are punished."

Sorrow and frustration scratched at her soul. "I'm just a social worker. I can't *do* anything. Couldn't even keep them safe. I have to face Emma's parents. They haven't returned any of my calls."

The SUV stopped. Clay jumped down and walked around the back. He opened the passenger door and pulled Madison out, wrapping his arms around her. "It's just us, babe. You and me. Let it go."

The safety and understanding Clay offered enveloped her. All the emotions Madison had carried alone burst to the surface.

The nights she couldn't sleep, worrying about where they were and whether she'd speak to them again.

The countless days, over copious amounts of coffee, she'd spent trying to convince them to pursue a different life.

The times Madison had emptied her gun's magazine into a paper target at the shooting range, wishing it was one of the men who had hurt the women she considered her friends.

She cried for the women who'd be buried where she had grown up. And for the five women who, a year later, were still missing.

Clay reached into the glove compartment and handed her a pack of tissues. She stared up at him, wiping her nose. "Not the first time I've cried in your arms."

He pressed his lips to Madison's forehead. "No, but now, I understand. You should've told me about the DNA collection. A database? I don't know what to call it, you haven't said enough."

"The less you know, the better. I guess Gina's boss will not be as accommodating with me evading questions as she was."

"No chance of that happening. Captain Wilson doesn't take prisoners. Well, he does, but you know what I mean."

Madison laughed, pushing onto her toes, and kissed Clay's cheek. She ignored the sting of his stubble. "I love you, Clay Davis. Thank you for always being you. I wouldn't be where I am today, if not for you."

"I call major BS. You're much stronger than you give yourself credit for. Don't you remember? You called me and invited me to go to the shooting range with you when you got back to Shadow Bay. That Monday, you were back at work. I didn't testify at his trial – you did. No, you're not allowed to use the closed court spiel. Maddie, *you* faced Foster. And here you are, still facing and fighting monsters." Clay brushed his lips against hers.

Madison pulled back as bile rose in her throat. "Clay, how did Adam know about Foster?"

***

Tuesday, 14 December, 7:00 p.m.

Mrs Johnson escorted Declan to the study before leading Natalie upstairs. Natalie appeared calm, as if she was breathing for the first time in years. Declan had said little during the drive to Captain Johnson's farm. Clay wondered if Doctor O'Reilly would lose his job, even though he'd been the linchpin to saving the women.

Captain Johnson asked Clay and Madison to join him in the dining room, where everyone else waited. Captain Wilson, Gina's boss, Clay knew only by reputation. Detective Shepherd he'd worked with during the take down of the trafficking ring on Friday. He hoped Shepherd didn't see the children's faces every time he closed his eyes. Not the way Clay did every night until Madison moved closer and wrapped an arm around his waist.

Both men stood and greeted them. Gina's smile appeared strained and filled with exhaustion.

"Miss Taylor, you have some serious explaining to do. I want the whole truth, not the sugar-coated, evasive nonsense you gave my detective." Captain Wilson moved his chair closer to the table.

Madison took the chair Clay pulled out for her. "I have some questions of my own for you, Captain Wilson."

Clay dropped his head to his hands, trying to hide the pride he felt.

Captain Wilson gestured for Madison to continue and rested his arms on the table.

"First, I want it in writing that none of the women, or the other person I got involved, will be prosecuted or held responsible."

Wilson rubbed a hand over his mouth. "I gave you my word before you spoke to Detective Larson this afternoon."

"No disrespect, Sir, but I don't know you. One of your detectives is involved and under police guard in the hospital. We have no way of knowing if more law enforcement personnel are involved or not. I'll answer your questions as soon as the state prosecutor and a judge sign the document."

Laughter bellowed deep from within Captain Wilson's stomach. It ended in a pack-a-day-cough. "You, Miss Taylor, are your mother's daughter." He shook his head and drank a sip of water.

Darla Johnson knocked on the door. Captain Johnson walked out and returned with a tray filled with mugs and freshly brewed coffee.

"How are the ladies doing?" Madison asked Darla and thanked her for the coffee.

"As well as can be expected. A lot of tears and hugs are going on upstairs. They were worried sick about Natalie. I'm going to take Doctor O'Reilly up to see them." She lifted a hand as both Captains opened their mouths. "They asked to see him. And yes, I know, I have no idea who anyone is under our roof or what this case is about."

Darla rolled her eyes and huffed. "I swear you police are all cut from the same damn cloth. A cloth I love, by the way. Call me if you need anything." She reached for the sliding doors when Gina spoke.

Gina played with the mug's handle. "Thank you again for opening your home on short notice." Captain Wilson and Detective Shepherd agreed.

Darla smiled, despite the sadness filling her eyes. "They are welcome to stay as long as needed. Even after all this is over and they don't have a safe place to return to."

Captain Johnson smirked, resting his arms on his belly. "I should've known you'd find a way to fill the house again. I was just getting used to the quiet."

"Tomorrow morning, you're taking our guests out and showing them around the farm. Teach them a thing or two about country living. None of them have been on a farm before." Darla pursed her lips.

"If you don't mind bossing me around during my vacation later, we're in the middle of an important meeting," Captain

Johnson said, with no irritation.

Captain Wilson's phone rang. He stepped out to take the call. He returned, holding his phone towards Madison. "Signed, as requested. Pardon my rudeness, Darla, but we need to get back to the reason for this meeting."

Tuesday, 14 December, 7:43 p.m.

Madison gave her email address to Detective Shepherd and asked that a copy of the document land in her inbox before the meeting ended.

She reminded herself what she had done wasn't completely illegal.

It did nothing to settle the turbulence in her core.

Clay leaned closer and whispered, "I'm right here."

She turned to him, grateful she wasn't alone. "Thank you, but it isn't as bad as it sounds. I just had to ensure there wouldn't be consequences for anyone else."

Captain Wilson sighed, running a thumb and forefinger over his moustache. "The floor is yours, Miss Taylor."

"Please call me Madison. Shortly after the women disappeared last December, I gained entry to their apartments or rooms and retrieved items which could be used for DNA testing. If I knew the person who lived with the missing women, I asked for the items."

Captain Wilson leaned forward. "You're admitting to breaking and entering?"

Clay opened his mouth. Madison silenced him by patting his leg. "No, Sir. I'm admitting to obtaining items which can be used to identify the women should their bodies turn up. I believe the Potters Park Five are five of the women who went missing last year. That's why I gave Angie's hairbrush to Evans."

Madison looked at every individual seated at the table. "He doesn't deserve to be called *detective*. And I refuse to dishonour what all of you do every day by calling him that. He isn't your peer."

She continued, "Detective Larson informed me Evans logged the hairbrush into evidence. Because of the backlog at the state laboratory, it could take weeks before we have the results confirming Angie's body is one of the Potters Park Five."

"The forensic investigators are still working through the rubble at Evans's house. The person who called in the tip implied there might be bodies buried in the backyard."

Madison shook her head. "I'm not in a position to give you my opinion, but it seems odd that he went through all the trouble to bury five bodies in Potters Park, five in Paradise Beach, and then bury the others at his house."

Everyone nodded.

Detective Shepherd placed his mug on a coaster. "From what the men told me when I interviewed them, I believe we might have another victim. The first year they had their get together, Angie was there, and again last year. One specific gentleman, who we won't name for obvious reasons, was very disappointed she wasn't there this year."

"I don't understand how Evans got Angie to work for him. May I talk to Natalie after we end this meeting?" Madison asked.

"As long as I'm present, I can't see it being a problem. If that's in order with you, Captain?" Gina asked.

Captain Wilson agreed and turned his attention to Madison. "The illegal entering aside, how did you obtain DNA evidence, which, according to you, proves Evans raped multiple women?"

Madison closed her eyes and reminded herself this wasn't the illegal part. They had taken her breaking and entering well. "Have you ever wondered what happens to condoms after the act?" Her cheeks heated.

"Can't say that I've ever given it much thought." Captain Wilson shrugged.

"See, that's the thing, no one does. Not even men who

leave their DNA behind. Since I started working with the women, I kept hearing stories about some of their clients who wouldn't take no for an answer. The public, and to an extent many law enforcement officers, don't think of sex workers as actual human beings. They are invisible. That is, until arrest figures need to be upped before an election, or when they're recruited as confidential informants, which they do at significant risk to themselves. Not all of them are drug addicts trying to earn enough money for their next fix. The women I work with didn't see an alternative way to survive. This is where the difference between forced prostitution and sex workers becomes a grey area. Not to me, but to most in law enforcement and the general public."

Detective Shepherd lifted a hand into the air. "Madison, I think I speak for all of us when I say we all view the women upstairs, as well as those who are missing, as actual people. You don't need to soften us to them. We realise they each have their own stories about how they ended up in this line of work."

Madison felt a weight lift off her shoulders. "I'm so used to protecting them and explaining to people why I want to work with them. Force of habit. The point I was trying to make – men throw their DNA away. Either in a hotel or wherever they meet for *dates*. Once discarded, it's free for the taking, which the women did. I gave them Ziploc bags for collections. And I'm the garbage collector." Even Captain Wilson smiled. "The difference is that my *dump* is a state-of-the-art laboratory. We're keeping all the discarded items in a fridge, located inside an actual vault. It's accessible from the owner's office. Few people are even aware of the vault."

Captain Johnson winked at Madison and nodded.

Detective Shepherd caught the exchange. "Captain Johnson, is there anything the rest of us need to be aware of?"

"Nothing which is of importance to this case." He glanced at Madison.

Bile covered butterflies fluttered in her stomach. "At some point, they'll find out. They might as well hear it from the horse's mouth. The owner of the laboratory is my sister-in-law's father."

Captain Johnson cleared his throat and gave Madison a compassionate but stern look. "Doctor Davenport has processed evidence for us before, when our laboratory was backlogged and time was of the essence. As it is now. Wilson, I recommend you make the necessary calls and get approval to outsource the evidence processing in this case to his facility. We had an independent forensic expert oversee evidence handling and processing as a precautionary measure, due to the importance of that case."

Clay turned to Madison and whispered, "Maddie, *you* need to make the request. Tell them."

Chapter 38

The women watched him with concentrated expressions. Darla sat on the daybed to his right. It reminded Declan of being on the witness stand. He leaned forward, lifting the mug from the coffee table. While everyone else had asked for coffee, Darla had given Declan one look and told him his options were either chamomile tea or water.

They'd all hugged him when he'd walked into the living room. Even Dakota. Declan had told them his name and explained the reason he'd been on the island.

"Now that it's almost over, what about Vegas?" Tiffany asked, placing an arm around Natalie.

"Natalie. Her name is Natalie." Declan smiled at her.

All the women turned to her. She nodded.

Tiffany asked again, "What are your intentions with *our* Natalie?"

Declan fought against the laughter threatening to erupt from his stomach. They took care of each other. Declan realised they were a family. "If it's okay with the four of you, and with Natalie, I wish to pursue a relationship with her. Whatever happens between us going forward is up to her. I want nothing more than for her to be happy."

Natalie bit her bottom lip, gazing at him. He had said this to her earlier in the afternoon as they'd laid on the bed, holding each other. Then too, she had bitten her lip, a gesture which made him yearn to graze that very lip with his teeth. *In her time, not mine.*

Kayla leaned forward, looking past Tiffany at Natalie. "Do you want him?"

"Ladies, we just escaped death. Literally. Yet here you sit badgering poor Declan. He's the reason we're safe. Let's focus on that – we're safe. Adam can't hurt any of us again. The police are meeting downstairs, discussing this investigation. There's more to this. So, if any of you can think of anything that might be important, or something weird that happened, or anything you remember, ask Captain Johnson to contact Detective Larson."

"What was he planning to do to us?" Dakota asked, knees pulled to her chest, looking younger than her eighteen years.

"The police are still investigating. But sex trafficking, rape and whatever else they can charge him with, depending on any evidence they can find during the investigation."

"Murder?" Dakota asked.

Declan nodded, grateful that Natalie didn't mention anything about organ trafficking. "Yes. If the police can find a gun in his house which can link to another murder through ballistics testing, or if they discover it on another property, but it has Adam's fingerprints on. Things like that."

He didn't know how much they knew about forensics, but realised they were perhaps more knowledgeable than the average rookie police officer.

"And if someone saw him shoot somebody? Say one of us. Would a judge listen to a whore?"

Declan stood and moved to sit on the coffee table. He held his hands out to her, palms up. Dakota glanced at Natalie, who nodded with a smile. Dakota placed her hands on his. "What's your name?"

She closed her eyes and whispered, "Mia."

"Mia, look at me." Declan waited, unsure of his next words. When she looked at him, words no longer mattered. Light returned to her eyes. "No one will ever call you the name *he* gave you, including you. You're no longer the person who did what you had to do for *Mia* to survive. Your entire life is ahead of you and you can be whoever you want to be. You, Mia, can decide what your future holds. I won't lie and tell you it's going to be easy, but I promise you, it will be worth it. One day soon, when you come to visit Natalie, I'll tell you my story. About the reason I became a medical examiner, and how I paid for my studies. Some of us have stories not that different from yours."

Tuesday, 14 December, 8:15 p.m.

She never returned after her break. He didn't miss her company or shrill voice, but she was always at work. What bothered him the most – Evie also hadn't shown up.

If they left him in this place, their names would go on the list. Emily/Noa and Madison still shared the top spot. The muscle monkey second.

Whoever the SWAT officer who had carried Madison away from him, as soon as Foster knew his name, he would go on the list.

Both bitches couldn't have left him here to rot.

Could they? Evie might.

Charlotte? No chance in hell. Not after the life he'd promised her. With her desperate need for adoration and acceptance, Charlotte was easy prey.

Foster could carry out the plan without them, except one key item remained on the outside.

If Charlotte didn't come in tomorrow, he'd ... what? Nothing. He was locked up in hell. He didn't have any power unless they were in the room with him.

Hands behind his head, Foster stared up at the unremarkable ceiling. *She'll be back.*

Tuesday, 14 December, 8:15 p.m.

The others trickled back into the dining room after stepping out to make calls. Gina had gone upstairs to fetch Doctor O'Reilly.

Madison turned in her chair, dropping her head forward until it rested against Clay's chest. She breathed, letting his scent fill her, calm her as it had when Clay had taken her away from Foster. Her nails dug into his sides, not realising she was hurting him.

Clay tilted her head up. "Maddie, I understand why they kept your name out of the papers."

"It's not that. I'm trying to figure out how this leads back to *him*. Maybe it's nothing more than Evans getting hold of a report he shouldn't have. It could've been a fear tactic to get me to back off from asking questions about the missing women." Madison brushed her lips against his, oblivious to the people in the room. "I'm not afraid of *him* anymore. If this is an extra nail in Evans's coffin, or leads to his partners' arrest, then I'll shout my name from the rooftops."

Clay's mouth moved close to her ear. "I prefer when you shout my name."

Madison shivered and opened her eyes to find an audience watching them.

Captain Johnson stared at them, a whimsical smile on his round face. "That right there is what makes this job worth it. Not to diminish all the death and destruction that monster caused, but that something this good has come from something that bad."

Captain Wilson glanced at them. "What are you talking about?"

Under the table, Clay lay a hand on Madison's.

With her other hand, Madison reached for the glass of water and took a sip. She cleared her throat. "Please investigate the possibility that Evans had contact with Foster Ericson."

"The River Valley Killer?" Detective Shepherd frowned.

"Yes. We all suspect Evans attacked me on Friday night and broke into my apartment. During the attack, he said, 'Just because one serial killer was soft on you doesn't mean the next one will be. No one cares about whores, Madison'. He also sprayed a pink dildo on my bedroom wall and stole the letters Foster sent me."

Captain Johnson's big hands moved up and down his red face. "The information about the dildos, and your name, wasn't made public."

"That's why I'm asking that someone dig into it. I doubt it's related to this investigation, but they kept my name out of the media for a reason. The last thing I want is a copycat targeting the women I work with."

Gina tapped a finger on the table. "I'll look into it and will report back. I agree it might be nothing, but the fact Evans knew about the letters makes me think there's more to this than him accessing a report he shouldn't have had access to."

"Thank you." Madison smiled at Gina. The woman was growing on her.

Doctor O'Reilly cleared his throat. "Am I here as the medical examiner who performed the autopsies on the five bodies discovered in Potters Park? Or am I here as one of the men from the island?"

Captain Wilson leaned back in his chair. "On the way here, my detectives and I compared notes. Detective Larson informed me you went this year looking for answers, and last year you weren't aware the women were paid to be there. I've known you for years, Declan. I respect you as a professional and as a man. It might be best if you brief Doctor Seymour for when this case goes to trial. She is conducting the autopsies on the remains discovered at Paradise Beach."

Declan nodded, his expression grim yet determined. "As you know, I conducted the autopsies of the Potters Park Five. You have access to my case files. When I noticed the post-mortem injuries to the bodies, I realised that it pointed at the men I spent two weeks with last year in December. Archer, Torch, Crush, and Trigger. And also, to me – Blade. The man who had welcomed us upon our arrival gave these names to us. The other men had been there the year before, the first year based on what they said. What happened to the fifth man from the first year, I don't know. They called him Ripper."

"Ripper is Adam." Madison pushed to her feet so fast the chair fell backwards.

Captain Wilson turned to her. "Miss Taylor, I think it's time you leave. To be honest, I hear your name so often I forget you're not one of us. I take it you haven't seen the women. Why don't you head upstairs and check on them? Detective Larson mentioned they're determined to change their lives around. You have your work cut out for you."

Gina squared her shoulders. "Sir, with all due respect, Madison isn't *any* civilian. She's put herself in danger more times than either of us can count. The information we received from Madison in the past has proved crucial to bringing various criminals to justice. And despite what you may think, she keeps the women working the streets as safe as one can in her position. Not forgetting what she survived a few months ago. Madison knows the women. She knows the streets. If anyone can help us get information, it's her."

"Detective, why do you think I asked Miss Taylor to check on the women? They will tell her far more than they told you." He turned to Madison. "Madison, if you don't mind? The same goes for you, Officer Davis."

Chapter 39

Clay reached for his phone and called the one person who had answers.

"What's wrong?" Jamie asked, her breath coming in short.

"Why are you panting? Are you in labour?"

Jamie laughed so loud that Clay was forced to hold the phone away from his ear. "No, I'm not due until February. What's wrong? You never call me, just send the odd meme for laughs. Not once, in the six months you've been a part of this family, have you called me."

Clay took a deep breath. "If you can answer my question, I promise to call you every day. And I won't tell Luke you peed a little on the forbidden couch."

"You made me laugh."

"Semantics, James." Clay bit the inside of his cheeks to keep from laughing.

"Call me *James* again and Madison will have to find herself a new boyfriend." A door slammed on Jamie's end.

"Are you slamming doors because you can't punch me?"

"If you were standing in front of me right now, I'd punch you in the throat. I'm stuck with *two* brothers now. And *two* boys growing inside me. We need more girls in the family."

Clay leaned against the front door. "Is Spencer working on your nerves?"

"Not at all, but he's coming to sing for the boys soon. They're going to kick me." Jamie sighed. "It hurts, Clay."

He laughed without malice. "Suck it up, Mommy. It's all

part of being pregnant. A few more weeks and you'll hold them in your arms."

Jamie sighed and cursed. She apologised to her unborn sons for her foul language. "Damn my parents for approving of you. Damn Madison for falling in love with you. Damn Luke and Spencer for respecting you as a friend. And damn me for loving you like a brother. So, *Slay*, why did you call me?"

The corners of his mouth lifted as Clay stared across the dark landscape. In the Taylors, he'd found the family he never had. Clay wanted his own family with Madison.

"You told Maddie you stopped keeping tabs on Foster when you resigned. I want the truth, Jamie. It's just us talking."

"Foster hasn't had any visitors. Not a police officer, a lawyer or a friend. Not a single person since he was sentenced. Foster's lawyer refused to handle his appeal. Last I heard, the state hasn't appointed a new lawyer for him. Why are you asking?"

Clay reminded her of what the attacker had said to Madison, the graffiti on Madison's bedroom wall, and the letters Foster had sent being stolen.

"Why isn't Detective Larson or someone on her team looking into this?"

"Madison asked them to, but with the primary suspect being a detective, I'm not sure who we can trust. This is more than sex trafficking and a pissed-off pimp. I can't keep Maddie safe when I don't know *what* I'm up against, or *who* I need to protect her from."

Jamie gave a long exhale. "I think it's time we called Luke and Noa. Foster will talk to Noa if she goes to see him."

"No. Madison will never forgive me, and Luke won't allow it. Neither will I if it means Madison has to be in the same room as that piece of shit. Asking Foster for his help, after what he did to them, to all of you? No."

"Then I'll go."

Clay shook his head hard and realised Jamie couldn't see him. "No. It'll be too stressful for you and the babies. I'll go."

"He doesn't know who you are, Clay. If Foster can't play a

twisted game with someone, then he isn't interested in talking to them."

Clay pushed his fingers through his hair. "I'm the man who took Madison away from him. In every way."

The front door opened. Clay spun around, thanking Jamie for taking his call, and ended it. Captain Johnson stepped onto the porch, holding a tumbler towards Clay.

"You can't go and see him." Captain Johnson lifted the tumbler to his lips. Clay did the same. "The warden doesn't allow prisoners in the infirmary to have visitors. When we took a break earlier, I spoke to the warden. Ericson has had no contact with the outside world since the day of his sentencing. Before that, he had contact only with his attorney. I've made some calls. His attorney has retired and moved to Wild Bay. And I highly doubt that it's any of the prisoners. Their interaction with Foster is limited and focused on putting him in the infirmary."

Clay drained the contents of the tumbler, almost crushing the glass in his grip. "We need a list of all personnel working at the prison."

Captain Johnson nodded. "Way ahead of you, Slay. The list is in my inbox."

"Are you going to share it with Captain Wilson?"

"No, but I sent it to Detective Larson." He placed his big hand on Clay's shoulder. "I don't know if Larson's trustworthy, but I've heard good things about her. It appears Madison trusts her. That says a lot."

Clay kept it to himself that Madison still loathed herself for trusting a serial killer. "I've known Gina for years. She can be a hard-ass, but I trust her. Thank you, Captain, for the brandy and contacting the warden."

Tuesday, 14 December, 8:48 p.m.

She shook out her hair, grinning at her reflection in the vanity mirror. Her natural colour always suited her best. "Hello gorgeous, I haven't seen you in years."

Pouring another glass of Dom Perignon, she savoured the taste. *Success.*

On the other side of the floor-to-ceiling glass sliding doors, life continued. She opened the doors, stepping out onto the balcony. She lifted her eyes to the penthouse suite. People scurried along the street below, living their miserable lives.

Birth. Exist. Death.

Birth. Soul-crushing pain. Death.

The corners of her mouth lifted. This was the first night of her new life. She'd lost count of how many lives she'd already lived. The part between her birth and death wasn't filled with the banal existence others accepted as their fate.

Adam was laying in hospital, chained to a bed like a caged animal. Animals she liked. Homo sapiens? Only if they served their purpose.

Charlie the homeless. She sank her teeth into her fist, afraid her laughter would travel all the way up to the poor thing's floor.

"If only someone loved you," she whispered into the night. Foster tolerated her because of their plan. *Foster.*

To her, Foster Ericson was nothing more than another tick on the bucket list spanning all her lives. Even as a teenager, she'd wondered what it would be like to have sex with a serial killer. Specifically, one who murdered women. Now she knew – nothing to write home about. Not that she had anyone to write to.

No home. No family. Nothing.

Just this life, the new one, until it was time for the next.

Tuesday, 14 December, 8:48 p.m.

Madison's arms weren't long enough to hug the four women pressing against her from all sides. "Okay." She laughed. "I'm grateful you're safe and I get to see your gorgeous faces again, but I can't breathe." The women stepped back, allowing her to take a deep breath. "I missed you too."

Madison hugged each individually and gave them a once-over. With Dakota in her arms, she smiled at Natalie and mouthed, "You did this."

Natalie shook her head, mouthing back, "Declan." Her smile reached her eyes.

Dakota tightened her grip on Madison. "My name is Mia. I realise now I never told you because he named me *before* I met you."

"Mia." Madison pressed her lips to the young woman's hair.

Darla stepped closer, holding a tissue out to her. Madison thanked her with a slow blink and a hint of a smile. "I haven't cried this much in months."

Mia stepped back, appraising her. "Why were *you* crying?"

They took their seats, all eyes on Madison.

"When this investigation is over, we'll have a picnic on my family's farm and I'll tell you what I should've told you months ago. Now we need to focus on the matter at hand so that we can get started with your new lives. Better lives. Actual lives and no longer merely surviving."

"Vegas is moving in with Blade." Mia rolled her eyes. "Sorry, *Natalie* is moving in with *Declan*. Doctor something."

"I haven't decided yet." Natalie shrugged, staring at the coffee table. "I don't know him. Vegas and her way of life is all I've known for years. It's time I figure out who I am, who Natalie is."

The others nodded, lost in their own thoughts.

Darla broke the silence. "Well, you're all welcome to stay here as long as you want. No, you won't pay rent, but you'll help around the farm. I don't care how much you work on my husband's nerves or keep him on his toes. He might protest, but after the kids moved out, the silence was getting to him. No matter what he claims."

Madison reached for Darla's hand. "Thank you, Doctor Johnson. It means the world to me, and I know to my friends as well." She turned to Natalie. "You do whatever makes you happy. And taking a bold step out of your old life is perhaps the move you need."

Natalie drew her legs to her chest. "I can't pack up my apartment. I'll have to see Angie's stuff."

"What do you mean, *see* Angie's stuff?" Kayla asked.

"About two weeks after she disappeared, her landlord contacted me and told me to fetch her stuff. She'd listed me as her emergency contact. Of course, I went and packed all her things and kept it at my place. Back then, I was sure she'd return for it at some point. Her whole life fit in three boxes. The apartment she rented came fully furnished."

Madison leaned forward. "May I go to your apartment tomorrow and take Angie's things? That way, you don't have to see it, but also, the police suspect she worked with Adam."

Five women spoke at the same time, denying Angie's involvement.

Madison waited for them to get it out of their systems. "Think about it. Angie approached Declan. She even approached some of you. She went on the *vacations* two years in a row. Why was Angie spared that first year when five women were murdered? Who is the other woman?"

There was no point in softening the reality of the situation. These women had lived every day not knowing if it would be their last, always telling themselves and Madison that – at least they weren't on the streets.

Jersey stood and walked to the window, keeping her back to the others. "Angel wasn't scared of Adam. Not once did I hear her say anything bad about him. We compared bruises and cried on each other's shoulders. Never Angie the Angel. I remember one day Tiffany came to my place and she was there."

Jersey turned to Tiffany, whose real name they now knew – Samantha. Samantha closed her eyes and nodded. Jersey continued. "Adam had forced Sam to have sex with two men while he watched. Their fantasy was to have a threesome with a married woman while her husband watched. Adam had told them she was his wife."

Samantha swallowed hard. "Halfway through, Adam started mocking them, saying they weren't doing it hard enough. Because I didn't scream like I screamed with him. He laughed at them. Both men got pissed off. When they moved to beat him up, Adam shot them." She gagged and ran out of the room.

"I'll finish the story for her because I don't want her to have to tell it. She's been through enough. Adam raped her. Their bodies were still on the bed, their blood and brains were all over her. When Sam told us, Angie laughed." Jersey punched the wall, sank to the floor, and cried.

Madison walked to her and sat down on the carpet, pulling her friend into her arms.

Chapter 40

The SUV's taillights disappeared into the darkness. The sound of crickets and frogs drowned out the quiet. Declan drew her closer and rubbed Natalie's arm. She pressed her face to his chest, hoping to forget everything she had heard. *Angie was never my friend.*

"Will her hand be okay?" Natalie asked, wrapping her arms around Declan's waist.

Darla had called Declan to look at Jersey's hand. Darla's medical expertise didn't extend to humans whereas Declan's didn't treat the living.

"It will be sore for a few days, but I don't think she's broken anything. Darla will monitor it for swelling and discolouration." He pressed his lips to her hair.

"I'm tired." Natalie didn't yawn.

"I know. Me too. I'm glad we're here, despite the circumstances. It gives us time to process and breathe."

Natalie's smile faded as fast as it filled her face. "I haven't breathed in ... I don't know how long."

Declan held her tighter, pressing her ear against his heart. "Can you hear it?"

The rhythmic thumping filled her head. Natalie's shoulders sagged, and she rested against him. He bent down, scooped her up, and carried her to the bed.

Declan eased her down and pushed the hair from her face. "Whenever it gets too much, we will listen to each other's heartbeats. As long as there's life in us, there is hope that tomorrow will be better. Waking up next to you, no matter whether it is here, on the island, or wherever, if you're with me and I get to see your beautiful smile when I open my eyes, then it'll be a better day than the day before."

Natalie reached for his face, trailing his jaw with her fingertips. "I want to move in with you. We can discuss sleeping arrangements later. For now, I just want to lie here and breathe. Declan, I want to hold you."

He brushed his lips over hers, smiling down at her as she lay with her eyes closed, a smile on her face, despite the sad rage he had felt suffocating the room when he'd tended to Jersey. "Then that's what we will do. Hold each other and breathe."

Thunder echoed through the night sky.

Tuesday, 14 December, 10:38 p.m.

King ran through the front door and jumped on the couch, leaving a trail of muddy paw prints behind him. Madison shooed him off and wiped his feet before drying him with a towel. King pressed up against her until Madison fell backwards onto the hardwood floor.

Clay's laughter filled the house. Madison turned to look at him and her breath caught. His shirt clung to him. The perfect lines of his torso were visible. She pushed to her feet, grabbed another towel, and closed the distance between them.

Clay moved to take the towel from her. Madison slapped his hand away and tried to pull the soaking shirt over his head. Her eyes fell on his stomach. *Six perfect wet squares.* Madison stepped back and stared, drawing her bottom lip between her teeth.

"How did Jersey hurt her hand?" Clay asked, pulling the wet shirt over his head, not realising Madison's mind was far from the events of the night until he saw her face. "Maddie? What happened?"

She moved closer, inhaling his scent as Clay wrapped his arms around her. "I wanted to forget for a while. And you're wet. And this body of yours. And it's you. After months, it's us. All these months, I had no idea what he was putting them through, the things Adam did to them. They never told me. How can I protect them if they don't tell me?"

Clay rested his chin on her head, cradling her to him. "Maddie, you did what you could. And you gathered evidence. Claire reached out to you using the safe words you put in place, which led to the police realising we're looking for one of us. They told you things tonight I suspect they haven't even mentioned to Gina."

Madison's cheek brushed up and down against his chest.

"He's under arrest. He can't hurt them again."

"How did no one realise he was killing people all over the city? How many other people has he murdered that we don't know about? Who helped him? He sat there, right in front of me at the police station. I had my gun on me that night. I could've killed him."

"On Friday, you had no way of knowing *what* Evans is."

Madison's voice caught. "Because they didn't tell me everything. Why don't they trust me enough?"

"They trust you, Maddie. But they feared him."

Madison stepped back and stared up at Clay. "Why didn't Adam kill me on Friday night? He could've shot me, staging a drive-by. I've made my fair share of enemies on the streets."

Clay cupped her face in his hands, pressing his lips to Madison's forehead. "He's had no contact with Foster."

"How do you know that?" Madison asked.

"I'm not the only person looking out for you."

Chapter 41

Wednesday, 15 December, 5:07 a.m.

Ignorant fool. From the beginning, she had thought this was her plan. Killing her wouldn't be nearly as much fun as bashing the life out of Noa and Madison. But she didn't deserve a spectacular death.

Foster glanced at the clock against the wall; fifty-three minutes until he'd have to look at her horrible face for the last time. *One last Oscar worthy performance in this shithole.*

Voices boomed down the passage. A stampede of feet rushed past the infirmary's door. The guards headed towards the section that housed the awaiting trial prisoners. It was too early for a riot. Then again, Foster hadn't spent enough time with the other prisoners to know what hours they kept.

Glancing around the room, he erased every item from his memory. Not even his brilliant mind had room to hold more than one sight. Noa and Madison. Bound for eternity … in their deaths.

Foster wondered who'd pay first for their treason. Perhaps it would be Emily Gallagher for becoming Noa Morgan, gutting him and scarring his magnificent stomach. How dare she stab *him* when he'd done nothing but love her. Or maybe Madison would meet the cricket bat first. Hard choice.

Too early in the day to make such a big life and death decision. And even earlier for a riot.

Again, Foster looked at the clock. A miserable five minutes had passed since he last checked. As long as he remained caged, all he had was time.

Soon, he'd live again. Free of schedules, clocks and other people calling the shots.

If Charlotte didn't show up for her shift, he'd have no choice but to make *pruno* with whatever life threw at him.

Foster Ericson never cared for lemonade and even less for prison wine. *I've got to get out.*

Wednesday, 15 December, 5:50 a.m.

The smell of coffee pulled her from a deep sleep. Madison opened her eyes to boxer shorts riding low on hips and a v-line so perfect it begged to be licked. She stretched her arms above her head, forcing her eyes to his face.

"Uhm, your top moved." Clay's eyes didn't meet hers.

Madison glanced at her bare chest, reached for the duvet, and pulled it to her neck. Clay placed the mugs on the bedside table and sat on the edge of the mattress.

Madison scooted up, clutching the duvet. "How long were you standing like that before I opened my eyes?" Her fingers trailed along the inside of his thigh.

"Your coffee might be cold." Clay grabbed the teasing hand and pressed his lips to her wrist, placing her palm against his cheek. "I wish we could stay here forever. You and me, together. In an actual house and not a cramped city apartment. It would've been amazing to stay here until Christmas, but Luke and Noa will kick us out as soon as they find out Jamie peed on the couch. Not to mention the things we did on their forbidden couch."

Madison pushed herself up, leaning back against the headboard. "My sister peed on the couch?" She laughed until she struggled for air and wiped tears from her eyes.

Clay grabbed her hand. "If you say a word to her about this, I will have to break up with you. Jamie threatened to punch me in the throat."

"You, Clay Davis, scared of a short, pregnant woman?"

Madison loved teasing Jamie about her being the oldest, yet the shortest. As if the five-centimetre advantage Madison had was a personal accomplishment and not down to genetics.

"Jamie Edwards has a short fuse and she won't be pregnant forever. Madison, I'm serious. If you mention it to anyone, I'll tell your parents what you did when they were at the wine expo in France."

Madison yanked her hand from his and, in a single move, leaped onto his lap. "Are you blackmailing me? After spilling Jamie's secret about her little spill on *the* couch?" She stared at him through squinted eyes.

"Yes. With your family, I'd rather blackmail you than make an enemy out of any of them. Your parents will love me more than they love their darling, youngest daughter, when they hear all about the weekend you—"

Madison kissed him hard, locking her arms around his neck. Her lower body moved against Clay's until he throbbed against her. Madison eased back, an eyebrow raised. "If you want me to touch *him* again, you'll promise to never ever bring that weekend up again."

She thrust her hips forward. "Am I making myself clear?"

"Yes, ma'am." Clay grabbed her hips, keeping her pressed against him. "If you want me to touch *him* again, you'll promise to never fix your top again. And that I'll never have to wake up without you."

"You drive a hard bargain, Slay." Madison rolled her hips.

"And you're making me forget words." Clay closed his eyes, a boyish grin on his face. "Promise me."

Madison showed him how to seal a deal without using words.

Wednesday, 15 December, 6:01 a.m.

The day arrived. In a few hours, she'd start a new life. Far away from this shithole, and even further away from *them*.

New is always better. Charlotte pushed the door open. The room was as empty as the sinkhole forming in her stomach.

A guard passed behind her. She spun around, grabbing his arm. "Where is he?" Her nails dug into the guard's skin.

He yanked his arm out of her grip, staring at her as if she was as crazy as she felt. "Listen, I just came on shift. We walked through the gate together."

She stormed off, heading towards the warden's office. As she lifted her fist to pound against his door, she realised he wouldn't be in until much later.

Voices heading towards the locker room drew her attention. Charlotte sprinted down the corridor. "What happened to him?" she called out.

The guards whose names she'd never bothered to remember stopped and turned to face her. The older one spoke first. "Who?"

"The patient." Charlotte hid her trembling hands behind her back.

"Boogeyman? The head of the trafficking syndicate? They took him to Shadow Bay Hospital about half an hour ago. Heart attack or something. Who cares as long as he dies on the way there?"

Her hands balled into fists. "Not him. Foster Ericson. Where is he?"

"He was transported in the same ambulance," the younger guard said, turning towards the locker room.

"Why? He was fine yesterday."

Both guards laughed. "He wasn't when the paramedics rushed him out of here. The dumbass set himself on fire. I guess he couldn't wait to get to hell to pay for the things he did to those poor women."

Charlotte pushed past them, running for the locker room to grab her purse and belongings. Today, she wouldn't bother offering the warden an excuse for being absent. She wasn't coming back.

Chapter 42

Duke placed a mug next to Gina's hand, startling her awake. "You never came to bed." He bent down, pressing his lips to the back of her neck.

Gina willed her eyes to remain open. "Passed out here. My back's going to hurt like a mother today."

She had spent the night scrolling through the list Captain Johnson had sent. There was no definitive link between Ben Adam Evans and any of the prison's employees.

Duke gazed at her. "You need to ice your eyes. I'll fetch some peas."

Peas. Gina remembered when Clay had handed a pack of peas to Madison. It felt like months ago, not days. "I like her." She reached for the mug.

"Who?" Duke took the seat next to her, turning the laptop to see what had kept Gina up all night.

"Madison. Slay's girlfriend."

"She's nothing like any of the women Slay's dated." Duke pursed his lips. "Sorry, you know what I mean."

"I do, and you're right. Madison's a much better person than Penelope ever will be. Unlike Madison, Penelope is selfish and feels entitled." Gina had always wondered how those who shared DNA could be such different people.

"What are you looking for?" Duke took the mug from her hands and brought it to his lips.

In the early days of their relationship, it had irritated Gina endlessly to share her first cup of coffee. After almost losing him years before, she now committed those moments to memory. In their line of work, no one considered the possibility of losing a loved one in a car accident.

"You knew about Madison, what happened to her. Not once did you let her name slip or mention anything about Slay becoming friends with a victim." Gina stared at him, admiring Duke even more. Trustworthy, strong, and the one person who had never disappointed her.

Duke handed the mug back to her with a shrug. "It wasn't my story to tell. *Why* do you know?"

"We believe Foster Ericson was in contact with our suspect. I can't see how. Foster didn't have any visitors. Evans never signed in at the prison. How could Evans have known the things he said to Madison? How did he know about the letters? Foster has spent the better part of the last four months in the infirmary."

Duke hugged her to his chest. "If there's anyone who can make sense of this, it's you."

Infirmary. Gina reached for the laptop and scrolled through the employees' names.

Again.

Wednesday, 15 December, 6:30 a.m.

Traffic is the nemesis of any paramedic when every second is crucial.

Even with the sirens on, cars didn't move. There was nowhere for the drivers to go.

"It won't be a loss, but if we don't get him to the ER soon, he won't make it," Jenkins called out to his partner. They'd been riding together for almost a year. He enjoyed working with Richter.

Jenkins stared at the other patient, checking that his vitals were stable. This wasn't his first rodeo transporting violent criminals to the state hospital. He ensured their restraints were still in place. *Violent and volatile go hand in hand.*

Richter glanced in the rear-view mirror. "Are you okay back there? Looks like the traffic is being redirected. We should be able to head home after dropping them off."

The heart rate monitor's shrill beep filled the ambulance.

"He's coding. I need to defib. Going to cut his shirt, just keep it steady." Jenkins reached for the scissors.

Wednesday, 15 December, 6:45 a.m.

Gina eased onto the freeway, heading to River Valley. She had asked Madison to go with her to Natalie's apartment to retrieve Angie's belongings. She struggled to comprehend the things Madison had told her after Madison met with the women.

Captain Wilson had agreed to take it up with the higher powers to have all the evidence sent to Richard Davenport's private laboratory. Due to the mayor's involvement, they couldn't risk sensitive information being leaked. The same employees who had worked the River Valley Killer case would process the evidence in this case. When Doctor Davenport had heard Madison's name, he gave all his other employees early paid leave.

People liked Madison; Gina was beginning to herself.

The call came over the radio.

She switched on the strobe lights, made a U-turn, and pressed the accelerator against the floor.

Wednesday, 15 December, 7:00 a.m.

Clay tossed his phone on the kitchen island, gripping the edge of the granite top. His angered voice and curses carried through the house.

Madison ran down the stairs, taking them two at a time. She grabbed his shoulders. "Go. Hunt that sonofabitch down and kill him. I don't care who says what, or what orders you get. Today he dies."

He spun around, pulling her to him. "I can't leave you."

Madison cupped his face in her hands and stared up at him. "I'm safe here. Declan and Natalie are coming over for breakfast. King is here, somewhere. Go Officer Davis. Slay this fucking demon." She pressed her mouth to his for a hard kiss. "Come back to me."

"I love you, Maddie." Clay kissed her forehead.

Madison stepped back, a hint of a smile on her face. After six months of pretending to be friends, to hear Clay say it and to say it back was now the most natural thing. "I love you. Be my hero to someone else. Make those kids feel safe again. Kill him."

Clay grabbed the keys and ran to his SUV. He understood Madison's bloodlust. They'd both witnessed the suffering caused by the hands of monsters.

Today he could end one monster and give the children, whose faces still robbed him of sleep, their sleep back. *You're dead, Boogeyman.*

Wednesday, 15 December, 7:15 a.m.

The carnage mirrored a scene from an action movie. Jenkins sat on the kerb. Blood covered his face, clothes, and hands. Most of it wasn't his. A fellow paramedic tended to the wound on Jenkins' forehead.

Gina did a three-sixty, taking it all in. The piled-up cars. People screaming. Firefighters cutting through metal, desperate to free those still trapped. A thick black smoke cloud filled the sky. Flames reached towards the heavens from the fuel tanker down the street.

Two bodies lay next to the ambulance. Blankets hid the faces of the dead.

Captain Wilson stepped up behind her. "This is a mess."

Understatement of the year. "How did this happen? We worked our asses off to bring him to justice. Three officers are still recovering in hospital and now he's gone?"

"I've called in SWAT. We've launched a nationwide manhunt. We will find him. Off the record, I hope whoever gets to him first empties a magazine in him."

Firefighters placed another body next to the others and ran off.

"Where is he?" A woman stood behind them.

Gina guessed the woman to be around her age and noticed no wedding ring when the woman fidgeted with her sunglasses. "It'll take a while before everyone is accounted for. Give the name of the person you're looking for to the police officer standing outside the coffee shop. The officer will assist you." Gina pointed towards the coffee shop and returned her attention to Captain Wilson.

The woman tapped Gina's shoulder. "The prisoner? Where is he?"

Captain Wilson moved closer with his hands behind his back. "And you are?"

"Is he alive? Whose bodies are those?" Tears slipped past the dark rim of her glasses.

Wilson stepped forward, squaring his shoulders. "Again, who are you? Identification." He held a hand towards her.

"Just tell me he's alive and where you've taken him." Her body trembled.

Gina waved two officers over. "Ma'am, if you don't mind going down to the station. We'll answer all your questions there, but not out here on the street. Not within earshot of the already terrified public and the media."

The woman stepped back, scanning her surroundings. Her eyes fixed on the officers approaching. "I just wanted to know if he's okay. I'll go now. My apologies for wasting your time."

A hysterical voice called out, "Is someone a doctor? My baby isn't breathing. Please! Help."

The woman spun on her heels and ran in the direction

where the frantic voice came from. Gina instructed the officers to follow and not allow her to leave the scene.

She turned to Captain Wilson. "She might be the mother of one of their victims, but something tells me she wasn't asking about *Boogeyman*."

Boogeyman – the code name they'd given their investigation into the head of a human trafficking ring who stole children from the streets or bought them from their supposed parents. It baffled Gina that an estimated eight million children were abducted every year. Not all of them by strangers.

Gina stood to the side when Commander Voight gave instructions to his team. At least Duke and Slay would work together. It always brought her a sense of relief knowing that they had each other's backs when they were on duty.

She listened while Captain Wilson called Detective Shepherd, instructing him to focus on finding Boogeyman and whoever had helped him escape.

Gina's orders were to remain focused on the Evans investigation. Someone had to interview him now that he was awake.

She walked to where paramedics were busy loading the infant into an awaiting ambulance. Jenkins stood next to the ambulance, talking to the baby's mother. Gina had met Jenkins as soon as she arrived on the scene.

"How is your head?" she asked after he closed the back doors.

"I've seen worse. Will I be arrested for killing him?"

Gina's focus shifted towards the strange woman, who had run to the child's aid, marching in their direction.

"No, you won't. It was self-defence. Besides, no one cares how Foster Ericson died. I saw his body when I got here. My personal and unofficial opinion – you did a decent job of slicing up the sonofabitch. Can't believe you did all that with a scalpel. If it makes you sleep tonight, what you did doesn't compare to the savagery Ericson inflicted on his victims. Most people will call you a hero, myself included." She patted his shoulder. Her attention turned to the woman standing too close for Gina's comfort.

Sunlight glistened on the pair of scissors clutched in the woman's hands. Her eyes met Gina's. She turned around and headed towards more cries for help.

"Doctor Hughes, you saved that baby's life," Jenkins called after her.

"Doctor Charlotte Evelyn Hughes?" Gina asked Jenkins, looking at him over her shoulder.

"Yes. She works at the prison."

Gina reached for her gun, turning in the direction Doctor Hughes had taken.

Chapter 43

Madison's stomach lodged in her throat. "Clay?" she asked, terrified of the answer.

"No, but you might need to take a seat. They can wait on the porch." Captain Johnson tilted his head back.

King ran to Natalie, his tail wagging. He fell at her feet and waited for a belly rub.

"Don't mind us. We'll sit out here on the porch and play with King." Declan bent down to pick up King's ball.

Madison hugged Natalie before walking to the living room. She needed the physical reassurance that one of her loved ones was safe.

Captain Johnson eased down next to her on the couch.

Clay is safe. This isn't about him. Madison took a deep breath, dreading whatever Captain Johnson had to say.

He met her stare. Relief and joy filled his face. "Foster Ericson is dead."

Fear rolled off her shoulders with every violent beat of her heart. "Dead?"

"Yes. The ambulance transporting him, and another prisoner was attacked on the way to the hospital. The other prisoner escaped, but Ericson is dead."

"How?" Madison asked. Disbelief and relief played tug-of-war inside her.

"With all the commotion during the attack, Ericson tried to make a run for it. The paramedic grabbed a scalpel and managed to slash Ericson's carotid artery. I doubt you need to hear all the details. But after what that sonofabitch did to you, I'll tell you, the damage to his hands, face, and throat was extensive."

"I should call Noa." Madison stood, her legs steadier than they had been in months.

Noa answered on the third ring. "Maddie, what's wrong?"

"He's dead, Noa. Foster is dead." Madison took a deep breath and slowly exhaled. "It's over. For all of us. His victims' families, you, me, and our family."

Tears streamed down Madison's nodded face. Laughter carried into the house from outside. *Natalie.* Not everyone's nightmares were over, not yet.

"I thought you deserved to hear it from me. Enjoy the rest of your honeymoon. I'll see you when you get back."

"Maddie, wait. Are you okay?" Noa asked, followed by a louder voice in the background on her end.

"Maddie?" The sound of her brother's voice broke her heart.

Madison managed to hold it together. "I'm fine. King is doing great. The horses are happy. The house is still standing. Enjoy skiing and don't break anything. I love you, Luke."

"Madison Taylor, where's Clay? I need to speak to him." Luke's voice filled with fear. He knew when she was lying.

"He got called to help track down a prisoner who escaped. I'll ask Clay to contact you as soon as he arrives home." This wasn't their home. The thought revealed an ache inside her to have a home to call their own.

"Who is there with you?" Luke asked.

Madison rolled her eyes at the ceiling. "Did Jamie call you?"

"No, I called her. What's going on?"

"I'll tell you when you get back. Enjoy your honeymoon. Don't worry about me. I'm safe. Captain Johnson is here and friends are spending the day here. I'll introduce you to them sometime."

"Why is Captain Johnson there? Give him the phone. Now."

Again, Madison rolled her eyes and wondered if a day would ever come when she wasn't considered the baby in the family. She doubted the twins' arrival would change anything.

Captain Johnson took the phone when Madison sat down next to him. "Luke, how's your honeymoon?"

Madison couldn't hear Luke's every word. She focused on Captain Johnson who he nodded, then shook his head. Clearly, Luke was busy with one of his overprotective rants.

"Now listen to me, young man. Madison is safe. Focus on this time with your wife. Noa deserves it. We can catch up when you get back." He listened again. Madison could've sworn Captain Johnson rolled his eyes. "Yes, Luke, you have my word. Clay hasn't left her side. Him being involved in a manhunt is irrelevant."

Captain Johnson ended the call and gave Madison the phone. "Your brother doesn't take no for an answer."

"No, he doesn't. I'll send Noa a text and ask her to keep Luke distracted. Otherwise, he'll be on the first flight back and there's no reason for them to be here."

Madison sent the text to Noa, hoping they'd return on the scheduled date. She wasn't ready to leave this place, or to no longer live with Clay.

Wednesday, 15 December, 8:02 a.m.

A nurse stepped into his room, closing the door behind her. The first thing he noticed was her dark red hair. He didn't know the exact word women called the shade. Hair colour didn't matter as long as the woman begged him for more. Even better when she pleaded with him to stop.

The nurse kept her eyes on the floor, easing closer to the bed. A familiar scent filled the room. Her hand glided along the sheet covering him from his ankle to his thigh.

She lifted her eyes and smirked. "Good morning, my love." Eva's smile was as insincere as the coo in her voice.

"You did this, you fucking bitch." Adam thrashed. Metal scraped on metal, making a sound he once craved.

She stepped around the bed and closed the curtains someone had opened for him earlier. "The sooner you get used to not seeing the outside world, the better." Eva leaned back against the wall. She pushed a hand into her pants, removed it and rubbed her hand over his mouth.

The blood leaking into his mouth tasted vile as he sunk his teeth into her fingers. Eva yanked her hand away.

A fist crashed into his face.

Guards stood outside the door. He could scream. Adam opened his mouth, but before a sound erupted from his throat, a silver piece of tape covered his mouth. There was a time he'd enjoyed and marvelled at his wife's agility.

"Adam, thank you for the time we spent together. But as with all the best things, it has to end." She shifted her gaze to his crotch. "You're so predictable, darling. I won't miss this horrid little thing."

Eva's fist connected with his erection.

Adam coughed behind the tape, curling into himself.

Eva sneered, leaning over the bed. In a low voice, she said, "It's quite a predicament you're in, my love. You had so much potential, but you are your own worst enemy. Well, your dark side is. This peanut-sized brain doesn't help much either." She tapped a finger on his forehead.

Adam controlled his breathing, swallowed the taste of egg yolk, and met her cold eyes.

"I should've shut you up a long, long time ago. That's basically a summary of our life together. I never went down on you, whereas you lived on your knees in front of me." Eva shuddered. "Strange, your mouth is the only part of you that gave me any pleasure. Oh, and of course, the money you made me. I wish I could thank you for my new life, but an employer never thanks an employee."

Nostrils flaring, Adam tried to reach for her. Eva pressed his arms down on the bed.

"It's time for a bedtime story; it's my favourite. Once upon a time, there was a man with a very tiny dick. He loved money, almost as much as he loved raping women. One day, the man met a queen. Out of the goodness of her heart, she showed him her queendom and invited him to stay in her world. The man worked hard to prove himself to the beautiful queen. The fool tried to hide what he did to the peasants, but the queen wasn't dumb. When she learned *what* the man was, she put him to use, adding more gold to her coffers. The man thought he shared in the spoils of the war he raged upon the inhabitants of the queendom. Yet, he never kept an eye on the treasure room. His tiny brain wasn't made to rule."

Eva trailed the back of her fingers over the duct tape. "The queen ensured the man had his own gold, enough to keep him from asking questions. And enough to show the sheriff that the man was a very bad and evil man. For years, the man did as he pleased. The queen allowed it, until one day."

Eva pressed her lips to Adam's clammy forehead. "And then, *one day* arrived. You see, the sheriff will find gold in the man's bank accounts. The queen was kind enough to register the castle in the undeserving man's name. The man will spend the rest of his miserable life in a dungeon. As for the queen? That's a story for another day."

Adam stared up at her, sweat trickling down his face.

"Darling, I'm going to remove the tape from your mouth. Forever, I'll be your fondest memory." Eva ripped the tape from his mouth. "The fuck you is in the details."

When she reached for the door, Adam said, "Eva, I won't go down without you."

With her back to him, she laughed softly. "Who is Eva?"

Chapter 44

Madison stared out over the lawn, towards the river where it passed at the foot of the mountain. King chased after the Egyptian Geese. Why the pair still bothered to land on Luke's farm had become a joke at their family dinners.

Natalie touched Madison's arm. "Who was that on the phone?"

"Detective Larson. She's at your apartment collecting Angie's things. She will pick up Doctor Seymour on the way here." Madison turned to Declan. "You understand Doctor Seymour is putting her career on the line by sharing her findings with you?"

Despite the professional risk, Doctor Seymour had agreed to do whatever was necessary to bring those responsible for the deaths of the five female victims whose skeletal remains they'd uncovered at Paradise Beach to justice.

Declan leaned back in the chair. "This is an absolute mess for all of us. Have you heard from Clay?"

Madison folded and unfolded the napkin on her lap. "No. Gina also hasn't heard anything."

Declan stood, collecting the dirty plates and cutlery. King's barking made him look up at the lawn. The geese flew away when King closed in on them, only to land a few metres away seconds later. The ritual continued.

He laughed. Natalie touched his back. He smiled down at her and turned to Madison. "We all need a dog like King in our lives." Declan disappeared inside the house.

Natalie placed a hand on Madison's, stilling her fidgeting. "He'll be okay. Before you know it, Clay will be home. This place is amazing. It feels like you're in a different world."

Madison sighed. "Yes, it does. I wish this was our home."

Natalie twisted in her chair to face Madison. All three of them had sat next to each other during breakfast, enjoying the view of the beautiful vineyards and the momentary escape from their dark realities. "How does it feel to make love to someone?"

Madison dropped the napkin on the table and turned to her friend. "I always thought sex and making love were different names for the same physical act. And then I slept with a man, who I, at the time, considered was the best thing since the invention of mobile phones." Bile rose in her throat at the memory of that weekend and how it had ended. And the murderer Madison had allowed inside her.

Natalie touched Madison's hair. "Don't go there." She shook her head and dropped it forward. "If *you* struggle, how the hell am I supposed to make peace with what I've done?"

Madison hugged her friend. "My story isn't finished. He's dead. *Dead.* I can live without the constant fear of him sending another letter, of Foster getting out of prison, or ordering someone to come after me. Freedom is a strange feeling."

Natalie laughed. "I understand exactly how you feel."

"I'm sorry. Sometimes I forget who I'm talking to when I'm with you. Always have. Thank you for allowing me into your life. I hope we remain friends."

"Oh sweetie, you're not getting rid of me that easy. We're friends. Always will be. You don't share a nightmare like this with someone, only to have them vanish from your life. We've done the lows. It's time we get to experience the highs together as well."

Madison pulled Natalie closer, their faces wet. They laughed, wiping each other's tears. Declan placed a box of tissues on the table and retreated inside the house.

"You're a remarkable human being, Natalie King, and I'm honoured to be your friend." Madison whispered *King*. This wasn't the time for him to come and beg for a belly rub. "What I was getting to, before we vowed our undying friendship to each other, was when I met Clay and we started spending time together, everything changed. We share this strange calm, yet it's exciting and mind-blowing and what I saw other people find. I never dreamt I would. When we're together, we don't need words to understand each other's needs or emotions. It's been like that since the beginning. And when we make love, it's the same. I feel full with him."

"I bet you do." Natalie grinned.

"Yes, I do. Damn." Madison failed to hide the smile at the memory of the feeling of him inside her, but more because of the fullness in her heart. "Clay gets me, and I him. When you connect on every level, love and respect each other, it makes you realise none of the people you were with before compare to the connection you share. Sex is sex. This is something I can't explain. All I can do is hope that you have found it with Declan."

"I want everything you said, but I don't know how. I've missed it since the first time I opened my legs to a stranger. Years ago, I was in love and thought we had something special. But we were young, and the relationship ended. So, I have a frame of reference, but I'm not the same person I was then. I'm damaged."

Madison cupped Natalie's face between her palms. "You're not *damaged*. Declan doesn't see you as dirty, or less of a woman. I've noticed how he looks at you, the way he speaks to you. Natalie, he opened his home to you. With no conditions. Allow him to get to know you, as you rediscover who you are. Let things happen when you are ready for it. I doubt the delicious Doctor O'Reilly will pressure you when he has mentioned *your* room more than once, but said *our* house."

Natalie glanced at the patio door. "He's amazing, but I can't help worrying that someone better is going to come along, and

Declan will regret asking me to move in."

"I'm hearing way too many *buts* from you today. Take it one day at a time. You don't know what the future holds for you as Natalie, or for the two of you. The most important thing is that you have a future."

Natalie pressed a tissue to the corner of her left eye. "Do you really think he killed all those people? Is he a serial killer?"

Madison sucked in her cheeks. "Let's focus on what we can do to help with the investigation. Gina should arrive soon. Are you ready to go through Angie's stuff? The boxes might not even contain anything important."

The wind tugged at Natalie's hair. She pushed it behind her ears. "She's a stranger to me. How could Angie laugh, hearing what Adam did to Samantha? Sure, she had a dark sense of humour, but I never expected her to be this cruel. Twisted. Sick."

An alarm tone sounded on Madison's phone. She reached for it and stood. "Come, Gina's here."

Wednesday, 15 December, 10:09 a.m.

Clay holstered his Colt M4 and thanked Duke for the bottle of water. Every available officer was out on the streets, hunting the Boogeyman. Even the officers who were on leave had come to assist.

Duke patted Clay's back as he walked past. The house was nothing but a meth lab, like most of the others in the neighbourhood.

Commander Voight strode in their direction. Clay respected the hell out of him for flying out to the island without permission. The man was an enigma. Hard on his team, harder on criminals and soft towards his family and friends. How Doctor O'Reilly had become one of his boss' friends wasn't a question Clay dared to ask.

"How difficult can it be to track down this sonofabitch? No

offence to his mother, although I doubt a loving mother raised someone capable of the shit he has done." Voight crushed the Styrofoam cup and tossed it into a nearby dustbin.

"Sir, we should consider other possibilities and not focus on his known associates. For all we know, he's in a hotel room somewhere in the city," Clay said.

The airport, harbour and train stations were teaming with plain-clothed officers and private security personnel. It was difficult enough to have one suspect on the loose. Now they had two. "Any sightings of Doctor Hughes?"

"None." Voight stepped away to take a phone call.

"I wonder if Gina has interrogated that other piece of shit yet." Clay didn't need to ask who Duke was referring to.

"He's still under guard at the hospital. Evans isn't going anywhere."

"She hasn't slept since the call came through yesterday morning. Gina claims she slept a bit during the night, and passed out next to her laptop in the kitchen. If she did, it was fifteen minutes, max. I know how she gets when she's got a case like this. She's the lead detective on *Boogeyman*, but Captain Wilson said the other investigation is her main priority now because of the involvement of a certain someone we won't name."

Clay pressed a hand to his stomach. The familiar uneasiness had settled in his gut as he'd left Luke's farm and Madison. "There are too many unanswered questions. We don't even know who Evans has in his pocket assisting him."

Chapter 45

Three boxes stood in the corner of the dining room. Gina photographed each item as Madison lifted them out one at a time.

A cornucopia of sex toys lay on top of the sheet Madison had used to cover the table. It was a good thing Noa had convinced Luke to stay in Switzerland.

The last item Madison lifted out stood in stark contrast to the rest. This was no place for a child's toy. Gina reached for the teddy bear and turned it over. She asked for a knife and smiled when Madison pulled one out of her pocket.

White stuffing fell onto the black plastic-covered surface. Gina ripped the bear open and removed a mobile phone. Madison handed her the charger she'd found in the first box.

In the kitchen, the kettle boiled and someone opened and closed cupboards. The mixture of sounds and anticipation sent Madison's anxiety skyrocketing. She waited for Gina to switch on the phone.

"It's going to need to charge for a bit. It's been off for a while." Gina stared at the items on the table. "These are not from a catalogue or a store."

"Wouldn't have taken you for being into the lifestyle." Madison smiled at Gina, who shook her head.

"I'm not, but in my line of work, I've seen plenty. You'd be surprised what's out there, especially on the dark web. Some people resort to making their own instead of buying. Most of these don't look store bought to me."

227

Madison agreed with a nod. She knew enough to contribute to a conversation, but not to voice an opinion. "We could ask Natalie."

"Ask me what?" Natalie called from the kitchen.

Madison and Gina walked to Natalie, not wanting her to see the items in the dining room. Madison thanked Natalie for the coffee and waited for her to return from the veranda where Doctors O'Reilly and Seymour were comparing notes and sharing information.

"Was Angie into BDSM?" Gina asked Natalie.

Natalie frowned, pulling her hair back and tying it high on the top of her head. "Not that she ever mentioned to me. I realise now, I never really knew her, and I thought we were friends. Why do you ask?"

Madison put her mug in the sink and reached for Natalie's hand, leading her to the living room. "We found some items in her boxes. Who packed her things?"

"Her landlord." She frowned and sank to the couch. "I remember now. The landlord said he'd asked Angie's boyfriend to take it, but the boyfriend never came back. That's when he called me."

"What boyfriend?" Gina asked, pressing her hands to her sides.

"Angie referred to most of her regulars as *boyfriends*. That's why I thought nothing of it. I recall thinking that maybe one of Angie's regulars went looking for her and the landlord remembered his face. Did I screw up by not remembering this last night?"

Madison placed an arm around Natalie's shoulder. "No, not at all. We don't know whether this is relevant to the case, or *if* this boyfriend is important. We might be able to compare the DNA from the items in the dining room to the DNA you and the others collected over the past year. Maybe a name will come up."

Gina lowered her elbows onto the backrest of a nearby chair. "How can you link the DNA to a specific name? I won't discuss the legality of how you obtained it, as that's still up in the air."

"The women encouraged the men to take showers after they were done. Some did, some didn't. Those who didn't one day, sometimes decided to shower on another day."

Gina massaged her temples. "Madison, get to the point."

"The women took photos of their driver's licenses when the men left their wallets in the room. They wrote the johns' details on the Ziploc bags before I collected them."

"You realise none of what you said to me can be used to make an arrest?" Gina rubbed her neck. "However, if it leads to concrete evidence, we could use it. Maybe." She shrugged.

Madison realised she wasn't the only one dancing on the thin line between right and wrong. Perhaps there was more to Detective Larson than she had first thought.

"I'll bag the items and deliver them to Richard Davenport when I head back to the city."

"Have you interrogated Evans yet?" Madison asked.

"No, still on my to-do list today."

"You can leave as soon as you've had something to eat. Running on reserves won't help you at all. Don't even try to deny it. I grew up with a detective." Madison ignored Gina's protests.

Wednesday, 15 December, 10:19 a.m.

Gina waited for Natalie to join Madison in the kitchen before making her way to the dining room. She switched on the phone. Relief washed over her when it didn't request a password. With a case like this, even the littlest of things were appreciated. She opened the app for instant messages and scrolled through the conversations. One name stood out – Ripper.

Ripper had contacted Angel every day, as far back as the phone's memory went. Gina wondered when Angie had purchased the phone and made a mental note to ask Natalie.

She swallowed hard at the sight of the images shared between the two.

Photos of each of the women from the island, accompanied by a vivid description of their abilities. The horrific photos of an underage Dakota – Mia – would be seared into her mind forever. Added to the growing list of things Gina would never forget.

Ripper had sent Mia's photo to Angel.

She read their messages, bit back the curse words, and fought the bile rising inside her. Angel and Ripper shared a bond not even the best criminal psychologists could explain. It was a good thing Angie was dead *if* she was one of the Potters Park Five. *I'll kill you myself if you're still alive.*

Angie had masqueraded as one of them. Tricking vulnerable young women into believing she was their friend all the while coaxing them to the slaughter and offering them to Ripper to satisfy his disgusting and sadistic cravings. Angel had relished in what he'd offered her in return, with photos of his depravity. *Their depravity.*

Gina ran to the bathroom. Mia's haunted eyes, her broken and bleeding body, pushed everything out of Gina's stomach. She sank to her knees, not caring who heard.

The door opened and arms enveloped her. Gina hugged Madison and cried.

Wednesday, 15 December, 10:25 a.m.

The files lay in the middle of the table. The horrors within them were a stark contrast to the beauty of nature. Declan knew many deaths weren't natural, but this was something else.

"Anything about the remains found at Evans's house?" Declan lifted his eyes to Doctor Seymour's.

"No, my team – *our* team – is still there. So far, they've unearthed the remains of three females. It's strange though, the Potters Park Five were buried in one grave, and I believe he also buried the bodies we found at Paradise Beach in a single grave. That's the best explanation I can come up with as to why we found them close together."

"It's plausible. But why take the time to dig multiple graves at his home instead of one? Then again, why bury any bodies on his property and not in a remote location like the others?"

Doctor Jane Seymour studied him. "Declan, are you okay? Why didn't you come to me when you first realised something was going on?"

He smiled at her. "You have a family, Jane. I didn't want to involve you when bodies kept turning up. To be honest, I didn't want to tell you how I spent two weeks of my vacation when you stood in for me during the busiest time of the year. It was selfish of me, and I apologise. You deserved to be with your family."

"Cut the crap, Declan. You also deserve to have a life. I will never judge you. We've known each other too long to not call it as it is. Hell, I've known you longer than your ex-wife has." She glanced at her watch.

"I think we've covered everything if you need to leave. You should be there to oversee the retrieval of the remains and evidence processing. This time, you're going to be the one on the witness stand."

She reached for his hand and squeezed. "Glad to do it, as long as you're up there as a witness. I doubt you'll lose your job over this."

"I know, but it taints my credibility next time I have to testify. A good, or horrible, depending on how you look at it, defence attorney will be all over this. This isn't something I'm going to worry about right now. There are far more important things for me to focus on. In case you need me to clarify anything, contact me through Detective Larson."

Jane stared past him into the house. The light breeze was a welcome relief on such a hot day. "Why is one of the women here and not where the others are staying?"

Not even Doctor Seymour had been briefed on their location, or the mayor's involvement. Declan reached for the glass of water. Midway, his arm dropped to the table. "We met on the island, and I guess you can say we're involved."

She whispered, "She's a prostitute?"

The judgement in Jane's voice made Declan realise that they'd never be able to tell people the truth about how they'd met. It didn't matter to him. Natalie King was the most amazing, resilient, and caring person he had ever met. "She's a medical student who did what she had to do to survive and pursue her dream. Not all of us have parents who can pay for our studies and send us into the real world without lingering debt."

"I don't understand because I'm one of the lucky few you refer to. Declan, if you're happy, I'm happy for you. The two of you are coming over for Sunday lunch as soon as this case is closed. If she's going to be a part of my oldest friend's life, it's important that I get to know her." Jane pushed to her feet, stepped around the table and patted Declan on the shoulder. "I need to head to Davenport Laboratory. The sooner we close this case, the sooner we can all go back to our lives. Let's hope it's before Christmas."

Chapter 46

He's dead. The thought of never seeing his face, hearing his voice, or feeling his gentle touch again shattered her soul. After years of being alone, unwanted, and unloved, she had found him. Her soulmate. Ignorant fools called Foster a killer. *We're all something.*

Ice clinked as the vodka spilled into the tumbler. Doctor Hughes didn't drink alcohol. But Doctor Charlotte Evelyn Hughes had died along with the love of her life. Charlotte remained. Foster and her father were the only two men who had loved her. Perhaps her mother would've loved her too if she hadn't died while giving birth to Charlotte.

She walked through the penthouse, inside Foster's creation. The brilliance of his vision and imagination was evident all around her. Despair filled her as the vodka burned down her throat.

There wouldn't be a ceremony to say goodbye to the man she'd worshipped. Father and Mother Ericson had disowned Foster the second he was arrested. They didn't deserve to love him. But Charlotte had no right to bury him, no matter how much she loved and cared for Foster.

This wasn't what they had planned. What they had dreamed their life together would be like once Foster was free from the shackles of a barbaric society where people were labelled and punished for loving someone. Emily and Madison had never deserved Foster's devotion. *Where are you, Evie?*

Evie had claimed to love her, but now that Charlotte needed

her, where was she? In hindsight, she realised Evie was a bitch. She used whoever and did whatever she pleased. Lust had made her colour-blind to the red flags which surrounded Evie.

Charlotte grabbed her tablet from the bed. With a few dabs of her finger, she ensured Evie would run back to her. Not that it mattered anymore.

From the walk-in closet, she retrieved the one gift Evie had given her. The steel was cold against her skin, the weight of it in her hand reassuring. Charlotte swallowed what remained of the vodka and climbed on the bed. She scrolled through her archived photos until she found it. Foster smiled. He was young and carefree. Clearly, it was taken long before that whore had spat in his face. Foster Ericson was a remarkable, beautiful man. *He loved me.*

Tears dripped onto her chest. Her lips closed around the barrel. Foster stared up at her. Charlotte kept her eyes on his. *I will love you, even in death.*

Wednesday, 15 December, 2:23 p.m.

A strange odour hung in the air. That's what Gina always thought, walking into the interrogation room. To her, it was the smell of pure evil. Homicide detectives didn't sit in this tiny space for a chat and coffee with a wholesome friend.

Every day, for years, Gina had seen the face on the other side of the table.

A fellow detective.

A sadist. A rapist. A killer.

Underneath his calm exterior, a dark side lurked.

Detective Shepherd tapped a foot against the tiled floor. With her elbow, Gina bumped the pen from the table. Bending down to retrieve it, she placed a hand on Shepherd's leg. No one liked the idea of interrogating a colleague.

"You're in a ton of shit, Evans," Shepherd spoke first.

"Am I?" Evans leaned back in the chair and rolled his

head from side to side. "Let's not waste time. I know how this works. Shepherd is the bad cop. Larson is the good cop."

Gina rested her elbows on the steel table. "What does that make you?"

A terrible sound came from Evans's smirking face. "The one not saying another word until my attorney gets here."

"Okay, then we wait. We'll go grab some coffee. You lost the bet, Larson. I told you he'd be dumb and lawyer up."

Gina stood. "My mistake for assuming Evans would want to be out of here before dinner."

They left the interrogation room and went into the observation room.

Evans sneered at the two-way mirror. "Hey, *dumbasses.* I've stood on that side of the glass more than you. Do I look like a fish at the aquarium? Enjoy the show, kids."

"Schmuck." Captain Wilson crossed his arms over his chest.

Gina rubbed her temples. The ibuprofen she had taken when she arrived at the station wasn't working. "We knew this wouldn't be easy. Evans has nothing to lose. All five of the women said they'd testify against him. If only we could go in there with something irrefutable. Did they find anything in his car? It's the same make and model as the vehicle in the video footage from the marina. The day he murdered Claire."

Captain Wilson turned to her with a sly smile on his face. "Forensics found a blood smear on the front passenger seat. Evans doesn't need to know the DNA is busy being analysed at Davenport Laboratory. It's been seventy-two hours."

Gina considered kissing her superior officer, blaming it on sleep deprivation and crying in front of Madison. Gina Larson didn't cry in front of anyone except Duke.

Off-key singing came through the speaker. Evans was enjoying himself and putting on a show.

Gina downed the cappuccino Shepherd had bought at the coffee shop across the street. They'd never made a bet about Evans requesting legal counsel. And they never drank the vile caffeine paid for by the taxpayers.

Evans's attorney sauntered into the room, introducing herself.

Oh sweetie, you're shaking hands with the devil himself.

Gina turned to the men. "What do we know about her?"

"She graduated a few years ago and works for Legal Aid. It appears none of the criminal defence attorneys Evans called earlier want to represent him." Captain Wilson ran his thumb and pointer finger over his moustache.

Grown for Movember, kept for December. Gina smiled, remembering what Madison had said after meeting Captain Wilson.

"Don't you think it's strange a big shot defence attorney won't jump on this case?"

"Yes, but sometimes the cards are dealt in our favour. Don't question it, Larson. Get back in there. Force him into a corner. Make Evans slip up. You're a brilliant detective. Now is the time to combine everything you've learned from the countless interrogations you've conducted. Make it quick."

Wednesday, 15 December, 2:45 p.m.

This was the best part of a new life. The first day was filled with promise and endless possibilities.

Unlike the day you are born, you hold the power to decide who and what you want to be.

Tomorrow she'd be wherever she decided. A new life deserved to be lived in an extraordinary city, with a new name, a different past, and an improved her.

She crossed her ankles on the table and brought the Dom Pérignon to her lips. Whoever she was now, liked champagne.

The lighter's flame teased her, mocked her, reminding her that no matter who she became, some memories couldn't be erased. The lighter flew and crashed to the ground seven storeys below.

For a moment, she thought about Charlotte, Adam, and

Foster. The suffocating, yet intriguing, triangle she had put behind her.

All three had sex with her, but in the end, she'd screwed them all.

Criminals really should be less trusting.

Chapter 47

Fatigue wouldn't win. Not today. Leaning against the wall, Gina swallowed the yawn. "We found blood in your car. It matches the DNA of a young woman who was murdered at the marina on Sunday. Your car's paint matches what we found on the rear bumper of Madison Taylor's car. Remember the one you sent off the cliff? Did you really mistake Jenna Thompson for Miss Taylor? Apart from the blonde curly hair, they share no other similarities."

Evans didn't move a muscle.

Shepherd cleared his throat. "We found your fingerprints on the neck of a broken beer bottle inside a house registered in the name of a company owned by none other than Ben Adam Evans. Do you know which house I'm talking about?"

He stared at Evans, who remained motionless. "I'm not referring to your house on Ocean View Drive. No, this property is quite a stretch on your salary. Care to explain how a detective can afford one of only four very exclusive and luxurious properties on Seal Island?"

Not a word from Evans.

"Ben, give me the names of the women buried in your backyard." Gina shifted her weight from one foot to the other. "The medical examiner estimates they were murdered and buried at the same time as the Potters Park Five. Interestingly, the skeletons show the same post-mortem injuries as the Potters Park Five."

Shepherd placed photos of the victims on the table facing Evans and his attorney. The attorney flinched. Evans didn't.

"Same as the five skeletons found at Paradise Beach. Weirdly enough, one of the victims wasn't cut in half." Gina tapped a forefinger on her lips. "That's right because Blade joined the group last year. What is Ripper's signature? Then again, I guess all of it is *his* signature."

Still, Evans said nothing.

"We have DNA evidence linking you to multiple rapes. An eyewitness who saw you shoot and kill Jeffrey Baker." Shepherd returned the crime scene photos to the file.

Evans snorted. His attorney placed a hand on his arm.

"Ballistics matched the bullets from Jeffrey Baker's body, SUV and house to bullets retrieved from the body of Detective Paul Wallace." Gina fought the urge to slap the hint of a grin from Evans's face. "Did I mention the gun used to murder Jeffrey Baker and Paul Wallace was found inside the safe in *your* house? The house you blew up to destroy the evidence."

Shepherd leaned back, crossing his arms over his chest. "See, Ben, you don't have to talk. The amount of evidence we have against you speaks loud enough. Giving us the names of your accomplices doesn't matter. You'll be sleeping with the other awaiting trial prisoners. Doubt you'll get any sleep or survive until breakfast. You're going to know what it felt like for your victims."

The sound of hands slamming on metal bounced off the walls. "My wife, Eva, is responsible for all of it."

The detectives glanced at each other. Gina spoke, "Your wife? There's no record of you ever being married. There's no evidence anyone lived in the Ocean View Drive house with you."

"The fucking bitch. She set me up." The restraints kept him from standing up. "Eva Evans. She's a nurse at Shadow Bay Hospital. She came to see me this morning. There will be video footage of her. Look for a woman with red hair. Ask the dimwit stationed outside my room."

A knock on the door stopped Evans' rant.

Shepherd stepped out and came back in, shaking his head. "No employee named Eva Evans worked at Shadow Bay Hospital."

"That's bullshit." Evans slammed his forehead against the table.

"Do you think you should do that, seeing as you already have a concussion?" Gina smirked. "Creating an imaginary wife won't change the facts. You, Ben Evans, Adam as the women knew you, or should I call you Ripper? Or was Angel the only person who called you that?"

His head jerked up. "She killed her. Eva killed my Angel. It was all fun and games to her until I met my soulmate."

Soulmate. A peculiar word to use for two people who Gina doubted had souls. Not with the atrocities they'd committed.

"I read your text messages and saw the photos you sent each other. Your bond was rather *unique*." Gina stared at him, desperate to not remember Mia's photos.

"Angel and I were in love. I never thought someone so perfect existed. Eva refused to let me go, not as long as I served a purpose."

Shepherd shook his head. "Ben. Adam. Ripper. Whatever. There's no proof that this, *Eva*, even exists. Except in your imagination. You've created this *wife* hoping we'd think you're mentally unstable. A psychiatrist would have a field day with you, and I assure you, the outcome of such an assessment wouldn't be in your favour. Did you not hear the amount of evidence we have against you? Oh, I forgot to mention something else – footage of you raping a woman."

Evans laughed, the sound deafening in the small room. "A whore? You trust a teenager?" He continued laughing.

Gina turned to Shepherd. "Did either of us say who the witness is or their age?"

They both shrugged.

She addressed Evans. "No, not the young woman you defiled. A neighbour saw you entering her home and heard her screams. Even gave us footage from their security camera. Such a nice neighbourhood, an absolute pity they have so many break-ins. Worked out well for us. And the officers who'd responded to the neighbour's call, remember you being at the scene and claiming to have arrived minutes before they had."

"You're lying. Why is this being brought up now, years later?"

"Did you never bother to find out where your clients stay? A man you named Crush was at first reluctant to come forward with the evidence of his travel agent of sorts committing murder, seeing as he's a politician. People will do anything to save their own asses."

Shepherd grabbed the files and stood. "We're done here. I doubt we'll see you at trial. You won't survive the night."

"Wait." Evans sat up straight. "If I admit to my part in it, can you arrange that I'm held in solitary confinement?"

Wednesday, 15 December, 2:47 p.m.

Sweat rolled down his back. He wiped the moisture from his face with a gloved hand. *Where are you, Boogeyman?*

Clay walked out of the warehouse and headed to the Gurkha.

None of the teams had managed to track him down. How hard was it to find a man who'd recently suffered a heart attack? Then again, when money wasn't an option, you could buy whatever and whoever you needed to nurse you back to health. Buying and selling children was how Boogeyman had accumulated his wealth. *A sick, twisted spin on capitalism.*

"He either left the city or he's somewhere nice and cosy, waiting for us to call it a day." Duke's stride matched Clay's as their feet pounded the asphalt.

"I still want to know how he got away."

Commander Voight ran up to them. "The same way they always do. He had help on the inside. And outside."

Clay's hands drew into fists. These days it seemed everywhere he turned there was a corrupt government employee. "Who?" he asked.

"No idea. But there's going to be hell to pay for this. Five civilians died. Four were rushed to the hospital, including a child. And Richter."

Richter had tended to most of them at some point in their careers, or he was at a scene taking care of a victim or suspect. He would've retired in a year's time. Richter was in many ways a part of their team.

Voight grabbed his phone from his pocket. "Yes?"

Duke and Clay glanced at each other as the rest of their team moved closer.

"Heading there now." Voight ended the call and told them to get in the Gurkha.

The Boogeyman was no longer hiding under a bed.

Chapter 48

Wednesday, 15 December, 3:30 p.m.

The attorney nodded. Shepherd pressed the record button.

Evans cleared his throat. "I, Ben Adam Evans, admit to trafficking women for sexual and financial exploitation. And being an accomplice to organ trafficking."

"And what else?" Gina asked.

Evans lowered his eyes to the table. "The murders of multiple men and women, over a period of two and a half years, for organ harvesting. I can show you where I buried some. Over the past few months, whatever remained of the bodies were cremated. I wasn't privy to the name of the funeral home."

"You admit to murdering these people, removing their organs and selling them on the red market?" Underneath the table, Shepherd rubbed his hands together.

"I didn't commit all the murders. A surgeon removed the organs. Eva acted as the broker."

"What's this supposed doctor's name?" Gina asked. Doctor O'Reilly had said they were looking for a trained surgeon. Doctor Seymour had concurred.

"Eva brought her onboard. Charlie something or another."

Not wanting to appear unprofessional, Gina refrained from rolling her eyes. "Come on, Evans, you need to give us more than a nickname. Is she also a figment of your imagination?"

"Yous. Hues. Something like that."

Gina pushed her back to the chair. "Doctor Charlotte Evelyn Hughes?"

"That rings a bell." Evans's head bobbed.

Gina needed an answer to another question. "How does Foster Ericson factor into all of this?"

Deep lines appeared between Evans's eyebrows. "The River Valley Killer? He doesn't."

Tired of skipping around the gravesite, Gina cut to the chase. "Did you or did you not attack Madison Taylor on Friday night?"

Evans's shoulders lifted to his ears, then lowered. Gina pushed her butt down on the chair. He had to think he was calling the shots. It was a rather useless tactic when interrogating a fellow detective.

"If Foster Ericson isn't somehow involved, why did you spray paint a certain image onto Madison Taylor's bedroom wall? Remember when you broke into her home?"

"I admit to chatting with Miss Taylor. But as for breaking into her apartment? That, my dear Larson, wasn't me."

Instead of pointing out that a random *chat* never ended with bruises on anyone's neck, Gina allowed Evans to spin the web of lies he'd eventually catch himself with. "When and how did you learn about the link between Madison Taylor and Foster Ericson?"

"Women are such fickle creatures. Someone's always listening in on your conversations."

"Whose conversation were you eavesdropping on?" Shepherd shifted in his chair.

"Eva and Charlie's. Eva was screwing Ericson. Charlie wished she was. He played them. Think I need to shake his hand when I meet him."

"You can do that as soon as you get to hell. I'm sure he's waiting for you. Ericson died this morning."

"Wonder who killed him? Eva or Charlie? Eva had no reason to. Charlie doesn't have the guts."

Gina pushed her fingers through her hair and rubbed the back of her neck. "*Charlie's* existence, we have verified. Eva remains a figment of your imagination. How could Eva have had sex with Ericson if he was in prison and she, according to you, worked at Shadow Bay Hospital?"

"I can prove the devil is real. If you manage to locate Eva, compare her DNA to the hair I submitted to the lab on Friday. Dumb slut never realised I kept the hair I yanked out when we made love."

The bile rising in Gina's throat didn't give up until she swallowed hard for a second time. "I thought you only ever loved Angie."

"I always make love, Detective. Whether a woman calls it that or something completely different, it changes nothing. The act I perform is the closest they'll ever come to experiencing love." Evans laughed. The sound was harsh and putrid.

Wednesday, 15 December, 4:03 p.m.

Madison grabbed her phone and answered without looking at the screen. "Clay?"

"No, it's me." Gina sighed. "I always worry about them. I wish I could tell you it gets easier, but you've been a part of Clay's world for six months. You know the emotions by now."

"Any recent developments on your end?" Madison asked, trying her best to focus on the reason for Gina's call if it wasn't about Clay.

"I've sent a photo of a woman to you and Captain Johnson. Evans claims this woman is an accomplice in his operation. Her name is Doctor Charlotte Evelyn Hughes. Madison, can you show the photo to Natalie and Doctor O'Reilly? Let me know if either of them recognises her. Captain Johnson will inform me if one of the other women remembers seeing her. She was at the scene this morning where Foster died. She asked about him and acted strange from the moment she got there until she disappeared."

Madison asked Gina to hold on and looked at the photo. "I don't know her. Foster was a malignant narcissist, and he manipulated people for fun. He made a police officer fall for him and she spoon-fed him information about the investigation. It's not a stretch that he might've manipulated this doctor as well."

"This case keeps getting stranger and stranger. Evans admitted to several things, but he's adamant he isn't the only player. We're trying to verify the existence of a woman Evans claims is his wife, Eva. Meanwhile, Doctor Hughes is still in the wind."

Madison sat down hard on the closest chair. "While you were in the bathroom, I scanned Angie's phone for other messages. There was one from an *Eva*. It said: *Do you want to end up like your whore friends? Keep your mouth off MY husband's dick*." Madison gagged.

"My sentiment exactly. At this point, it could be anyone, but I'll have someone look into this Eva's number to see if we can trace it."

"I shouldn't have snooped. I'm sorry."

"You're apologising for snooping?" Gina laughed without malice. "It's thanks to your snooping and pushing that this horror came to light. Angie's hairbrush is being processed at Davenport Laboratory. It turns out Evans replaced the one you'd given him with his imaginary wife's hair. He even went as far as buying an identical hairbrush."

Madison rested her forehead on her palm. "This is a giant puzzle. Half of the pieces are missing and the other half are all the same colour. I hate puzzles."

Voices became louder on Gina's end. "I like you. I despise puzzles too. Long story. Madison, I've got to go. *Peas* show the thing to your guests and invite them for dinner. Either your boyfriend, or the person who made a huge error in judgement the day they met you, can drive the *pack* of them back to their hotel."

Gina ended the call. Madison smiled at her screen, understanding Gina's weird word choices. Maybe they'd bonded when Gina had cried in her arms. Time would tell if they became real friends and not merely the girlfriends of teammates.

Madison found Natalie and Declan in the living room, their lips almost touching. Coughing, she held her phone towards them as she walked closer to the couch. "Pardon the interruption. Do either of you know this woman?"

Declan took the phone and studied the photo. "Can't recall that I've met her. Who is she?" He handed it to Natalie.

Natalie stared at the screen before placing Madison's phone on the coffee table. "Never seen her face."

"Doctor Charlotte Evelyn Hughes. She works at the prison. Evans named her as an accomplice. If she's a doctor, I bet *she* removed the organs." Madison lowered herself onto the coffee table. "Detective Larson ordered that you stay here until either she or Clay take you back to the cottage later. Seeing as I interrupted what looked like a very special moment, I'm heading to the stable to prepare everything for the horses."

"You were at the stable before you came in." Natalie reached for her hand. "Clay's going to be fine."

"I know, but I feel so powerless. He's out there making a difference. Three of my family members are all former detectives. My mother was a social worker. Jamie gets her force of nature thing from Mom. Noa survived the hell Foster put her through. Maybe one day, I'll tell you the story." Anxiety made Madison's hands shake. She pushed to her feet. "I can't sit here and do nothing."

Declan stood and wrapped his arms around her. "Madison, you are doing something with your life. It's time you realise we all play a small part in a much bigger picture. The important thing is that whatever your part is, play it to the best of your ability. From what Natalie has told me, you're doing more than that."

Madison clung to him, wishing it were Clay's arms around her. It would mean he was safe. "I haven't spoken to my friend's parents. They refuse to take my calls. When my mother called them, they answered. How can they ghost me when I've known them since I was six years old? I grew up in front of them, for crying out loud. Emma and I, we're like sisters. *Were*." Pointless to fight it, the dam broke. Madison cried until she struggled to catch her breath.

Declan held Madison's trembling body. "Have you considered that you remind them of Emma?"

Chapter 49

Wednesday, 15 December, 4:15 p.m.

Death didn't want her. Charlotte's knuckles turned white on the steering wheel. Her foot pressed down on the accelerator. All of their conversations, their stolen moments together, had come rushing back as she'd lowered the pistol from her mouth.

There was only one reason for death to reject her – she still had a purpose.

Foster's soul couldn't rest in peace. Not until the two bitches who had betrayed him joined him in the afterlife.

Charlotte placed a hand against her heart. *He's here.* Foster's presence had been with her since the moment she pulled the trigger. Their bond was stronger than death.

"I will avenge you. They'll pay for what they did to you. I'll start with the bitch who rejected your love and tried to gut you. Then it's time for the one whose *name* made you hard." Charlotte's palms repeatedly banged against the steering wheel. "Last will be your parents, after Jenkins, of course. And then we can be together. For eternity."

Up ahead, Lamont Estate's sign came into view.

Wednesday, 15 December, 4:20 p.m.

With his back against the container, Clay scanned his surroundings through the scope of the Colt M4A1. He'd seen the surveillance photos when Commander Voight had briefed the team. Boogeyman was here.

Next to Clay, Duke crouched, protecting his six. The air around them charged with anticipation. It coursed through his veins. Clay realised he'd also felt it the first time making love to Madison, but in a good way.

Before long, he'd be home, cuddling with her on the forbidden couch. Most importantly – there would be one less monster roaming the streets.

The team's instructions were clear – by any means necessary. Words that Commander Voight didn't say often. *Bureaucratic bullshit.*

In the distance, seagulls cawed. Duke placed a hand on Clay's shoulder. They advanced towards the warehouse. The team approached from all sides.

Clay's heartbeat remained steady. This wasn't the first time he'd hunted the Boogeyman.

Keeping his head low, Clay dropped to a knee to the left of the warehouse door. He kept scanning the container yard through the scope. Clay waited for the order.

On the other side of the door, Duke held the stun grenade at the ready. He smiled at Clay. Clay said a silent prayer that they'd all be walking back to the Gurkha. And that Maddie was safe.

"Breach!" Voight's voice was loud in Clay's ear.

He yanked the door open. Duke threw the grenade.

They stormed in.

Commands shouted.

Rapid-fire erupted.

Clay dove behind a wooden barrel. He peered over the top. Bullets whizzed by his head.

To his right stood a forklift.

Clay ran, shooting in the direction from where the bullets came.

Behind the safety of the forklift, he glanced at his throbbing leg. Blood spurted from his thigh.

***

Wednesday, 15 December, 4:35 p.m.

King ran in circles, excited to chase the ball again. Madison waited for him to heel at her feet. When King did, she bent down and kissed his head. She threw the ball towards the river and ran for the house. Seconds later, she crashed to the grass, rolling on her back as Luke had taught her.

King's front legs rested on her stomach. He breathed with his mouth open. Madison could've sworn he was smiling for besting her. She showed him his ball. King pounced on her hand. She released the ball and pulled him to her, nuzzling his neck with her face.

Getting to her feet, Madison readjusted the bra holster and raced King towards the house. An unfamiliar car stood outside. Madison pushed her hands into the shorts' pockets looking for her phone. It was in the living room.

She patted her thigh and waited for King to follow. The front door wasn't the best point of entry.

The metal of the Glock Gen 43 felt warm in her hand. Madison pulled the slide back and made a mental note to tell no one in her family she wasn't carrying it one-up.

Madison crouched below the kitchen window and duck-walked to the back door. *Damn Luke and Noa for all the windows they installed during the renovations.* Her breath came in fast as she pushed to her feet between the door and the window. King stared up at her. His presence was far more comforting than the gun in her hand.

She peeked through the window with the barrel of the handgun pointed at the ground.

In the dining room, two figures sat with their backs to each other. An unfamiliar figure pointed a revolver at them.

Madison crouched down, pressing her face to the top of King's head. "Stay." She kissed him and stood, reaching for the door. Stepping into the kitchen, Madison's phone rang in the living room.

"You better tell me where she is, Vegas! Where's Emily?"

"I don't know who Emily is." The sound of skin connecting with skin echoed through the house.

"Charlotte, Emily isn't here. She's at the shooting range. Leave Vegas tied up and I'll take you to Emily. It's walking distance from here." The control in Declan's voice grounded Madison.

Using the kitchen island as cover, she crawled towards the living room. When she reached the end of the island, Madison pressed the button under the counter. *Don't come, Jamie.* With the silent alarm triggered, Madison estimated she had three minutes to gain control of the situation. She wouldn't risk having her pregnant sister walking in.

Footsteps sounded over the hardwood floor. *She's pacing.*
Madison waited.

Charlotte came into view in the mirror on the opposite wall as Madison peeked around the corner.

"We'll wait right here. She's going to beg for his forgiveness, and then we can be together forever." An eerie sound came from the dining room. Madison realised Charlotte was laughing. "You two would've made me a tonne of money. With all your passion, I bet the sex is mind-blowing." Charlotte made the disturbing sound again. "Now, I'm going to blow both of your minds. I wonder if one bullet can do the trick? Two for one."

"You won't get away with this. The police know who you are, Charlotte. Adam told them everything about how you butchered people for their organs." This time, Madison saw Charlotte slap Natalie. Not a sound came from Natalie.

Charlotte snorted a laugh. "Adam? The only woman he hasn't raped hasn't been born yet. She gave me this revolver to protect myself against him."

"Who gave you the gun, Doctor Hughes?" Declan asked.

"Don't patronise me." The barrel of the gun struck his forehead. "You cut up dead bodies and put their organs back. People like this whore of yours are nothing but spare parts. They don't deserve the air they breathe. They wreck homes. Spread diseases. Filthy, disgusting whores."

Charlotte moved to stand in front of Natalie, pressing the muzzle against her forehead. "Any last words? It's a waste that your organs will decompose. Your death could've saved lives. Instead, you'll rot like the piece of trash you are."

Madison's phone rang for the second time. She ignored it, focused on controlling her breathing, as her therapist had taught her.

Shooting to her feet, Madison rounded the corner. Her gun lifted to Charlotte's face.

"Lovely of you to join us, Madison. I wasn't planning to kill you first, but you'll do. Apologise to Foster. He's here, you know." Charlotte grinned, showing her nicotine-stained teeth. A tear rolled down her plump cheek.

Madison kept the gun steady, the sight focused on Charlotte's forehead. "No."

"He loved you, his precious *Maddie*. Foster killed for you. You're no better than this piece of shit. *Vegas*." She pulled a face as she said Vegas. "I always wondered how Adam decided on your names." Charlotte shrugged. "Guess it doesn't matter anymore."

She returned her focus to Madison. "Ask Foster to forgive you."

An unknown calm came over Madison. "Let me at least think of what to say. Uhm, okay. Good riddance, Foster. Your death is enough for me."

"You fucking undeserving slut." Charlotte's hands trembled, clutching the gun.

"Beg him to forgive you." She stared Madison in the eye and pulled the trigger.

Chapter 50

Gina ran into the house. She stopped in the doorway and assessed the scene. Copper along with a hint of a recently discharged firearm, filled the air inside. Gina focused on the dining room first. Two chairs stood with their backs to each other. Pieces of rope were discarded around the chairs. Dark red streaks on a wall and part of the table. On the floor lay a female body. A pool of blood surrounded the victim's head.

In the living room, Doctor O'Reilly held Madison's hands and nodded when his eyes met Gina's.

Madison turned as Gina stepped closer. "I didn't have a choice." Tears streamed down her face.

Natalie set a box of tissues on the couch and walked back to the kitchen. Jamie leaned against the kitchen island, talking to Luke on the phone. King lay with his head resting on Madison's lap.

"Madison, I ..." Gina put an arm around Madison's shoulders. "Captain Wilson and Shepherd will arrive any minute. Give them your statement and then we need to leave."

Slowly, Madison turned to Gina. "You can't arrest me for killing her in self-defence. She was shooting at me." Madison stared at her hands in Declan's. "Why didn't any of the bullets hit?"

Gina glanced at Doctor O'Reilly. He shrugged. "Ballistics will need to confirm it, but I suspect the firing pin is missing."

"Madison, you won't be arrested. It's going to take some

time for the crime scene investigators to process the scene and gather evidence. Doctor O'Reilly, can you stay here until I come back later? Or Captain Johnson can drive you back to the cottage. I don't want to ask Madison's sister to stay, not in her condition," Gina said in a low voice, not knowing Jamie never missed a word said about her.

Jamie marched into the living room. "My condition? I'm pregnant, not struck down with the bubonic plague. I'll stay. Under the circumstances, I think it's best for Doctor O'Reilly and Natalie to move into my parents' house for the night. The same goes for Madison and Clay. Once they're done processing the scene, I'll contact the crime scene cleaners. Luke and Noa can't return to this mess tomorrow night."

"They don't have to come home earlier because of this." Madison dropped her face into her hands.

"The silent alarm triggered the internal surveillance cameras. Luke and Noa saw and heard everything. As did I. Clay would've had access to it too. Why isn't he here yet?" Jamie asked Gina.

Gina's lips quivered. Tears flooded her eyes.

Jamie sank to the couch next to Madison, pulling her sister into her arms. Over Madison's head, she stared at Gina. "Why isn't Clay here?" Jamie demanded.

Dread swirled in the pit of Gina's stomach. There was no good way to say this. "Clay was shot. They're busy preparing him for surgery. Duke did what he could to stop the bleeding." She covered her mouth with a shaking hand. "He's going to pull through. Clay is strong. He will be fine."

She nodded and pushed to her feet. Gina touched Madison's shoulder. "There's nothing we can do while he's in the OR except pray. Let me finish up here and then I'll take you to the hospital."

"Did they kill him? Boogeyman?" Madison asked, her jaw tight. Rage filled her wet eyes.

Gina smiled. "Yes, Duke said it looks like the bullet came from Clay's rifle."

Madison wiped the tears from her eyes, unable to stop the flow. "Clay can't wake up without me."

Wednesday, 15 December, 6:15 p.m.

The setting sun cast a warm glow on a horrible day. Natalie leaned into Declan's embrace, rubbing her hands over his back.

Jamie waddled towards them, King on her heels. "You're sleeping at my parents' house tonight, just as a precaution. Guests don't have access to the house and my mother gave the staff the day off tomorrow." She waived a hand through the air. "She does this often, so don't bother saying anything about it being an imposition. The restaurant and cellars are on the other side of the property. No one will know you're there."

Natalie realised how much the two sisters looked alike. "Thank you, Jamie. I don't know how we will ever repay Madison or your family for everything you've done for us."

Declan nodded. "You need to sit down. This heat and the stress isn't good for you or the baby."

Indignation filled Jamie's face. "Two babies. Boys. They love to wrestle and kick my bladder." She pressed a palm to her lower belly.

"Doctor's orders. Sit. I'll fetch you a bottle of cold water and ask Detective Shepherd how much longer they'll be." Declan didn't wait for her to object.

Jamie eased down on the porch swing, asking Natalie to sit with her.

"How do I help her through this? It can't be easy to kill someone even when it is in self-defence." Natalie settled on the floor to let King climb on her lap. She grunted under his weight but smiled. "I thought Declan and I were dead. Then Madison came in. And that woman pulled the trigger. So many shots fired. Blood. Everywhere."

Jamie patted Natalie's shoulder. "Madison is a remarkable person. She's strong, courageous, fearless, and has overcome a lot in the past few months. This will be another thing she survives, making her even stronger. All we can do is to be there for her and treat her exactly as we did before."

Natalie nodded, wiping her eyes. "The bond between siblings is something I've always envied. I was my parents' miracle baby."

"As long as you are friends with Madison, it's as good as having a sister. She loves to a fault, although to an extent that has changed in the last few months."

"What did Foster Ericson do to her? That crazy woman kept telling Madison to apologise to him. Why would Madison need to apologise to the River Valley Killer?"

Jamie glanced towards the dining room. "He is dead. And nothing else matters. Madison survived him."

"You've seen gunshot wounds before, haven't you?" Natalie's hand stilled. King nudged it with his snout.

"Yes, a couple." Jamie refused to allow her mind to replay the images of the death and destruction she'd encountered.

Natalie asked, "Will Clay survive?"

Declan returned, handing them each a bottle of water, and placed King's bowl next to Natalie's leg.

Wednesday, 15 December, 6:45 p.m.

Fear pulverised her stomach, forcing Madison to swallow repeatedly. It was worse than being locked in that cellar. Not even having a gun pointed in her face compared. Madison paced the length of the waiting room.

"Madison, sit down. You're wearing the floor out. I'm going to see if they have some puzzles in the paediatric ward. It'll give us something to do."

Madison spun around and glared at Gina. "You wouldn't dare."

Gina sat back in her chair, placing her hands behind her head. "Try me. Tell me, why do you hate puzzles?"

Madison leaned against the wall. "Because I have an older brother and sister who considered it hilarious to hide pieces. Since I was young, I hated not being able to solve a problem or see something through. Why do *you* hate puzzles?"

"After my parents died, my aunt and uncle assumed it would be therapeutic for us to sit in suffocating silence and focus on anything other than their deaths." Gina returned her arms to the armrests and grabbed the edges.

"Thank you." Madison smiled briefly.

Gina leaned forward, rubbing her hands together. "For what?"

"Being here with me. I know Clay is your friend, but you didn't have to stay with me or try to take my mind off worrying by sharing a memory I can see is painful for you."

"Is this how our friendship is going to work? You trying to psychoanalyse me?"

"Ah, you like me. You said *our friendship*." Madison squinted, the smile more than brief. "My friends call me Maddie."

Gina rolled her eyes at the ceiling. "Yes, and I approve of you dating my friend. You're much better for Clay than my sister ever was. Penelope didn't deserve him. She never bothered to get to know or understand him. You just do, without trying."

"He makes it easy for me. Even though we both claim we were never friends, you get to know someone better, and on a deeper level, if you focus on the friendship before the relationship. Gina, I can't lose him."

A man opened the door, ducking his head under the doorframe as he walked into the room. "Clay lost a lot of blood, but according to the paramedics he has a shot." He grimaced. "Bad word choice."

Madison wrapped her arms around his waist before Gina could stand. "Thank you, Duke, for saving Clay's life. Commander Voight told us what you did when we got here."

Duke stared at his sleeves. His friend's blood wasn't visible on the black material, but Madison noticed a smear on his wrist. She stepped back, dread playing pinball in her stomach.

Gina moved closer and hugged Duke. "You did good. He's here, in surgery, and he's going to be fine. Even Clay would say the most important thing is that the Boogeyman is dead."

Duke lifted Gina off her feet and held her to him. He looked at Madison. "Are you okay? Commander Voight briefed me on what happened. I tried to call you, but I guess you were pretty busy yourself."

Madison swallowed hard. "I can't think about *that*. Not until Clay is out of surgery and wakes up."

The rest of the team stepped in, taking a seat after hugging Madison. Commander Voight's words brought tears to her eyes. She didn't hide them.

Around her, sat Clay's chosen family. His family was now hers.

The ringing of a phone cut through the deafening silence in the room. Gina reached for her phone and lifted it to her ear. "Sir?"

"I need you to come down to the station. Davenport Laboratory found a DNA hit. It's from the hairbrush Evans handed in at our lab," Captain Wilson said.

"Sir, that's impossible. It's been less than twenty-four hours. And we have nothing to match it to." Gina rose and stepped towards the door.

"Larson, get your butt down here. I'll explain everything."

"I'm fifteen minutes away." She ended the call and turned to face the room. "I've got to go. Duke, will you please drive Madison home? I don't know how long this might take. The system found a hit on the DNA."

Chapter 51

Richard Davenport settled in his chair after explaining the advances in DNA analysis and testing they'd made over the past year. They'd cut down processing times to a few hours, depending on the level of degradation of the sample. The hair Evans had submitted, must have been kept sealed in a plastic bag.

"It's impossible. She can't be involved in this." Gina rubbed her hands over her face.

"We can run further tests when she gives us a sample. I'm merely informing you of our findings. It warrants investigation," Davenport said, taking a sip of the liquid in the travel mug he'd brought with him to the station.

Gina turned to Captain Wilson. "I didn't even know she was here in Shadow Bay." She shrugged, the movement of her shoulders minimal. "I have no idea where to look for her."

Detective Shepherd stepped into Captain Wilson's office, closing the door behind him. "There's no record of her anywhere after the missing person's report was filed. Of course, the newspaper articles following the fire mentioned her name."

Gina winced. *Impossible.* Her sister couldn't be involved in this.

"Detective Larson, we're running the photo your parents gave the police when they reported her missing through facial recognition, and we'll also age it to what she might look like now."

Gina shook her head behind her hands. "She can't be involved in this."

Captain Wilson squeezed her shoulder. "Gina, people change. From what's mentioned in the file, it's clear Thea was often in trouble as a teenager."

"You don't know what things were like back then. She acted out. It's quite normal behaviour, considering what went on." Gina slammed her fists on the table in the corner.

Davenport softened the tone of his voice. "Gina, why don't you explain to us what happened? If we understand better, it will help us locate her. Thea can answer whatever questions you or Captain Wilson have. All things considered, there's a possibility she might've been one of Evans's victims. If your sister is a victim, we have to help her. We can only do that if we can find her." He brought Gina a glass of water and waited for her to take it.

"Thank you." She placed it on the table. "Penelope had childhood leukaemia. I was her only match. Thea got lost in all of it. Our parents were focused on the possibility of Pen dying, and me needing to save her. They barely had any time for Thea. She acted out because she wanted attention. Back then, none of us understood her erratic and delinquent behaviour." Gina didn't add that her therapist had helped her come to this realisation.

"No one has been arrested for the fire. The case remains unsolved." Captain Wilson again placed a hand on her shoulder, but she jerked away from him.

"Thea didn't set the fire. She left a few weeks before it happened." The fire had left Gina and Penelope orphaned.

"Why weren't you and Penelope home that night?"

She stared at him, shaking her head. "So what? Now either Penelope or I did it? She was seven. I was fourteen. We were all so focused on living and beating death. Why would we, or I if that's where this is going, kill our parents?"

"Gina," Davenport tried. "None of us are implying that you killed your parents. But the police report states a motorist saw a teenage girl walking down the street. The witness later realised it had been around the time of the fire."

"My aunt and uncle invited Penelope and me to spend the night with them, to give my parents a break. Pen being sick … Thea running away. It was taking a toll on them, and on their marriage. There's nothing more than that for the reason we weren't there that night."

"Could Thea, if she's responsible for setting the fire, have been aware you weren't home?"

Gina lifted her eyes to Shepherd. "No. It was a last-minute thing. My aunt and uncle arrived at our front door. The four of us went to see a movie, and by the time we got to their house, the police were waiting outside."

Shepherd kneeled next to her chair. "If you had been home, you would've died too. And Penelope. Whoever set the fire wanted to kill your entire family. Who hated you that much?"

Gina shut her eyes. "Thea."

Wednesday, 15 December, 9:30 p.m.

He kept his eyes closed, savouring the warmth of her gentle touch as her fingertips trailed along his face. Her voice soothed him awake. She didn't sing often enough. The corners of his mouth lifted.

"I missed you." Madison rested her forehead against Clay's.

"You should leave before my girlfriend gets here. She's not the sharing type, won't even share her food with me." Clay opened his eyes, expecting the light to blind him. It didn't. Madison must've switched off the overhead lights.

"Trust you to think about food the moment you wake up. My mother has already worked out a menu for when you get released and we will go stay with them. She's going to nurse you back to health in no time." Madison beamed down at him and pressed her lips to his forehead.

Clay reached for her face, his movement sluggish.

"Hey, you should rest. I'll tie my hair back if it tickles you because I refuse to stop kissing you. Ever."

He shook his head and grinned. This was the Madison he'd fallen in love with. No matter what, she always brought a smile to his face. "I wanted to feel your lips against mine again."

"That can be arranged when your doctor approves of it. Not before." She squinted, but Clay knew the smile reached her eyes. "Are you hungry? Probably too soon to eat after surgery."

"I'm famished, but not for food." He bit his bottom lip, so did Madison.

"In that case, I'll go tell your team to give us a few hours and then they can come see you."

"Hours? Maddie, I had surgery. Suffered massive blood loss, and I nearly died. I think we should keep it short. And oh, so sweet."

Madison straightened her spine. "Not until the doctor clears it. My orders."

"Have you never had fantasies about a hospital room?"

She rolled her eyes. "No, Slay, I have not. People die here." Madison gripped the railing of the bed. Her head dropped forward. "You almost died. Clay, I killed someone."

Chapter 52

Thursday, 16 December, 6:38 a.m.

Gina sat in the interrogation room, waiting for the prisoner to be brought in. It was a good thing they'd agreed to put him in solitary confinement. She had more questions, and no doubt he wouldn't have survived an hour among the other awaiting trial prisoners.

The previous night, Duke had thrown Gina over his shoulder and carried her to their bedroom. He'd held her until she stopped crying, cursing, questioning. She'd woken up feeling like a train had smashed through her brain, but at least her body felt rested.

Gina glanced at the digitally aged photo in the brown folder. *Thea.*

Behind her, the door opened. Gina didn't look at the prisoner or the guards escorting him. The rattling sound of chains offered a sense of security. *How did none of us see the monster hiding behind the badge?*

"Good morning, Detective Larson. It's bound to be a wonderful day if I get to see your pretty face this early."

"Doctor Hughes is dead." Gina didn't look up as the guards pushed him down onto the chair on the other side of the table.

"Okay, what do you want me to say to that? May she rest in peace? What a loss to humanity?" His laughter squeezed the air from her lungs.

Gina opened the file and stared at the face. A lifetime of memories flooded her mind. More questions bubbled to the surface. She turned the photo and pushed it across the table.

Evans tilted his head, picked it up with chained hands and grinned. "Ah, you've found Eva. Except she didn't have red hair. Did you add this little detail because of your delectable colouring? It's true what they say – redheads are absolute fire in the sack. Perhaps, if she'd looked like this, I would've enjoyed her more." He tossed the photo back at Gina.

"What can you tell us about *Eva*?" Detective Shepherd asked.

Evans faked surprise. "Didn't see you there, Sheppie. You're standing so quietly in the corner, like the good boy you are."

Gina returned the photo to the folder and closed it. "Answer the question."

"We met at a bar on the promenade, had sex in the bathroom, and had some more at my house. Eva realised she'd never find anyone better than me, so she never left. Well, she did for work and whatnot. But that's the short version of our super romantic story."

"You claim she's your wife," Shepherd said.

"We got married on the beach and asked two tourists to witness for us."

"Who performed the ceremony because there's no record of a marriage licence?"

"Eva's best friend did, the fickle little Charlie. What Eva saw in that woman only she can tell you."

Shepherd had found the hotel where Charlotte checked into the penthouse suite using the name Evie Ericson. The letter she'd scribbled on hotel stationery had been lying on the bed. Her handwriting was typical for a doctor and had taken some time to decipher. "You raped Charlotte."

Evans rolled his eyes. "The bitch is lying. She ached to understand the reason why Eva loved my dick so much. All I did was show her, gave her the honour of experiencing it for herself. To be honest, she should thank me for touching her." He shuddered.

Like everyone else who'd read Charlotte's graphic and

detailed letter, Gina wanted to beat Evans to death. Instead, she rested her elbows on the table and laced her fingers. "Where can we find Eva?"

"You can't. Eva no longer exists. She's long gone with *my* money. I already told you this when I gave my statement yesterday." Evans forced a yawn. "Are we done?"

Gina nodded and waited for the guards to take Evans back to his cell. The moment the door closed, she turned to Shepherd. "We're never going to find her, are we? Thea's giving us the finger, like she did when we were children. No matter how many times my mother scolded her, she kept on doing it. Thea always told me that: 'The fuck you is in the details.'"

Shepherd pushed his fingers through his hair. "We know she changes personas with the same ease other people change their underwear. Think about it, Larson. Who is the last person we'd look for?"

Gina's head jerked up. She jumped to her feet and headed for the door. "My mother." She ran to Captain Wilson's office with Shepherd on her heels.

As Captain Wilson's office came into view, she shouted, "Sir, we need to locate Althea Maynard."

Shepherd stopped at the nearest cubicle and yanked the officer out of their chair, offering a quick apology. He typed the name Althea Maynard into the search engine and waited. With his hands pressed to his head, Shepherd closed his eyes.

"Detective, you've got a hit," the young officer said.

"That's impossible. These things usually take hours." Shepherd glanced at the computer screen. The chair smashed into the officer standing behind him. "Send all available units to the airport. Shut every plane down. I don't care how you do it. Just do it."

Gina stared at him wide-eyed. Captain Wilson stood next to her and yelled at the officers to get to work.

Shepherd yanked his tie from his neck. "Let's go, Larson. Time to get your answers."

Chapter 53

What were the odds that of the eight billion people in the world, the one to arrest her would be Gina? Thea studied her nails, grateful she'd made time to have them done when she put Eva behind her. Red suited her, no matter who she was.

"I'm waiting," Detective Shepherd said.

He'd introduced himself when he entered the tiny room. Thea remembered the way he'd fastened the cuffs around her wrists in the airport lounge. They weren't metal handcuffs, but those plastic things police officers preferred nowadays. Except Eva's husband, he'd loved the bruises the metal ones left on his toys.

"Detective, whoever you think I am, you're wrong. Do I need to call an attorney? Perhaps it's best if I did. Your partner used excessive force and assaulted me at the airport. I'm sure there are enough eyewitnesses who will corroborate my story. And in case you didn't notice, there are security cameras in the lounge."

The older of the two men identified himself as Captain Wilson. "Thea. Eva. Evie. Whatever name you want to go by, it's pointless. You'll be charged and convicted based on the forensic evidence, and not your name. Evidence has a way of speaking for itself and, in your case, it screams."

Without a doubt, her sister was standing on the other side of the two-way mirror. Precious, lifesaving Gina. The ideal daughter, as their idiot parents had believed.

They'd never realised that she was the perfect one. Thea wasn't sick like the baby of the family. She knew better than to ask whether Penelope was still breathing. *Does it matter?*

It came as no surprise that Gina was a police officer. Even as a child, Gina had been a bitch and stuck to her moral compass. Rules and guidelines their parents had tried to drill into them. Thea had never liked following directions or rules.

Detective Shepherd's face made up for the dullness of the room. Thea wondered what it would take to get him to drop his guard. And pants. *Tears? No.* Not all men were as easy, or useful as Ben Adam Evans. She should've buried him a long time ago.

"Both of your lovers are dead. Your husband is alive and quite talkative," Captain Wilson said, busying himself with a stack of papers on the table.

"Pretty presumptive of you to think I have two lovers. The real number might surprise you, Captain. I don't have a husband, so whoever the canary is, he isn't mine." Thea reached for the Styrofoam cup and sipped the vile, mud-tasting liquid the police called coffee.

Detective Shepherd pushed a piece of paper across the desk. "Read it."

Fuck you, Charlie. The words echoed in her mind, but Thea swallowed her rage and controlled her expression. Trust the fat bitch to stab her in the back. *And after everything I did for you.* Charlie had been nothing but a miserable piece of educated shit when they'd met in a bar. At first, she'd lorded her medical degree over Eva's head, as if it meant anything. Too bad for Charlie that Eva had a piece of paper stating she was a qualified nurse.

With any luck, they'd end up in the same prison.

"Doctor Charlotte Hughes is dead," Captain Wilson smirked, staring into Thea's eyes as if he could hear her thoughts.

Orange had never suited her, no matter what colour she'd dyed her hair. Thea would rather die than spend the rest of her life in a jumpsuit. The chains around her wrists, ankles, and waist made it impossible to attack either of the men. To be killed by another inmate felt below her. If death was her only option, it would be when and how she decided.

"Why are you showing this to me? I've never met an Adam, Eva or whoever wrote that." She slid the photocopy of Charlie's letter towards Detective Shepherd.

Three knocks on the steel door. Her gaze flicked towards the sound and then returned to the men, who remained seated. The change in their expressions was unmistakable.

Phlegm moved in Captain Wilson's oesophagus as he coughed. After taking a sip of water, he cleared his throat. "Sex and organ trafficking. Arson. Multiple murder charges, including that of your parents. The attempted murder of your sisters. Fraud. Identity theft. Manufacturing and distribution of video footage showing minors being raped. Child pornography is a despicable phrase. Anyway, those are just *some* of the charges against you, Thea Larson."

Her heartbeat didn't quicken. Not a drop of sweat formed anywhere on her body. Neither of her pupils dilated. Around the time of Penelope's diagnoses, Thea had realised she wasn't like her family or friends.

It hadn't mattered to her whether her youngest sister survived, but her parents shifting their full attention to their other two daughters … Now, *that* had bothered her. Not in the way it would have most people though as Thea had come to suspect over the years. With their focus no longer split in three, Thea had learned how much she craved being in control.

The door opened and closed. Gina's presence filled the room. "It's like you always said, *Sis*. The fuck you is in the details."

Chapter 54

Laughter welcomed them into the house. "Thank you for going with me," Madison said, hooking an arm around Natalie's and pulling her closer.

"Thank you for arranging that they be buried on your family's farm. I wish they could've seen how beautiful it is out here. It's bittersweet."

Except for Detective Paul Wallace's niece, none of the other bodies had been claimed. Paul and his niece's ashes had been scattered at sea.

Madison stopped and inadvertently yanked Natalie back. "How is living with Declan?" Madison's eyebrows flashed. "Have you?"

Natalie pressed her palms to her darkening cheeks. "You were right. It's different. I'm happy. He's always smiling. Living together is much easier than I expected. Declan is calm, centred and naughty. I think I'm falling in love with him."

Madison grinned. "Tell him. It will be the perfect Christmas gift."

Aaron walked past carrying a tray full of mugs. "Are the two of you done acting like teenage girls? It's time to open the presents."

They followed him into the living room and made themselves comfortable on the carpet. Declan pulled Natalie closer and kissed the top of her head.

Madison placed her chin on Clay's knee and stared up at him, drawing her bottom lip between her teeth. The doctor had cleared him for physical activities the day before. They were making up for lost time.

"Stop looking at me like that." Clay pressed a finger to her nose. "I love you, Madison Taylor."

"Not as much as I love King." The dog rushed to her and climbed on her lap. She turned to Clay. "What do you think the chances are that Noa will give him to me for Christmas?"

"I heard that," Noa said from across the room. "Zero chance of that. King's mine."

King ran to Noa. Madison pouted and moved to sit on the couch. She squeezed in between Clay and Duke. "I guess I'll have to be satisfied with you."

Clay's breath tickled her ear. "Do you wish to change the statement you made this morning? You know, after waking me up with this incredible body of yours."

Turning to him, their lips brushed. "No. You're everything to me and always will be. I love you." Madison kissed him hard, forgetting they were surrounded by people.

A big, blended family. Their family.

"Seeing as the doctor gave Clay the all clear, you can sleep in your own room again, Maddie. There's no need to continue playing night nurse." Aaron crossed his arms over his chest.

Laura asked Gina and Natalie to help hand out the presents. It was a Taylor tradition that the youngest, in this case also the newest, members of the family did it.

Madison whispered to Clay, "I didn't have time to get you anything. Can I give you the same gift I gave you this morning?"

Clay thanked Gina for the package she held out to him. "No. No re-gifting. It has to be different every time."

Declan left the room and came back carrying a box. King jumped against his legs, tail wagging. Declan placed it at Natalie's feet. She kneeled and opened the box.

Tears streamed down her face as she reached inside. "A puppy. She looks just like King." She hugged the tiny black and white body to her chest.

King tried his best to sniff his new friend. Natalie laughed, rubbing King's head before putting the puppy down in front of him. "She is gorgeous. Thank you." She yanked on Declan's hand until he sat down next to her. Natalie pressed her lips to his mouth, cheeks, nose, and forehead.

"You mentioned that you never had a dog growing up, and, seeing as you have a home now, I thought it was about time you have one. What do you want to name her?"

She smiled at the pit bull puppy and lifted her up. "Blade ... because Blade saved me. I think I'm in love with you."

"Are you talking to me or the pup?" Declan asked.

Natalie snuggled the puppy to her chest, despite King's attempts to play with the other four-legged creature in the room. "You."

Declan grinned with one eyebrow raised. "You *think*? I know for a fact I'm in love with you."

Butterflies filled Madison's stomach. Her heart was so full of joy she thought it might explode. Natalie had a new life. As did Mia, Erica, Samantha, and Liza.

Mia was staying with Captain Johnson and his wife, helping Darla in her veterinary clinic while she'd finish her high school education.

Samantha, Erica, and Liza had moved in together. The Taylors had pulled some strings to get them all permanent employment.

Laura handed a gift to Madison. She flipped the card around to see who it was from and leaned her forehead against Clay's chin. "When did you have time?"

"I had some help. Open it. Everyone else has opened theirs." His own gifts could wait.

Tearing off the wrapping paper, Madison held a small box. She opened it. *A key?* She turned to Clay and frowned.

"We loved living at Luke and Noa's, being out of the city, yet close enough to Shadow Bay for your work and if I have to cover a shift for the team."

Duke shook his head. "We're going to miss you, Slay."

Clay patted his friend's shoulder and continued, "I bought a house in River Valley. Together, we can make it a home."

Madison jumped to her feet. "When did you buy a house? And you're telling me this in front of my dad, who might strangle you in your sleep?" She glanced at Aaron, who grinned from ear to ear. Next to him, Laura pressed a tissue to her eyes.

"You're a grown woman, Maddie. We want you to be happy," Laura managed between sobs.

Aaron cleared his throat, handing an entire pack of tissues to his wife. "Clay, this is a big farm. You break my daughter's heart ..." His shoulders lifted. "I don't want to hurt you, son."

Clay stared at them, opening his eyes as big as possible. Luckily, Madison was in shock and not paying attention to her parents. "Maddie, turn the box around and open it."

"My, my, aren't you full of orders?" Madison did as Clay asked and fell to her knees.

"Hey, I'm supposed to be the one on my knee. Damn bullet wound." Clay got to his feet with Duke's help. "Madison *Babe* Taylor, will you move in with me?"

Madison rolled her eyes at him. "We promised to never wake up without each other. A promise, I'd like to remind you, I kept while you were in hospital. My back is still buggered from sleeping on that chair."

Clay pulled Madison to her feet, taking the ring from her palm. "You fell asleep in the chair *one* time because you were too stubborn to sleep on the bed with me. A sore back is the price you have to pay for not listening to me."

"Hey, both of you. Get on with it. Some of us have our own news to share," Luke said, touching Noa's stomach.

Clay cupped Madison's face and pressed his lips to her forehead. "Madison, will you marry me?"

She pulled away, pursing her lips. "Isn't it a bit of a cliché to propose *now*? That's what Luke did after another monster was locked up and we were free to continue with our lives."

Luke laughed. "I warned you she'd say that."

Everyone, including Gina, told Luke to keep quiet.

Clay took a deep breath, ignoring the throbbing in his thigh. *Damn bullet.* "Babe, it's a simple yes or no answer."

Madison studied his face and turned her back to Clay. "You're in pain. Time for your medicine. I'll go get it."

A collective groan erupted from the people in the room.

"Yes or no, Madison?" Clay grabbed her hand, losing his balance and falling backwards onto the couch.

Madison remained on her feet. "What do you think?"

Acknowledgements

First and foremost, I want to thank you. Yes, you. The reader. To you, Silent Death might be just another book, but your support means the world to me. Whether or not you loved the story, thank you for taking a chance on my dark imagination.

Sgt. Will Dodds, Forensic Specialist. Your time is valuable, and your passion for your work is undeniable. I'm forever grateful that our paths crossed and that you always make time to help me ensure the authenticity of my writing. You're a real-life superhero.

To my beta readers – Amanda Jaeger, Jen Peterson, Nicolina Pieterse, and Yolanda Martins. Your excitement when I announce a new project and willingness to read the unedited version is always appreciated.

A special shout-out to Nicolina for helping to ensure I got the medical information right. I doubt I'll ever come up with a story idea and your first response won't be: "I'm so glad you're a good person."

Amanda, you went above and beyond with your feedback. I loved the extra notes you added and the discussions we had about specific elements. You're an amazing sounding board and friend. Not forgetting, a brilliant author in your own right. I owe you one.

My editor, Jessica Huntley. To refer to you as my editor seems wrong, as you do so much more for me than editing my novels. Thank you for your hard work, and the behind-the-page laughs we had about certain scenes. Being an author yourself, adds a special touch to your work as an editor. I couldn't do this without you.

Jana and Marc Barclay, for designing the cover. We all know books are judged by their covers. Thank you for ensuring mine is not only what I had in mind, but making it so much more. You've been my rocks in a very unstable world and I'll never be able to repay you for your love and kind-heartedness.

My family and friends. Your continued support truly means the world to me.

Every ARC reader. I know your time is valuable and your to-be-read list never ending. Thank you for making time to read and review Silent Death.

Most of all, to God, for allowing me to experience true love and carrying me through the hardest days of widowhood.

All mistakes are my own.

About the author

Mariëtte Whitcomb studied Criminology and Psychology at the University of Pretoria. Writing allows her to pursue her childhood dream to hunt criminals, albeit fictional and born in the darkest corners of her imagination.

When Mariëtte isn't writing, she loves reading psychological thrillers and true crime books or spends time with her family, friends, and two miniature schnauzers.

Connect with Mariëtte:
Sign up for her newsletter on her website:
https://mariettewhitcomb.com
Email: mariette@mariettewhitcomb.com
Facebook: @mariettewhitcombauthor
Instagram: @mariettewhitcomb
Goodreads: https://www.goodreads.com/
goodsreadscommariettewhitcomb
Bookbub: https://www.bookbub.com/authors/mariette-whitcomb

Also by Mariëtte Whitcomb

FINLEY SERIES

Orca / Book One

Deception / Book Two

Binding Lies / Book Three

Fortius / Book Four

STANDALONE THRILLERS

The Skull Keeper

DEATH TRILOGY

Death Isn't Enough / Book One

Silent Death / Book Two

www.ingramcontent.com/pod-product-compliance
Lightning Source LLC
Chambersburg PA
CBHW052033240626
47153CB00006B/2057